I0817839

TRUTH STAYS BURIED

TRUTH STAYS BURIED

A NOVEL

ALEXIA BOLAND HERRICK

Truth Stays Buried

ISBNs
Ebook: 978-1-7636340-1-5
Paperback 978-1-7636340-0-8
Hardcover: 978-1-7636340-2-2

Cover and interior design by Christian Storm

First edition (2024)

For Peter, Darcie and Eliza.

CONTENTS

PROLOGUE

HARRISON

THE NIGHT HARRISON MARKS DIED began with triumph. He was riding high as the leading crime and investigative reporter in the Sapphire Ranges, a thriving regional city on Australia's east coast, favoured by tourists for its mountain ranges and thick tree fern and bush covered valleys. The city's size had tripled after the COVID pandemic, becoming a trendy tree-change location of choice for many desperate to flee the concrete capitals.

Harrison was a British-born journalist and was drenched in the glowing spotlight that had shone so brightly upon him after years of unrivalled success in Australia. He was revered and recognised amongst his peers. After all, he had claimed several awards for breaking some of the biggest stories the region had ever seen. And the night he died, he had just collected yet another trophy, not knowing it would be his last.

Harrison was tall, intimidatingly attractive with trademark perfect flowing black hair. His suits were pristine, as though he had been styled by the latest issue of GQ. Everyone at the Sapphire Times had been waiting for his resignation announcement for years, expecting the 30-something would be snapped up by a bigger news outlet to solidify him as a national treasure, a star. Yet, he never left. The truth was Harrison enjoyed being a big fish in a little pond.

But below the surface, was a darker truth. The real Harrison Marks was a man both driven by his success and drowning in it. He was a slave to his craft and struggled to find any kind of balance between his personal and professional life.

No one really knew Harrison Marks, he didn't even recognise himself anymore. He had evolved into a grand manipulator. Everything he did had a carefully calculated angle, benefit, and purpose. And until the night he died, it had rarely backfired.

He lived in a state of waiting. A lion stalking, anticipating their moment to pounce in the tall grass, waiting to break the next story.

On the days he drank, he rarely stopped, disappearing for days on end from the newspaper, denying to himself that he was trying to escape from something more sinister. He got away with it, but only because he was Harrison Marks.

Harrison was struggling to keep track of the secrets and destruction he'd left in his wake. The sad twist in fate was that the night Harrison died, he had intended to go to bed and stay there. He had gone home, but wasn't sleeping next to his wife. The lies had become too much. And now he was paying the price.

He thought of his wife Cressida's strained expression that afternoon as they silently passed each other in the hallway. The love was gone from her eyes, and he didn't blame her. Deep down, he hated himself too.

Harrison rolled over. Even the spare room mattress was the best quality available, not too hard, not too soft. He had married into a life of wealth, thanks to his wife's family. He moved across the sateen sheets and pillows, searching for his half-empty bottle of whiskey reserved for these moments, when his second phone rang. It was his burner phone, exclusively reserved for his confidential sources. When it rang, he always answered, no matter when, even if it was 3 am.

As he sat up quickly, he held his head, feeling the rush of blood, throbbing from the bottles of champagne he had also drank earlier that evening. He rubbed his eyes, focusing on the chain of texts that flooded his phone's screen.

The journalist was careful and methodical. He changed his number every few months and encouraged his sources to do the same. He used shorthand, codes, and signals. These methods had helped him become the incredible, trusted reporter he was. After all, without the trust of his sources to fuel his award-winning stories, Harrison had nothing.

Within minutes of receiving the anonymous messages, he was dressed and had pulled on his thick wool coat, checking his alcohol-stained breath against his hand.

He had been chasing this source for weeks and his effort was finally paying off. His sources often demanded to meet at the strangest locations, everywhere from underground carparks to random park benches two hours from town. But Harrison didn't care. Breaking a story, delivering the truth, changing the world with just a few strokes of the keyboard was all that mattered to him.

He slipped out of the million-dollar white heritage home on the nicest street in the city, quietly sliding the back door closed behind him. Cressida slept in the master bedroom, large enough to be a standard home's living room. Harrison would never know that she had woken to the sound of Harrison's car starting in the driveway, listening to it creep onto the street outside.

He knew that Cressida wouldn't bother to open her eyes - it was what he always did - she would expect him to leave, always without an apology, and always without a goodbye.

As he drove further and further from his home Harrison wound the window down, allowing the freezing cold winter air to fill the car as he drove through the city streets, the only illumination from the streetlights reflecting onto the wet roads. He hung his head slightly out of the window to let the force of the icy wind hit his face, letting it burn his skin until it became numb. It made him feel alive. And it forced him to feel *something*.

Harrison sped through the red lights without stopping, his heart racing with excitement. He was determined to do whatever it took to get this story. And drink-driving at speed was the least of his worries.

There was something comforting about the dead of night. Almost every soul was sleeping, except for him, instead his mind was already back to work, racing to his next story.

Misted rain quickly filled the air again and the automatic wipers screeched as they moved across the windscreen. The rain reflected the lights above the road, creating a white, foggy haze that caught Harrison's attention longer than it would've if he had been sober. Suddenly, he slammed on the brakes, seeing a flash of orange before realising he had narrowly avoided a fox as it skittered past.

Harrison's car swerved on the lightly wet road, fishtailing for twenty metres before he finally regained control, slamming on the brakes. He laughed aloud and wiped perspiration from his brow. It had been another bloody close call. He felt the rush of adrenaline flood his veins and wondered if he would have survived if he had instead allowed himself to crash into the street pole. But giving up, even on himself, just wasn't in Harrison Marks' nature.

Sitting idle in the middle of the street, Harrison looked in the rear mirror to wonder if police would be patrolling at this hour. He smelled his breath as he considered turning around and going home to sober up and instead pushed down on the accelerator to continue his mission. And that was Harrison's final mistake.

He continued to drive towards the famous Ranges National Park, speeding around its winding mountainous roads where he would meet his source, and meet his end.

Within the hour, he would be dead.

HARRISON COULD HEAR the sound of his killer becoming quieter and quieter, like a dial controlling audio being turned down, before eventually fading to silence.

He couldn't speak or move while they dragged his body downhill along the cold, wet bushland for what felt like hundreds of metres. With a broken neck, he could not fight for survival. And then came a final blow to the head.

As the rain fell, his stinging pain disappeared. Then there was nothing but the sensation of the rain, heavy branches, dirt, and wet bush being thrown over him, covering his body.

In Harrison's last moments alive, he did not think of those he loved or of everything he had accomplished. Instead, he thought of everything he had left unfinished. Everything that would remain undone.

His story was about to end. And the truth would be buried with him.

CHAPTER ONE

TASMAN

TWO MONTHS EARLIER

TASMAN HILL'S EYES felt like were about to seal shut. It was his fourth consecutive graveyard shift this week as the night reporter for the Sapphire Times, one of the two last remaining newspapers in the Sapphire Ranges.

His mobile phone rang, buzzing across his desk. Tasman's eyes darted down and the intrusion forced him awake. He hesitated over whether to answer it or not. It was his mother, calling again – the fifth time in just a matter of days. But Tasman was not ready to talk, not yet anyway.

Instead, he furiously rubbed his eyes, willing himself to be alert, cracking his neck to the left, then to the right before continuing to proofread the articles written by his colleagues during the day shift – where Tasman wished he was.

The newsroom at the Times was filled with rows and rows of desks and chairs, most cluttered, stacked with old newspapers that had gathered dust, along with days old cups of tea sitting, long forgotten. The newsroom featured a barely used makeshift broadcast studio built in, affectionately known as 'the broom cupboard', along with a large glass walled meeting room with thick heavy doors. Eight stacked flatscreen televisions, each displaying commercial news channels were fixed along the main wall, separating the other side of the headquarters, belonging to the advertising staff, who were responsible for bringing in the revenue and keeping the lights on.

The Sapphire Times building had once been an architectural marvel for the city, a large concrete oval shaped building with floor to ceiling glass windows, peering out to beautiful green lawns and hedging to create a grand entrance. Over time, the building's colour had turned an off-white, damage to its roof left unrepaired, and the lawns had been taken over by weeds. It was a sign of the times for struggling newspapers battling for a budget to survive with an aging readership.

Thank goodness for paying online subscriptions, thought Tasman.

The keen reporter had only been on the nightshift for two years, and at 27 he was considered a late starter by journalistic standards. But he was determined and prepared to do whatever it took to succeed. After graduating from university, he had bounced from internship to internship, and knew he was lucky to have a job.

In fact, Tasman had delayed commencing his journalism degree for years out of sheer fear he would fail and disappoint his dead father even more. He instead chose to travel, but the holiday just never seemed to end. By his mid-twenties and his third trip to Thailand, he felt a jolt of shock when he realised all of his school friends were already well on their way in their own careers, some even starting a family. Their lives were in full-swing, and back then, Tasman was just floating, going nowhere.

'You got to where you wanted to be eventually darling, that's all that matters,' his mother had told him. 'As long as you're doing what you want, then I'll be proud of you.'

Except that he wasn't where he wanted to be, he thought as he sank into the old steel chair and sighed. He looked around the empty newsroom, it felt like he was just another ghost haunting the building at night. The last night shift reporter lasted just three months before they threw in the towel. Was he simply just floating again? Waiting for an opportunity to present itself?

It was Tasman's strongest desire to make it on his own, without any ties to his father - a former legendary news reporter at the Ranges Advocate well over twenty years ago. Now, the tabloid was the Sapphire Times' only remaining competition in the city.

Tasman knew keeping his family connection secret in the media world would be a challenge, but he was determined to try. That's the problem with journalists, they have a way of digging up the truth - even if it is buried long in the past, he thought.

Tonight, like many nights, was slow. Tasman's tall, lanky frame barely fit underneath the old, cheap wooden desk that forced him to hunch over slightly to face his computer. He turned his head towards the sound of the after-hours cleaner approaching and jumped from his seat far too enthusiastically to allow them to pass by.

'Good evening,' said Tasman, hoping for a conversation. He had tried to speak to the cleaner each night for months, but the same man in light blue coveralls never acknowledged Tasman, instead choosing to listen to the booming music pumping through his headphones as he pushed the vacuum by manoeuvring around Tasman as though he wasn't even there.

'I guess I really am a ghost,' he said aloud to the cleaner jokingly.

However, Tasman wasn't completely alone in the newsroom each night. The sound of the buzzing police scanner, the constant quiet chatter of the cable television news stations that had switched to late night home shopping, and the snoring of Rueben Griffen, was comfort enough.

Rueben Griffen, who everyone at the Times affectionately referred to as 'Griffo', was an elderly, chain-smoking sub-editor who had haunted the Sapphire Times' ageing brick headquarters for longer than anyone really knew. Tasman liked and respected Griffo, even if he was only ever awake for an hour or two at a time.

Griffo wasn't the only employee with a nickname in the newsroom, almost all the reporters in the city still referred to each other by surname only. It was a classic, quintessential trademark of print journalists.

Tasman glanced along the walls of the newsroom where portraits of the star reporters hung. The prime position was, of course, filled by Harrison Marks. Tasman rose from his chair and walked along the display. He stopped before Zaylee Edwards' black and white framed photograph, she wore a tailored blazer and her arms were folded, her blonde hair tucked behind her ears while she stared seriously into the camera. Tasman sighed loudly. He was happy for his friend, ecstatic even - after all she had her own round as the health and education reporter - and she was nailing it.

Tasman stared at the portrait, his mind flashing back to sitting next to Zaylee at university, she had always been exceptionally confident, brilliantly smart, and naturally beautiful. But most of all, she was the kindest person he had ever met.

He had been the last to arrive at their first lecture inside a packed-out theatre. Besides Tasman, Zaylee was the only other mature student in the room. She had watched Tasman hesitate as he searched for somewhere to sit and she dumped her bags from the seat beside her and offered it to him. They had become friends ever since.

Zaylee had even put in a good word for Tasman when the nightshift reporter position at the Times opened up. Now they both worked at the same paper, except they were separated by daylight. Put simply, Zaylee wasn't a floater. She went after what she wanted and never backed down.

Tasman stood over his old desk, resting on its edge to face the large glass meeting room, and sighed loudly.

Being stuck on the nightshift was not going to change a thing. He needed to be seen and he needed to be at the morning editorial meeting, hell, he would even settle for being in the room, he thought.

And that's when Tasman suddenly had a plan. He would stay on in the morning to attend the all-import editorial meeting, where the news agenda for the day was set. He would take a seat at the long boardroom table and at the meeting's conclusion, he would march up to the Chief of Staff Jet Townsend, or if he was feeling ballsy enough, the most important person in the building, Editor Victoria Stanley. He would plead his case. He might even beg.

The only minor issue was Townsend - he wasn't an accomplished journalist, but somehow rose through the ranks of the newsroom with speed. From what Tasman could see, his willingness to agree entirely with anything Victoria said had helped his accession greatly. The man had no backbone. But Townsend didn't care – he was desperate for power. And at least he had it.

'Well, I've got nothing to lose, right Griffo?' Tasman said aloud as he drummed his desk, looking around the dark, static room while the old fax machine and police scanner hummed loudly, before Griffo grunted and let off loudly to Tasman's disgust.

Tasman simply wasn't willing to wait another moment longer on the nightshift.

There was no more time to float. He would have to sink or swim.

CHAPTER TWO

DAYLIGHT STREAMED into the newsroom, a burst of light flooding through the tall floor to ceiling windows. The nightshift was finally over. And soon it would be time for the single most important meeting at the Sapphire Times. In the newsroom boardroom each morning, Victoria would plan the news agenda and call upon her reporters to pitch their stories accordingly. They decided everything in the room. And Tasman felt a sense of excitement that he was finally going to be inside it.

Tasman glanced at Townsend's desk and felt a wave of relief that the chair was still empty and Victoria's office door still closed. It had been so long since he had seen his bosses, he wasn't sure if they would even know who he was.

'We all know Townsend's on a sociopathic power trip most of the time,' said Zaylee to her boyfriend Peter and Tasman one night over drinks at Peter's bar, The Lonely Squire.

Tasman had encountered Townsend at work for the first time after he had signed his nightshift contract.

'No one takes him seriously. He's never even written a proper story in his life. Yet he somehow still acts like he's up there with Harrison,' said Zaylee gesturing above her head. 'I even heard him tell an intern he *trained* Harry. The man is a joke, just stay out of his way. Or you'll be on blast.'

'Am I supposed to know what that even means?' Tasman joked to Peter as he sipped a free glass of celebratory champagne, realising he hated its sour taste but didn't want to offend Peter's generosity. He gulped it down so he could be done with it.

'Isn't this also the same guy that sends out dozens of emails with nonsense tasks and directions but loops in the entire newsroom? Zaylee gets emails all day and night. I reckon you're actually lucky if you're on the night shift because the guy's gotta sleep at some point. You might make it out alive,' said Peter grinning as he simultaneously cleaned the shiny wooden bar and stepped towards his next customer to take their order.

'Remember, there's deadlines, and then there's *Townsend's deadlines*. The guy is insane. He needs every little thing yesterday,' said Zaylee, before she leaned across the bar to quickly kiss Peter on the cheek. Tasman couldn't help but turn away out of politeness, he always felt uncomfortable to stare at a public display of affection, even amongst his own friends.

Tasman admired Peter. He had dropped out of their journalism degree after one of Professor Ward's journalism lectures. The Professor had warned her students of the difficulties of being a member of the media, from the pay and conditions to the intense pressures of chasing the news. She had said matter-of-factly that in this day and age landing a job was near impossible. As soon as she uttered those words, Peter stood up in the lecture to address the whole class.

'Well, stuff that for a joke. I'm out.' And just like that, he quit university. Peter had the added advantage of having family money - within a few weeks he had already planned a new dream - opening his bar The Lonely Squire.

Peter was like that, he went after what he wanted, without any hesitation and full of confidence. No wonder he and Zaylee were a match. Peter looked like he belonged in a surfing advertisement, a body like a Hemsworth brother, complete with long bleached dreadlocks that he had been growing for so long that they had become part of his personal brand. He couldn't be without them now.

Tasman was happy for his friends, but from time to time, he also caught himself envying their relationship. He had never been able to find that kind of connection – not that his parents' relationship was a good model to follow.

'Morning Hill, you look like shit,' said Griffo. The gruff sub-editor woke up, fresh from an almost full night's sleep.

The old man always evaded the universal rule of no smoking indoors by throwing his cigarette out just before anyone from senior management walked into a room. It was as though his advanced age gave him a free pass to be left alone to do his job without question. Everyone adored him. Even Townsend.

'Right, morning, mate,' Tasman said, his voice croaked.

Tasman's desk phone rang. The caller ID showed it was Townsend, calling from his own desk just metres away within the newsroom.

'Hill, why are you still here? Didn't you finish an hour ago?'

So, he did know what he looked like, thought Tasman.

Tasman looked up from his screen at Townsend, who was avoiding eye contact with him entirely as he scrolled through emails. Townsend's ginger fringe that exposed his receding hairline fell across his forehead and he played with it as he spoke on the phone, twirling it around and around his finger.

'Actually, I thought I would stick around this morning for the daily, I thought we could chat... maybe after the meeting?' said Tasman, glancing at Townsend again still sitting at his desk facing away from Tasman on the call. 'I've also got a few ideas for stories to pitch to Victoria, plus that climate change piece, you know the one on the upcoming extreme weather — with the severe rainfall predicted this month and...'

Tasman quickly flicked through several pages of his notebook filled with shorthand, a coded guide barely legible to anyone other than Tasman, hoping he could offer up something else to show his worth. 'Did you get my emails on that? I thought I might run it past you in person so we can get it up online today, you know, get in first,' he offered hopefully. Townsend remained silent for a moment.

'Okay. You know it's unpaid time, right?' said Townsend, dropping his curled fringe. Townsend's eyes were fixated ahead on his screen, ignoring Tasman's gaze. 'What was that climate or rainfall story or whatever?'

Tasman could tell he was barely listening, but he desperately persevered.

'I've written a piece on a climate research report that's about to be released. They're expecting we are going to have something like a year's rainfall in just a month or two - they're predicting landslides and flooding across the Ranges—'

The silence at the end of the phone returned. Tasman wondered if he should just hang up and walk over to Townsend and have a proper conversation in person and be done with it.

'Who is saying this again?' Townsend repeated.

'It's the Ranges University's climate science professor…,' Tasman let his words trail off and stopped talking. He knew he had lost him.

'Look, I'm just not sure it's *worthy*,' Townsend finally replied, as he nodded hello to a young female reporter who walked by his desk.

Tasman was confused.

'Yeah, it's definitely newsworthy,' said Tasman enthusiastically, believing Townsend had misheard him. 'I mean, it's topical, it's political, there's the new environmental advocate's campaign for the government to lower emissions and –.'

Townsend cut him off. This call was a trainwreck, thought Tasman.

'No, Hill, it's *not* worthy. It's not worthy enough,' Townsend snapped as he spun his chair around to face Victoria's office windows, away from Tasman's view.

'But this incoming rainfall could lead to landslides, local economic downturn, and tourism suffering?' said Tasman, continuing to fight despite knowing the effort was useless. Tasman had waited all night for his chance to speak to Townsend and he didn't want to just give up that easily.

'Look, how else do you want me to explain it, mate? We're not running a story on that,' said Townsend. 'It's not the right time. Let's just sit on it for a couple of days and see where it lands, right?' he said.

Tasman suppressed the urge to scoff into the receiver as he searched for the words to move the conversation to how Tasman could be considered to move to the day shift, but the line was dead. Townsend had already cut the call and was walking into Victoria's office.

Tasman's mouth was agape, 'what an absolute –.'

'Prick,' said Griffo, interjecting. 'Big weather system brings rain. It is utterly groundbreaking stuff, Hill,' said Griffo as he struggled to pull on his tattered tweed coat but got there eventually. 'Thank goodness that idea tanked. I don't want to write the headline for that crap,' he laughed, his husky voice coming through as he coughed into his old patchwork handkerchief.

'The risk of landslides is real, though. I mean, we've got hikers, campers, and all the residents up on the mountain, all there for the rainforest. All that rainfall could bring it all down. Can you imagine what would happen if this place cops that much rain for weeks or months?' As Tasman spoke, even he knew he was boring himself.

'Look of course climate change is a solid story. But you know this business, Hill. When someone's killed by a flood from extreme rainfall in the Ranges, then I reckon you've got a shot,' Griffo grinned. 'Go out there and give the people what they want. They want news that's affecting their lives right now, then pack your punch with the science behind it,' he offered wisely.

Griffo leaned over and whispered, his breath rancid with the stench of cigarettes. 'Look, I know your old man was a big deal,' he said, avoiding eye contact with Tasman in an attempt to be discreet. 'I respect that you're trying to make it on your own - and trust me, there's a few around here that could use that same lesson,' he said as he looked at an intern scrolling social media. 'But if I were you, I would use your name to get you as far as you can.'

Tasman nodded and smiled politely at the advice, although he could never imagine a scenario where he would be desperate enough to use his father to get what he wanted.

'Oh, and one more thing,' Griffo continued. 'Don't forget the golden rule. Remember, "If it bleeds, it leads", right? Honestly, what are they teaching you kids at university? It's like I've got to train you all from scratch,' he laughed, coughing into his elbow.

Tasman cringed at the expression, but he knew Griffo was right. The news could be a heartless business, often someone's worst day was a media outlet's strongest day in readers or viewers. It was the nature of the beast.

Tasman's mind instantly recalled the death of three pedestrians killed by falling glass windows from the construction of the city's first skyscraper around a year earlier – it had filled the newspaper for weeks.

The City Council had controversially approved the skyscraper, despite the conflict of interest with one Councillor, Glenn Mosca, owning the construction company building it.

Police had ruled the deaths as an unfortunate freak accident, with extreme winds blamed for the large section of glass falling from the building, dropping to the street below and striking the three innocent victims as they crossed the road. It was a tragedy that rocked the region and local media covered the story relentlessly.

The families quickly launched a civil lawsuit that was still underway. It looked as though the whole thing might settle for a few hundred thousand dollars for the loved ones left behind.

Councillor Glenn Mosca expertly managed the media, issuing heartfelt condolences and demanding an independent review. He even dedicated the top floor of the skyscraper in memory of the victims. He knew how to wrangle a media opportunity, and the media ate it up. After a few months, life in the city eventually moved on, and so did the news cycle.

'You'll get your story sorted, don't you worry about that,' continued Griffo, packing his satchel while giving Tasman a reassuring grin.

The old man must have seen the deflated look on my face, thought Tasman.

'Timing is everything in this place. And you never know what will happen next, that is of course unless you've sat on a story for too long and someone else snatches it right out from underneath you,' Griffo laughed staring at the newsroom's TV wall.

Tasman followed Griffo's gaze to the television screens, each rolling through the morning news headlines. And that's when he saw it. Appearing on the bottom right-hand corner screen was Professor Julian, the climate researcher who had given Tasman his upcoming extreme weather report as an advanced exclusive weeks ago. He was warning residents that the climate change fuelled big wet was coming.

And just like that, a competitor news outlet had broken Tasman's story.

It turned out it *was* worthy, after all.

CHAPTER THREE

TASMAN STOOD in the men's bathroom and looked at his tired reflection in the mirror, smoothing his scruffy, slightly knotted brown hair across his face and checking if his breath was passable.

Tasman was attractive, but he was blissfully unaware of this. He lacked care in his personal appearance and often looked rather shabby, as though he had just rolled out of bed minutes earlier. But today, Tasman knew he needed to impress. He fiddled with a necktie, awkwardly placing it around his collared shirt, fussing with the string of material before abandoning the idea completely when he realised how ridiculous he looked.

Tasman walked into the newsroom boardroom, hesitating for a moment as he decided where to sit before settling on a chair near the head of the table. After all, he was there to be noticed, and Victoria was known to commence the daily editorial meeting by 8am sharp. Townsend would close the door, locking it behind them should anyone dare be late.

Tasman held his breath as Kevin McAllister strutted into the room, as though each step he made was a carefully curated movement under the direction of a television producer for the best camera angle.

McAllister stopped and stared at Tasman in his seat, raising an eyebrow to display his disapproval that Tasman was there at all.

Tasman knew all about McAllister, he was one of the only reporters at the Times who almost never filed a story each day and constantly missed deadlines. Now in his 50s, McAllister was a good example of the cut-throat nature of journalism. His television news network had dumped him after a twenty-five-year career. He was the same vintage as Tasman's father, Eric Gleeson. They had even crossed paths back in the day. Naturally, from what Tasman had heard, they hated each other. It was one of the main reasons why Tasman kept his famous journalist father a secret. Throwing the Gleeson name around was not going to earn him that many favours, especially at the Times, despite what Griffo thought.

Zaylee appeared in the doorway and instantly gestured to Tasman to move further down at the other end of the boardroom table.

'Good to see you during daylight, Hill,' said Zaylee as she sat next to him. She casually leaned towards him in a whisper 'Wait, didn't you work last night? What the fuck are you doing here?'

'Edwards,' Tasman nodded to Zaylee with a smile. 'Actually, yes I did… and here I am, still going strong,' said Tasman, eagerly checking his watch. He didn't even want to calculate how long he had been at work. 'I'm starting to get worried that I've been on the night shift for so long that I am a bit out of sight and out of mind,' Tasman explained, nodding towards Victoria's empty chair at the head of the boardroom table. 'If this goes on for any longer I'm going to be as old as Griffo before anything changes.'

'Ahhh, well then. Tasman Hill is finally ready to take the next step in his life and chase down that promotion, I'm proud of you!' she smiled, teasing him. 'I'm sure they didn't forget about you; they've probably kept you on the graveyard shift because you're such a bloody good worker. They wouldn't want to lose you, it's not exactly the easiest shift to fill.'

Tasman's phone rang again, he fumbled with the device to silence it. His mother had been relentless with calls since she announced her latest engagement, in what would become her third marriage since Tasman's father.

Tasman didn't know how much time he needed to mentally prepare for her next marriage, which would of course soon lead to the next inevitable separation and divorce soon after. For once, he wanted to focus on himself.

'Still ignoring her, then?' said Zaylee, watching Tasman's phone screen continue to flash.

Tasman nodded, avoiding Zaylee's bright brown eyes because he knew what was about to come next.

'Hill! It's been how many weeks now? Don't you think you should at least hear what she has to say?'

He knew she was right. Zaylee had that endearing but equally irritating quality of being that one friend who was always right.

Before Tasman could answer, the room fell silent as Harrison Marks quickly walked in, wearing a much-too-tight blue suit, most probably crafted from fine European fabric. He stood at the head of the table where Victoria would sit, as though it was his chair. His expression was livid.

'Right, who the fuck is in my space?' yelled Harrison, as he threw down his satchel that slid a little across the polished wooden table. He looked around the room in frustration as the reporters silently exchanged looks of confusion. No one dared speak.

'Okay, seriously. Who did it? Who parked in my space? You know, the reserved one with my name on it,' he said raising his voice again.

Zaylee coughed and nudged Tasman, and it took a moment before he finally realised, he had forgotten to move his car last night. Tasman had parked in the closest space to the entrance of the Sapphire Times — Harrison's – and had promised himself that he would move it in the morning, but the nightshift had clearly got the better of his memory.

Tasman rose slightly from his chair, breaking the tension. 'Sorry mate, it's mine. My car in your space, I mean,' said Tasman apologetically. 'I just finished the night shift and I'm not usually still around this late in the mornings, it completely slipped my mind,' he continued before Harrison interjected.

'Right, and you are?' demanded Harrison as he looked Tasman up and down, assessing him.

'Tasman – Tasman Hill, I'm on the night shift' Tasman replied adjusting his suit jacket and standing taller.

'Yeah, night shift – I got that. Well off you go then, night owl,' Harrison replied sarcastically, pointing towards the boardroom doors.

Tasman felt as though he was being dismissed by a primary school teacher.

'But the meeting is just about to start,' said Tasman, checking his watch, his eyes wide. 'I'll move it right afterwards,' he said as he sat back down.

Harrison scoffed, and walked over to Tasman's chair, grabbing onto its back to swing it around to face him. Tasman rose from the seat and matched Harrison's stare; they were face to face.

Tasman told himself he wasn't going to be intimidated by the golden child star reporter in front of the entire newsroom. The standoff reminded Tasman briefly of how his own father would act when he was challenged. And Tasman wasn't the type to back down to him, or to anyone else for that matter.

'Listen, Hill, was it? Here's some advice, if you want to continue working here, let alone ever working during daylight hours, I would get the fuck outside and move your car, right now,' threatened Harrison.

Tasman considered his words knowing that if he left now, he risked being locked out of the room altogether or sacked if Harrison had his way. This wasn't a fight he could win.

'You better run, before those doors get locked,' said Harrison, still standing firmly in front of Tasman. 'We all know how much Victoria hates timewasters. You know, journalists need to have basic time management to meet deadlines and what-not,' Harrison grinned. He looked around the room, as though he was garnering support from the watching audience.

Zaylee looked at Tasman apologetically. He knew this was a fight he couldn't win. Tasman pushed passed Harrison to make his way out of the room. He walked with haste, snatching his keys from his desk.

'Yep. Bye, bye!' said Harrison loudly, waving behind him.

Tasman rushed towards the car park, passing Victoria and Townsend as they walked to the boardroom, before locking the door behind them.

The sting of Tasman's failure and embarrassment hit him hard. How could he have thought he could change his entire future in one morning, by attending just one meeting?

Tasman turned the key to his father's old station wagon, a rusted piece of scrap metal that had far exceeded its own life expectancy. He turned the key again, waiting once more to hear the engine roar to life. But there was nothing. Tasman pleaded with the car aloud, willing it to start, gripping the wheel harder and harder, with no result.

Of course, this would happen now, he thought.

After what felt like an endless minute, he turned the key a third time and the engine reluctantly started.

'Thank you!' he yelled. Slamming his hands on the wheel triumphantly.

The car reversed a few metres out of Harrison's space before it backfired, and then rolled to a stop. The old car had granted Tasman mere seconds before it clapped out for good.

Spitting profanities, Tasman got out and attempted to push the car out of the entrance. He prayed no one was watching him. As the car slowly inched forward, Tasman struggled as he tried to steer while leaning inside his window.

A car slowly approached Tasman, crawling beside him. It was the Sapphire Times receptionist who looked utterly bewildered at the sight of Tasman helplessly trying to control the car.

Christine Andrews was an older woman with peroxide blonde hair dressed in head-to-toe pink, complete with over applied eyeshadow almost touching her eyebrows. She reminded him of his own mother, and he hated that.

'Oh honey, you know that's not how you do that, don't you?' said Christine, looking at him with sincere pity.

Tasman had never actually spoken to Christine, but she was the type of person you met, and you felt you had known them forever. Within seconds she had got into his car, slammed its old, tired gears into neutral to allow him to push it into place off to the side of the packed carpark.

'You're going to need a tow truck. How old is that... thing? It looks like it should've died before you were born,' she quipped.

'Thank you. Christine, right?' said Tasman. 'Yeah, you're not wrong... it's done a few kilometres.' Tasman was grateful for her help while equally irritated that he didn't know how to do it himself.

'And you're the night guy,' said Christine. She began clicking her fingers as she chased the memory of his name, as though she was working through a mental Rolodex. 'Hang on, it will come to me in a second.' She paused again, still clicking. 'Tasman. You're Tasman Hill! I knew it would come to me eventually,' she laughed.

Tasman nodded, trying to be polite as he mentally extinguished an image of himself haunting the newsroom as a ghost again.

'Do you want me to call someone for you, honey?' she offered as she looked over Tasman.

He knew he looked tired; he could feel the bags under his eyes. He tried to straighten his creased white collared shirt as he noticed.

'You look like you've had enough for one day already,' she said.

'No, all okay,' Tasman replied, forcing a smile. 'I'm all good. Thanks for helping me back there. I'll sort that tow truck out,' he said as he turned and stared at the bomb of a car.

Christine hesitated, as though she was about to offer him some more motherly advice but thought better of it. Instead, she offered him a kind wave goodbye before she disappeared through the sliding glass doors, leaving an exhausted Tasman behind her.

Waiting for the receptionist to be out of view, Tasman sighed deeply as he allowed himself to slump onto the grass of the Sapphire Times' lawn.

A text beeped on his phone from Zaylee.

'Don't take it personally. Everyone knows Harry is a total fucking arsehole.'

Tasman threw the phone beside him on the grass and laid back, staring up into the bright sunlight for a moment.

Zaylee was right, Harrison Marks was a fucking arsehole.

TASMAN WALKED BACK into the Sapphire Times' foyer, realising his bag was still at his desk, long forgotten after the eventful morning. As he walked through the doors, he immediately felt the eyes of the receptionist, Christine.

'So, your car is all sorted then Mr Hill?' she asked with a knowing stare, while Tasman glanced back through the floor to ceiling windows with the tow truck leaving the property, its tray empty. He had sent it away knowing he could never cover the bill. The humiliation of the day already felt like it was a fast-spreading stain.

The salary of a journalist wasn't great. If Tasman had paid for the tow truck, he wasn't sure how he would swing his rent for the week, let alone what the cost of the service to resurrect the old car would be, knowing it was better off as scrap metal.

'Yeah, something like that. I might just be racking up a few parking tickets at this rate, I'll work it out,' he said.

Christine's smile dropped. Without hesitation, she swung around in her chair and began rummaging around in a desk drawer amongst what sounded like a mixture of papers, pens, and keys.

'Ah, I knew it was in here somewhere. For a second, I thought I had lost them,' she said.

Christine peered up from the desk and was confused by Tasman's blank expression, as though he ought to understand what she was talking about. She smiled her warm, motherly smile. And with another word, she tossed him a car key.

'It's yours for as long as you need it. Within reason, of course. Just take it until you get back on your feet... whenever that might be.'

The exhaustion and stress of the day was hitting Tasman hard. He looked at the keys she had thrown him and realised she had just gifted him a Sapphire Times corporate car to borrow. She was an angel.

'I'm actually meant to give it a run from time to time, you know, to make sure we get our advertising dollars' worth,' Christine winked. 'No one will miss it, as long as you know, you don't crash it or anything.'

The reception phone rang, and she waved goodbye to Tasman as she answered the call.

Tasman walked outside back into the parking lot and clicked the remote on the keychain, searching for the car. His spirits were lifting, stunned at the kindness Christine had shown him.

When he heard the car unlock, he realised what Christine had meant. The car she had gifted him was the old Sapphire Times news van. In complete irony, Harrison's face and a group of reporters from long ago, were printed in larger-than-life advertising for the Times across the van's side.

Tasman found it hard to swallow, advertising the smirking Harrison Marks with his folded arms and serious, smug expression as he moved around town. But he couldn't afford to be picky. He had no car and had no options.

The old news van reluctantly slid into gear as he drove towards his apartment in the city centre. After the long shift he had been through, he could not wait to get home and walk through the door of his neat little apartment. It wasn't much, but it was home. As he drove, he replayed the sting of the events of the morning.

Tasman thought of Griffo's advice again. It would be so easy to drop his father's name. Harrison and Townsend may even respect him a little. But Tasman didn't want the easy way out. He didn't need the name. He needed to succeed on his own. It was for this reason Tasman took his mother's maiden name to sever those ties and to start fresh. It was something that they had shared after his father left them, back when all they had was each other.

The old news van clanged and rattled, as though it was travelling off road. Its stereo system had long been broken, but the crackling police radio snapped the silence as he drove. Tasman didn't turn it off, instead he adjusted the dial as the radio buzzed a familiar static sound, like an old friend who had kept him company on so many night shifts before.

He came to a stop at an unattended portable traffic sign, flashing golden yellow lights signalling for a detour. Tasman had known about the planned upgrades to the main roads leading to his end of the city, in fact he had published the story overnight reminding residents to detour to avoid long delays, but he knew his exhaustion had got the better of him.

As he turned around, he hoped the news van's old built-in GPS would redirect him to another way home, but instead it continued to stall, the recalculating warning frozen on screen.

'Why won't this day just end?' he said, as he brushed his hair from his face, his fingers sticking to the knots. Tasman tapped the GPS, as he navigated the turning, inclining roads leading him towards the tourist scenic route at the base of the Ranges National Park.

He looked up at the brilliant green fern-covered mountains surrounding him. The Ranges were beautiful, and famous for that reason.

After almost twenty minutes, he finally reached the Black Spur, one of the most treacherous sections of winding road near the base of the mountain.

Tasman could feel fatigue setting in, wanting nothing more than to close his eyes. He was fading. Rolling down the stiff windows of the van, he let the cold air hit him like a hard slap in the face. The moment he did, he snapped back into clear awareness just in time to slam on the brakes. An overturned truck lay across the highway. It had rolled and remained half off the road on the sharp bend, its trailer dangling down the Ranges Mountain cliffs.

Another metre and he would have crashed into the truck, following it and its trailer down the mountainside. Tasman's skin chilled and goose bumped at the sight, his breath vanished for a moment as he imagined how quickly he had avoided his own death had he taken the bend just a fraction faster.

Maybe luck was on my side after all, he thought.

CHAPTER FOUR

IT WAS EERILY SILENT. Tasman could hear nothing but the wind ruffling the ferns surrounding him. He quickly ran the length of the truck to the cab, calling for the driver, for anyone, but there was no response.

He could see it was a tanker transporting fuel, and its sour, unmistakable smell grew thicker in the air. Carefully climbing the overturned cabin's steps to peer into the window, he called again.

The twisted steel wreck creaked and groaned at his weight in response. Tasman wasn't religious, but in that moment, he was praying the whole thing wasn't about to slide back into the depths of the valley below. There were specks of blood, shattered glass, half eaten takeaway boxes, and an empty bottle of tablets strewn across the seats. The driver was gone.

The balancing truck wreckage again screeched as it swung in the wind, causing Tasman to jump back to the road.

Tasman read and re-read the name emblazoned on the tanker Emerald Trucking & Logistics Co, the name sounded familiar, but he couldn't place it. He was more concerned that the entire thing could go up in flames at any moment and he needed to step back, to move as far away as possible. But he didn't. Fighting the urge to run, his breath quick and fast, Tasman fumbled for his phone, calling the emergency services while considering that he needed to capture this event – to call it into the Sapphire Times. It was a story that had delivered itself right to Tasman and he wasn't going to miss that chance.

'Was the driver ejected from the vehicle?' asked the emergency dispatch operator.

'I can't see anyone. The cabin is empty,' Tasman replied, looking around furiously at the crash scene. 'But I can smell fuel – it's a fuel tanker too,' he added.

Tasman looked across the road, searching for the leak, the unmistakable smell of fuel filling the air.

'Move away from the truck,' directed the operator. 'There is a risk it could explode or catch fire. Move as far away as possible and stand by. Police, fire, and ambulance are on the way now.'

Tasman jumped down from the wreck and stood along the steel guard railing on the side of the highway. He looked down the cliff and wondered if the driver lay somewhere below, hurt and unconscious, desperate for help. The edge of the cliff was far too steep to navigate on his own, he knew there was nothing he could do but wait for help.

Tasman began photographing the scene with his phone for the story he was already planning in his head, his hands shaking from the adrenaline, he took dozens hoping for something usable. As soon as police and ambulance arrived on scene, he would call it in and offer an eyewitness report to Victoria – and maybe he would slowly earn back some of the credibility he had lost that morning.

Tasman moved towards the news van, and the police radio sprung to life again, startling him. He tried to make out the voices relaying commands and details through the static buzz. He leaned into the window to listen, wondering how far away help would be. By now, the Sapphire Times and the Ranges Advocate would know too if they were listening.

'Police, fire, and ambulance requested immediately to a single truck rollover. Location Black Spur, Ranges National Park. Called in at 09:34 am. Driver is unaccounted for, possibly ejected from the vehicle upon impact,' said a voice.

'Possible fuel spill and/or unidentified potentially hazardous material. A witness is on the scene. Prepare crews urgently for immediate response,' the voice continued through static.

Tasman took his phone to call Townsend but stopped when he felt a presence and the sound of movement behind him. He had no time to react as he turned to face it. All he could feel was searing pain as something struck his face hard.

Tasman lost balance and looked up to see him. It was the driver of the truck.

The truck driver grabbed Tasman to punch him again, this time lifting him up by the neck and shoving him up against the news van. The man had tears in his eyes and rage in his face. He was in deep shock and Tasman was at his mercy.

'Mate, please stop. I'm trying to help!' Tasman begged.

The driver pushed him hard into the side of the van, directly on top of the image of Harrison and the reporters. Tasman didn't even feel the sting of his eye socket as his mind raced to make sense of what was happening. Tasman was powerless to push the driver away.

'You parasite. I know who you are. I know where you're from. You're going to twist the truth, just like your mate there,' the driver yelled, as blood from a large cut on his forehead dripped onto Tasman. He was talking about Harrison.

'Mate, I was just driving home. I'm not here for this. I'm not here for... you,' Tasman struggled. 'I just want to get home, please, mate.' Tasman pulled desperately at the truck driver's hands that gripped his neck. This might be it - the moment I die, thought Tasman as stars swirled in front of his eyes.

The driver's eyes were wild, as though he had become possessed. 'I can't lose my job. You'll tell them you saw the pills! If I lose my job, I will lose everything, my family, my house, and it will be on *you*.'

'Mate, I know nothing about any pills,' Tasman gasped. 'I don't know what you're talking about. Let me walk away, okay? Please.'

'They'll find out,' said the truck driver, speaking even faster, looking past Tasman. 'It's over now.'

Tasman struggled to breathe – the dark stars were getting worse. The driver's hands remained tight around his neck.

'Listen, I'll help you,' Tasman pleaded, struggling to speak. 'I can...,' he uttered, before stopping at the sound of sirens wailing in the distance. The truck driver flinched.

I need to keep him focused so he doesn't kill me before help arrives, thought Tasman. Can I hang on? He wondered, dazed and limp but Tasman was fading.

Through a haze, Tasman's eyes saw a police officer run towards the driver. No, he was hallucinating. She couldn't be real. But she was just in time.

Suddenly the driver jerked his head arching his back, his hands dropping from Tasman's throat at last. Tasman sucked in great gulps of air, watching in disbelief as the officer rolled the driver over and cuffed him. She wasn't a mirage after all.

'It was an accident. They made me overload the trailer. They made me do it. And now - my truck, fuck!' he yelled as two male officers appeared and moved the driver from Tasman's view.

'Are you okay?' the officer who had saved his life casually asked, looking over Tasman's face, bloodied and bruised. 'Looks like we showed up just in time,' she said placing an arm on his shoulder in comfort.

Tasman nodded silently, still in shock. He slid down the side of the van, rubbing his throat. He eventually caught his breath, pulling his clothes down off his chest and back into place. His blood felt like it was racing throughout every vein in his body.

Seemingly out of nowhere, Tasman realised that more police, firefighters, and ambulance crews had appeared, surrounding him and the turned over truck. Drivers who lined the snaking road were out of their cars, filming the scene on their phones.

A paramedic moved him into their van and began assessing him, but Tasman was more concerned with the scene outside. He could see another paramedic assessing the truck driver nearby, while police stood guard.

Tasman, feeling as though he was in a dream, looked again at the truck's branding, Emerald Trucking & Logistics Co, and the penny finally dropped. It was the same business at the heart of Harrison's expose on logbook tampering in the trucking industry. The driver's hatred of the media made sense. He thought about how he would include this in his story before he jolted upright as he realised, he still hadn't called Victoria to claim it. He couldn't let another opportunity slip away and he didn't care he would sidestep Townsend to get it.

'I need you to take a seat, okay? We need to monitor your breathing after what's happened,' said the female paramedic.

She looked back at her younger male colleague with a diagnosis who was filling in a form on a clipboard.

'Definite strangulation, no loss of consciousness, but he couldn't have been far from it,' she concluded. 'You've got a bit of a nasty cut, and you'll bruise up nicely, expect to see a lot of black and blue.'

The female paramedic wiped blood from Tasman's eye socket, still throbbing from the attack.

Tasman nodded. 'Look, I'm a little stiff, but I'm totally fine,' he said, moving towards the edge of the ambulance to see what was happening outside. 'I'll be okay. He didn't finish the job though, did he?' he said in an attempt at humour.

The paramedics exchanged a glance between them. The joke was in bad taste, thought Tasman.

'You'll be okay. We're just making sure you're breathing okay and there's no other damage,' said the woman. 'You should be fine in a couple of weeks. The adrenaline will wear off in the next few hours and that's when you'll feel it,' she warned.

'Great. Thanks. I'm sure I'll be fine. It looks far worse than it actually is,' he said as he searched for his phone.

Tasman moved to the edge of the steps as the young paramedic stopped and watched him, realising he was attempting to leave.

'Mr Hill - we just need you to sit down,' he said.

But Tasman wasn't going to listen. As soon as he stood up, he heard the yells of firefighters to stand clear. Tasman, his phone in hand, clambered out of the ambulance and began filming as emergency crews ran for cover. An unforgiving screech of metal thundered throughout the valley as the rest of the truck began to slip backwards.

He had got the vision. He had captured the truck disappearing down the unforgiving, vertical cliffs of the Ranges National Park. There was silence throughout the valley after the sound of it crashing through the trees.

Tasman watched as police spoke to the truck driver, officers drafting notes and taking his statement. The driver was staring into the space where his truck once was. He had truly lost it all now.

Tasman wasn't about to press charges. But he had something else in mind.

He walked back to the news van, opened the door and found the police radio still buzzing loudly.

Wiping blood that had seeped from his eyebrow, Tasman prepared to make the one call that he was convinced would be his big break, his magical opportunity to finally earn a place on the daily round, to become a fully recognised journalist at the Times.

Staring at his blood-stained hands, he thought of Griffo's golden rule - "if it bleeds, it leads", and just like that, he knew exactly what to say to Victoria Stanley.

'Victoria, hi, it's Tasman… Tasman Hill. Yeah, that's right, the night reporter,' he began confidently. 'Listen, something's just happened, and I've got a story for you.'

TASMAN HAD GIVEN HIS STATEMENT to police and finally made it home, dragging himself up to his third-storey apartment. He lived in the dodgy end of town, where the sirens of emergency services often echoed throughout the night, Tasman didn't notice them so much anymore, he was barely ever home to hear them. Each step up his apartment stairs was a challenge; he ran out of breath and took a moment to regain himself on the way up. Touching his neck, the skin burned intensely in response.

He lay down on his squeaking, half-broken steel bed. It was the biggest piece of furniture in his tiny apartment. The moment he opened the door, he felt instant relief.

I finally made it, he thought.

Tasman hadn't bothered to decorate the apartment since he had moved in. Brown moving boxes remained stacked along the wall, waiting. It was white and sterile, and he liked it that way. It felt like a blank canvas, a fresh start. The bathroom, kitchen, and living space were all just steps apart.

Desperately, he tried to sleep. But every few minutes, the pain and discomfort thrust him back into consciousness, his eye socket throbbing, his neck sore to the touch. The adrenaline had finally worn away, just like the paramedics had warned. He searched his bedside table for paracetamol when his phone rumbled, the screen flooded with notifications from his news feed. His story had broken, his bloodied and bruised face was everywhere.

CHAPTER FIVE

TASMAN KNEW THE REPORTER should never become the story, but he couldn't deny it. It felt great to be seen, and to be on Victoria's radar.

Tasman's mind replayed the moment he had turned around as the truck driver throttled him, clasping his hands around his throat, to then the entire truck sliding backwards down the cliffs, collecting the metal guard rail with it. The anger of the truck driver was stopped the moment the police stepped in. He couldn't help but wonder what would've happened if they were a few seconds late to save him. It still sent his mind spinning.

Tasman's eye socket had swelled and turned black and purple, but he would never call in sick for his shift, even after the ordeal he had been through. Journalists at the Sapphire Times rarely did, it was another unspoken rule of the newsroom. The only person who got away with not showing up – was Harrison.

The news didn't stop, so why should I? he thought. He would rest today and go back to work that evening.

He touched his head and moved his hand back quickly; it throbbed in pain. Tasman lay on his bed and thought to himself how simply missing the morning editorial had set off a chain of events that he could never have expected, and now selfies showing his cut, bruised face and neck featured on the Sapphire Times' website, covering the truck rollover and attack.

Tasman's phone rang, and he knew who it would be without even glancing at the screen. He knew he had punished her enough with his extended silence since she announced her engagement to David.

Since his father had abandoned them, Tasman had always thought of his mother and him as a team, bonded forever in what they experienced. He didn't understand himself why he expected her to continue living in limbo, especially after he left home to go to university and then the Ranges. He knew he was being unfair.

He answered on the last ring and was relieved she had already hung up. He let the voicemail play out, one of more than a dozen he had left unopened over the last few weeks.

'Honey, it's me - it's Mum,' she began, forgetting caller ID already displayed who was leaving the recording. 'I just saw the news - I can't believe it - are you okay, darling? What an absolute nutter to attack you! David and I are going to drive down tonight to see you to make sure you're okay. I've been worried sick. Please call me back,' she pleaded before the message ended.

Tasman knew he would have to call her back to avoid a random appearance from his mother and her new fiancé. He swallowed to prepare himself to at least try to be nice, he knew she deserved that. She answered the call immediately.

'Mum, hi, it's all okay. I'm fine, it looks worse in the photos,' he lied as he touched his eye socket, still stinging from the pain. 'There's no need to come down, I'll catch up with you both another time,' he continued.

There was no way he wanted to see the man that wanted him to call him 'Dad'. The thought made him want to vomit. He already had a father, and the experience was traumatic enough the first time around. Let alone the second or third time she walked down the aisle since. His mother's marriages were always trainwrecks. And it was always up to Tasman to pick up the pieces when they inevitably crashed in spectacular fashion.

'Honey, I wish you would put all of this behind us. If you took the time to get to know David, you would like him, he's different from the others - I'm telling you,' she said, her voice reaching a higher pitch. Tasman knew his mother could sense his reluctance to see her, and as always, she had cut straight to discussing the underlying the issue.

'Yeah, soon, Mum. We will work it out,' he winced, stopping himself from rubbing his eyelid again. 'I'm actually tied up with work right now,' he lied, hoping to excuse himself from the call. 'I'm dealing with all the fallout of this thing, but I'll talk to you soon, okay?'

'Okay, darling. I love you, Tasman,' she said, her voice disappointed, accepting she would not win him back at that moment.

Tasman always appreciated the way his mother never pushed him. She knew him and knew it would take time.

CHAPTER SIX

IT WAS EVENING when Tasman arrived back at the newsroom, ready for his shift. He sat in the old news van and lingered for a moment before getting out, considering if his close call with death that morning was enough to credit him with becoming a permanent on the day shift. He had surely earned it now, he thought.

Tasman walked into the grand foyer and glanced at the wall of television screens behind Christine at reception — the story was still splashed across them all with images of the overturned truck Tasman had taken, then his bruised and battered selfies that Townsend had insisted upon in order to give the story 'context' for how serious his injuries were.

Tasman placed his satchel onto his desk and noticed he was being watched by the remaining reporters who were still at their desks rushing to meet the evening deadline. As he sat down he was quickly greeted by Zaylee wearing a bright yellow pantsuit, she had stayed late to see him.

'I've been waiting all day to talk to you about all of this,' smiled Zaylee as she went to touch his taped eyebrow and black and purple eye socket. 'Ouch, it doesn't look good. I mean, shouldn't you have at least taken the day - sorry I mean the night - off, you know just this once? Even everyday heroes need to take a day off once in a while, Hill,' she teased.

'Not this hero, especially ones who are trying to get promoted,' laughed Tasman. He adored the small amounts of time he spent at work with Zaylee. It was bittersweet, always a reminder he was never quite at her level, but it motivated him to keep trying.

Tasman looked past Zaylee and watched as three men entered the reception at pace, one wearing the same branded Emerald Trucking & Logistics Co high-vis shirt the truck driver from the crash at the Black Spur had worn. A man with a neatly trimmed short cut white beard wore a suit while holding a manilla folder filled with documents, and another, aged in his 40s looked serious and tense. It was Councillor Glenn Mosca. Christine rose from her long, winding reception desk, arms folded as though she was defending herself against an angry mob. Tasman moved closer towards the foyer, approaching as if he were backup, followed closely by Zaylee behind him.

'Good afternoon. We demand to speak with Victoria Stanley. Immediately. She knows who I am. And she will know what this is about,' said Councillor Mosca belligerently.

Mosca impatiently adjusted his blazer, buttoning and unbuttoning it as he glanced at the reporters left in the newsroom, ignoring Christine.

What an absolute arsehole, thought Tasman. Councillor Mosca was clearly looking for an audience. This was a man who wanted to put on a show, he was the star performer and Christine was the unfortunate patron with a front row seat.

'Sir, can I ask you to please-,' said Christine as she moved from behind the desk, blocking the entrance to the newsroom.

Councillor Mosca abruptly cut her off. 'I'll ask again,' he said impatiently tapping the palm of his hand on the counter. 'Get me the editor. Victoria Stanley. Now. Thank you,' he said as he rolled his eyes, shaking his head at the two men standing awkwardly behind him.

Tasman was stunned by his blatant display of rudeness. It reminded him of his own father and the way he treated wait staff at restaurants. It was embarrassing to watch, yet his father was never apologetic for the scenes he caused.

'Is this guy for real?' he whispered to Zaylee. The entire newsroom fell silent, now also watching.

Tasman looked at the large man standing with his arms folded behind Councillor Mosca. His face was bright red, but he remained silent. He wore a bright yellow shirt from Emerald Trucking, far too small for his protruding stomach, and tight blue shorts.

It wasn't unusual for members of the public to complain about stories in the Sapphire Times. Christine fielded calls and emails constantly. But for complainants to appear in person, was rare.

'Sir, unfortunately Ms Stanley is not available right now. You'll need to schedule an appointment,' said Christine firmly.

This wasn't her first rodeo, thought Tasman as he took a step back to lean against the foyer wall.

'No. No appointments. We will speak to her now. Thank you,' replied the Councillor.

Christine pursed her lips tightly, as though swallowing her natural reaction to swear in response to the rudeness of the men standing before her.

'Sir, you will need to take a seat and -'

The Councillor laughed, cutting off Christine as he shook his head in disbelief. 'You know I've dealt with your paper for years and years, right? Tell Ms Stanley that I represent this fine city, and it is in her interest to have a conversation with me. I'm here supporting a fine local business - the same business this newspaper continues to target, week after week,' he said, gesturing at the larger-than-life image of the truck crash on the foyer screen behind Christine. 'Now, I'm sure the last thing you and Ms Stanley would want is for me to refuse to work with you altogether, right?'

Tasman and Zaylee looked at each other in disgust. The politician was playing hardball. Christine looked back towards Victoria's office for a moment, wondering if the editor had yet seen the exchange or could overhear what was going on.

'Mr Goldsworthy here and his business have been the victim of several targeted and defamatory attacks by this publication... and Mr Marks. We are demanding your biased media coverage against Emerald Trucking & Logistics Co cease immediately.'

Tasman turned to see Harrison sitting on the edge of his desk, chewing on the tip of his silver-plated pen as though he were enjoying himself. Tasman could tell that the reporters still in the building were now only there to see how this would all play out.

Surely Harrison would stand up and say something? After all, he was the target of their attack, and they had a point. Harrison had made it his personal mission to continue to investigate the conduct of Emerald Trucking & Logistics ever since the logbook scandal story had broken.

Harrison had uncovered how the trucking employees had been tampering with logbooks to increase their performance times and profits and the story had made national news, with politicians vowing to toughen up on greedy business by taking advantage of the safety of its employees.

Harrison had started digging for the story after the death of one of its drivers. A grain harvest transporter who had fudged his logbook hours under the direction of company management - he ended up dead after driving fatigued, crashing into a group of trees one summer night.

That story broke months ago, and now the same company's truck had overturned, and now one of its drivers had considered killing Tasman to prevent media coverage.

Tasman touched his neck; it was even more stiff and sore than this morning.

Christine appeared poised and calm while he continued to shout, the two men accompanying him standing silently watching on.

'Now, Councillor Mosca,' she began, her voice stern as though she was speaking to a toddler mid-tantrum. 'Perhaps you did not hear me. You will need to take a seat. If you continue to shout at me, I'll be calling security, or the police. Do I make myself clear?'

Christine balanced sweet and sharp perfectly, thought Tasman. Tasman wondered what the Councillor's next move would be. He was clearly unbothered by the threat of police.

'There's no need to get the police involved. Although, speaking of the legal matters, please mention to Ms Stanley that Mr Barriano - our lawyer - is also here. With a cease-and-desist order,' said Mosca, indicating to the man standing behind him in a suit with a nod.

Townsend had finally appeared, Tasman could see fear in his eyes, as though he had never actually been forced to deal with a dispute of this kind while being the Chief of Staff. He stumbled over the legs of his chair, before composing himself, brushing his fringe from his face, before jogging to knock on Victoria's glass doors to alert her.

The three men moved towards the long bench seats lining the glass foyer windows. The truck company boss stood; his arms folded. Christine pressed the buttons on her desk phone hard, calling Victoria, whispering to evade the listening ears of the visitors nearby.

'That's the guy that completely hijacks the Council meetings each month, right?' said Tasman recalling the stories he had published during the nightshift. 'As soon as he knows there's a journalist in the room, he takes it all into overdrive,' he said to Zaylee who had been joined by the young intern standing closely behind her listening.

'Yeah, last week he threw the Council papers proposing a restriction on the height of high-rise buildings into the air and walked out of the room,' said the intern as he scrolled his phone. Zaylee and Tasman were surprised at his offering to the conversation.

'How did he even get elected?' questioned Tasman, turning back to Zaylee.

'It was a shocker to most of us, especially after the whole "deadly skyscraper fiasco", it was his construction company behind it. But money talks around here, and Mosca has plenty of it,' Zaylee shrugged as she pulled out her phone to respond to text messages.

Tasman had published dozens of stories during the nightshift featuring the antics of Councillor Mosca. He was the builder of the high-rise apartments in the city, but he had also made a name for himself as the spokesperson for local businesses doing it tough, including Emerald Trucking & Logistics Co.

'Surely Harrison is going to say something, right?' said Tasman to Zaylee in a whisper to avoid the eavesdropping intern.

'It looks like he's enjoying the drama too much,' she nodded in Harrison's direction, the man was smiling as he leaned back in his chair and chatted on the phone while watching the room.

Tasman and Zaylee watched as Christine led the men to Victoria's office, where the editor stood, her arms folded at the door, flanked by Townsend.

'I don't know. Victoria looks like she's got them covered,' said Tasman.

'It's Townsend I'm worried about,' Zaylee said as Townsend nervously closed the door to Victoria's office, drowning out the shouting from Councillor Mosca.

'SHOULD I CALL SECURITY?' asked Tasman, unsure if the Sapphire Times security guards were still on the payroll, after all, it had been weeks since he had seen a security car drive past at night during the graveyard shift.

'I'm pretty sure they slashed the security patrols a few budgets ago,' Zaylee said, laughing nervously.

'Well, that's reassuring,' said Tasman.

Five minutes had passed by, and the shouting from the office grew louder before Victoria suddenly opened the door, confidently gesturing the men towards the foyer and exit.

'Unfortunately, Councillor, it's time for you and your party to leave,' she demanded.

The lawyer, Mr Barriano, handed her a letter as he passed.

Another cease and desist to add to the pile, thought Tasman. Legal threats were as common as toilet paper at a major news publication. And with the seriousness the Sapphire Times gave to them, it may as well have been.

Councillor Mosca seemed satisfied with his performance and looked to the newsroom to survey the reactions of the remaining staff still floating around. He moved towards the door, along with Mr Barriano, but Mr Goldsworthy, the owner of Emerald Trucking & Logistics Co, refused to move, despite the Councillor pulling him towards the exit.

Goldsworthy scanned the newsroom and zeroed in on one desk, it was Harrison's.

'You!' Goldsworthy yelled moving toward Harrison, standing in front of him. 'I'm warning you, bloody vulture!' he continued, his face burning bright red as he waved his finger wildly in the air. 'Leave my company out of your stories, you got it?' he shouted through gritted teeth, resembling a fairy tale ogre.

'That sounds like a threat,' Harrison replied, completely unfazed. With the eyes of the newsroom upon him, Harrison smirked. He wasn't the only one who enjoyed being part of a spectacle.

Councillor Mosca stepped forward, tugging on Goldsworthy's arm to signal again that it was time to leave, they had made their point. Goldsworthy moved even closer to Harrison, he towered above the journalist, casting a furious stare.

'Keep this up and we will see you in court,' said Goldsworthy, lunging forward to intimidate Harrison, who remained still. Victoria and Townsend stood at the glass doors, watching along with the rest of the newsroom.

'That's an interesting speech,' said Harrison coolly. 'But here's the thing Mr Goldsworthy, I only write what's fact. And mate, I've seen all the evidence I need, and it's just the tip of the iceberg,' he continued, leaning forward to his foe. 'And let's not forget about your poor driver? You know, the one who ended up pinned between his own truck and those trees, all to meet your company's demands? His poor family.'

'That's enough!' Goldsworthy shot back. Harrison had struck another nerve. 'Don't you dare use my company to sell your bloody papers!'

'Actually, we're online now, broadcasting across all the platforms and, even a touch of livestreaming on social media -,' said the intern.

Victoria shot a deadly stare at the young, hipster intern who fell silent, quickly getting the hint that he was out of his depth.

'He won't last the week at this rate,' whispered Zaylee to Tasman while rolling her eyes in the intern's direction.

'And you - what's that saying about glass houses, hey?' said Harrison, gesturing towards the Councillor who placed his expensive silver ballpoint pen back in his suit pocket. 'That's right. Glass,' Harrison continued. 'Councillor Mosca. It is always so good to see you. How are your skyscrapers going... losing any more windows lately?' he said sarcastically.

Councillor Mosca remained silent but scowled at the question. He had met his match.

'So go ahead, send in the lawyers,' dismissed Harrison, flicking his hands to banish them from the newsroom.

Goldsworthy had heard enough. He lunged towards Harrison, who stepped sideways leaving the man to fall forward, slamming his hand on his desk, before Councillor Mosca and the lawyer pulled him back.

'We don't need to resort to anymore violence, at least not anymore today, Gents, my colleague already has a rather sore neck thanks to you,' said Harrison, smiling as he straightened his shirt and looked from the lawyer to Councillor Mosca. 'Let's just see what buried secrets get dug up at court then. After all, the truth always comes out, right?' he scoffed.

Councillor Mosca's expression was one of disbelief, he looked at this lawyer as though willing him to speak. Harrison was now challenging them all.

Harrison was both fearless and insane, thought Tasman. He was putting on a show for the entire newsroom to witness, and Tasman couldn't help but admire him for it at that moment.

Goldsworthy's face was piping red with anger, he turned to leave, pushed from behind by the men he had arrived with, before taking a second look back at Tasman's blue and purple bruised face and neck.

Victoria had seen and heard enough, stepping forward she raised a finger to Harrison to silence him, while turning to the three men that had created the scene.

'Gentlemen, you are now trespassing on private property so we will give you this opportunity to leave now freely, before we call the police to remove you,' Victoria said in a low, calm and unaffected voice.

Goldsworthy had been three times her size, yet he did nothing to intimidate her.

Councillor Mosca again pulled at Goldsworthy's arm, who shrugged him off as he stormed out of the building, leaving the lawyer to trail behind them.

Tasman looked back at the stunned newsroom, journalists began filing out after long overstaying the end of the shifts.

Tasman sat down at his desk, watching Harrison walk out of the newsroom.

As he stared, he couldn't help but wonder who exactly Harrison had been speaking to, who he was threatening with the truth not staying buried for long. What were they hiding? And was he talking to Goldsworthy? Or to Councillor Mosca? Maybe it was both.

CHAPTER SEVEN

THE NEXT EVENING, Tasman walked into the newsroom ready to begin his shift, his bruising had worsened to an even darker shade of blue that made him look like the victim of a serious car crash.

As soon as he entered, the atmosphere of tension and drama of yesterday had vanished, replaced by one of excitement. If decorations were allowed, there would already have been streamers hanging from the light fittings and banners congratulating Harrison on his fourth Golden Quill victory, and the awards hadn't even happened yet.

Tasman nodded to himself, stifling his feelings of jealousy. He had completely forgotten that the Golden Quill Awards were tonight, and instead of joining his colleagues at the shiny, bright awards night, revelling in their achievements, he would be in spending the evening here, watching the live television feed alone, while Griffo napped on the couch.

Reporters stood around dressed in gowns and suits, as Harrison stood on his desk, opening a bottle of champagne in pre-emptive celebration, while Tasman logged onto his computer.

It wasn't surprising Harrison was in high spirits. He was likely about to win his fourth Golden Quill. Win a Golden Quill, and they considered you an excellent journalist. Harrison Marks had won the last three consecutive years and had become a living local legend in the Sapphire Ranges. And he knew it, thought Tasman.

In his tuxedo, Harrison resembled a stunt double for a younger Daniel Craig in James Bond. Harrison jumped from his desk, he was drunk already. He stood with Victoria, her cascading black bob haircut complete with fitted violet gown looked to be the epitome of fashion, her style broadcasting her power and beauty all at once. Tasman watched them. It was obvious the respect and favouritism she held for Harrison. Victoria listened to Harrison, providing her undivided attention when he spoke, as though she was holding onto each word with careful consideration.

Tasman envied Harrison's respect, his career, and power. He glanced down at his tired collared shirt and suit pants, if he was ever going to step up to Harrison's level, he knew he had to eventually spend the money on a proper work wardrobe. Tasman jotted down the simple reminder to go shopping in his notebook, underlining it three times before he was interrupted by Zaylee.

'One before you start?' asked Zaylee, holding her own freshly opened bottle of champagne, offering him a glass.

'You've got to make the most of it when Victoria opens up the bar cupboard,' she laughed, straightening her red sequinned gown.

'Thanks, but I'll pass - on the clock - you know how it is,' Tasman joked. Tasman had always worn his emotions on his sleeve, and the disappointment that the Golden Quills marked another year he had not progressed in his career was hard to swallow.

'Don't worry Hill,' said Zaylee, reading Tasman's faked happy expression. 'After what happened on the mountain, you know, your whole "near-death experience", there's no way you'll be passed over for the next opening,' she patted him on the back. 'I actually heard there might be some movement with Tamra moving on to start some fashion blog,' she said excitedly, hoping to lift Tasman's spirits. 'In all honesty, you aren't missing anything tonight. These things always end up being totally shit,' she said checking her matching painted red nails as she spoke. 'It's literally just another Harrison Marks appreciation awards night,' she said, doing her best to fake her lack of interest in the evening.

Zaylee squeezed Tasman's shoulders apologetically as she made her way towards the foyer to leave. The cabs had arrived simultaneously and began to line the entryway of the Sapphire Times.

'Looks like you're my date for tonight then, Hill,' joked Griffo, as he sat down opposite his desk. 'Sorry I didn't dress for the occasion,' joked the old man as he opened up a Tupperware container with his dinner. 'I can see you didn't bother, either,' said the old man, looking at Tasman's tired, dated suit.

ONLY A FEW HOURS had passed but the night felt as though it was dragging on longer than usual. Griffo was in his second hour sleeping slumped in his chair, while Tasman updated copy on the storms and record rainfall expected to hit the city from tonight, drenching the region over the coming days and weeks.

There was unusual silence in the building, even the police scanner and Griffo's snoring were silent. There was nothing but the sound of Tasman's fingers hitting the keyboard when a bright crack of lightning lit up the dark car park outside, a sudden burst of violet, white light. The storm was approaching, and rain was beginning to lightly fall, Tasman could see it sticking to the newsroom's large glass windows.

Tasman forced himself to watch the Golden Quill Awards live. He watched as Harrison stood at the podium, clenching a trophy while he made his fourth consecutive award acceptance speech to a room of his fans and peers all applauding his success.

Tasman threw down the TV remote on his desk, which startled Griffo for a moment before he returned to his sleep. He got back to work, checking the storms maps online and monitoring the emergency services internal radio.

He was determined to find his next, great story, and this time, he would not let it go.

IT WAS JUST PAST MIDNIGHT when Tasman looked up from his computer screen, he had been so busy making calls to chase down new leads while furiously typing up copy that he had not even noticed if the late-night cleaner had been and gone. It felt good to be in the zone, he thought, to be focused and determined to find a new story.

Tasman stopped as he heard the echo of voices coming from the other side of the newsroom. The main entrance was always closed at night, so it had to be staff, he told himself as the hairs on the back of his neck began to tingle as he considered who would be at the Times after hours.

He swung around in his chair to face the growing noise that was becoming so loud it was even more audible than Griffo's snoring. In the dimly lit newsroom, he could see the bright lights from the offices beyond the kitchen shining through the doorway.

Tasman slowly stood from his desk, searching for anything he could actually use as a weapon to defend himself. He took an empty bottle of champagne left on top of an office bin to arm himself and silently moved towards the sound of the voices.

He turned the corner holding the bottle tightly in his grip before stopping himself from entering the kitchen area, realising none other than Victoria and Harrison were standing there, appearing to be mid-fight. Tasman hesitated, considering to turn back, but instead stood still in the shadows.

'That's convenient, isn't it?' Victoria said to Harrison, visibly angry. 'You come back here after another success and all you want to do is to pick a fight. You're a child, you know that, right? You are always looking to destroy something, anything that's good,' she said, her voice breaking.

Tasman had never seen Victoria show any emotion at all. She was raw and real.

'If you think I have a problem, just say it,' Harrison hissed. 'Trust me. You wouldn't be the first to give me this sad speech.'

'You're flying a little too close to the sun, okay? Come back down to earth for a minute and you'll see things more clearly in the morning. It's time you took sobering up seriously, you can't keep this up. And I can't keep covering for you,' she said, offering him a glass of water he ignored.

Harrison moved towards the sink, instead pouring another round of whiskey into his glass, before undoing his bowtie and beginning to laugh.

'It's funny. You know, I know *you* need me. But I don't think you understand how much you actually need me,' he hissed, slurring his words slightly.

Tasman could see Harrison's eyes were narrow, fixated on Victoria.

'Do you think this fucking rag would be where it is without me? Do you really think it would still be around without me? Without my stories? Lose me and you lose the readership - simple. And what would they think?' he said, pointing at the formal executive portraits hung on the wall.

'Harry, please,' Victoria said, rolling her eyes. 'Not this again. I told you, if you don't feel as though your talent is being recognised, then you know where the door is. And I thought I had made my thoughts about you, about us, more than clear. I'm not the one refusing to move on.'

Harrison scoffed in response. 'Oh, that's right. Thanks for the reminder. If you're not careful, you might lose me in more ways than one,' he said, his voice low and harsh. His eyes were still watching Victoria, like a hawk, waiting to strike at its prey once more.

Harrison seemed to be enjoying the fight, thought Tasman. He knew he risked being discovered at any moment but couldn't look away.

Victoria raised her hands, standing tall and confident. She had heard enough.

'You know what? This has gone on for far too long. And I'm tired of babysitting you. Leave,' she said. She had had enough of his performance. Harrison had been aiming to wound, and Tasman could tell he had been successful. And without another word, Harrison threw his golden glass award to the tiled floor, the award smashing into hundreds of pieces.

Tasman knew he had to make his presence known, and the sound of the smashing glass was his only plausible excuse for entering the room. He placed the empty bottle on the floor and waited a moment.

'Is everything okay?' asked Tasman, carefully stepping into view from out of the shadow of the dark hallway. Tasman pretended to look confused and unaware of what was transpiring, faking his urgency as he walked into the light. But he had heard too much, and Tasman had a face that showed every thought, every emotion – just like his mother.

Victoria's eyes flashed wildly as Tasman appeared, startling her. She struggled to find the words to speak, clearly unable to place Tasman's name, before she eventually recalled.

'Hill! What are you doing here?' she screeched, piecing together that he was her graveyard shift reporter as she spoke. 'Of course, the night shift... everything's fine,' she said, attempting to maintain her composure as she looked to the floor, glistening from the smashed pieces of Harrison's award.

Harrison faced away, leaning himself over the sink, staring into his drink. Tasman had heard enough to know what he had stumbled upon and overheard; Harrison Marks was not just fighting with his boss, but he was fighting with his lover too.

'I'm sorry to intrude. I heard voices and then the smash... it's pretty unusual for anyone to be here at this time of night, so I thought I better check it out. I thought it might've been the afterparty of the awards or something, but I can see that I was wrong,' he paused, painfully aware of the awkwardness of the situation.

'Thank you, Hill. Everything is perfectly fine. I'll organise the cleaners to come by first thing in the morning to sort this out.'

'Are you sure?' Tasman asked again, hesitating as he stepped forward some more. He had seen his own mother and father at war and knew that sometimes a third party could change the temperature of the room just enough, to stop things from escalating. Sometimes, anyway.

Harrison finally turned around and leant on the kitchen bench still cluttered with cups and plates left to airdry. His face looked swollen and bloated. He stared at Tasman. His bright green eyes relayed so much more than his silence. He was letting Tasman know he had no place being here. It was time to go.

'Just a little too much to drink. Accidents happen. That will be all, thank you, ah Hill,' she said, dismissing him again.

Tasman collected the empty champagne bottle from the hallway and began walking back to his desk when he felt Victoria's hand tug at his arm from behind in the shadowed light.

'How long were you standing there?' she asked, in a lowered tone so only Tasman could hear, looking at the bottle in his hands. Victoria held his arm tightly as she spoke and didn't let go. Tasman had never seen her more serious or desperate for information.

'No time at all,' he lied. Tasman knew she didn't believe him. But she had to trust his word.

'Good,' she said surveying him, as she dropped her grip. 'Oh, and Hill, we wouldn't want to spoil Harrison's big night with stupid office gossip, would we?'

'No, of course not,' Tasman replied, shaking his head slightly, faking indifference.

'Excellent. Enjoy the rest of your shift,' she said, watching him suspiciously.

Victoria turned back towards the kitchen only for Harrison to charge into the hallway, shoving past Tasman as he rushed past. Harrison was completely out of control, thought Tasman.

Tasman watched Harrison leave, pushing through the Sapphire Times' glass doors to walk out into the light dusted rain and get into his car.

Tasman wondered if he should run out to him, offering him a ride home or to call a cab, after all, Harrison was beyond inebriated. The rumours of Harrison being a high-functioning alcoholic were true. But that didn't mean he could drink and drive. He could kill himself, or worse, someone else.

As Tasman hesitated, Harrison's car roared to life, and within an instant the screech of its tyres against the wet driveway echoed loudly, the car fishtailing out onto the road. He was gone. Tasman considered calling Harrison back, to try to reason with him. As he reached for his phone Victoria appeared at his desk.

'Victoria – Harrison just left. I don't think he's in any state to-,' he began, but Victoria waved her hand dismissing Tasman, taking his phone and gently placing it back down onto the table.

'Like I said, we wouldn't want anything to ruin Harrison's big night, would we?' she said calmly. Tasman was speechless. 'Oh and one more thing, Hill. Excellent work with that truck rollover story,' she said, faking a smile as she looked at Tasman's swollen eye and down to his bruised neck.

Tasman knew she was being suspiciously attentive and overly kind towards him, which only cemented that what he suspected he had witnessed between Harrison and her and was right. It was an illicit affair.

'I trust we will see you at tomorrow's editorial. Don't be late,' she said casually as she walked towards the foyer.

Tasman considered her offer for a moment before he answered. 'Ah, yes, absolutely. I'll be there,' he replied, feeling completely astonished at what had just transpired.

'Good. Welcome to the day shift, Hill,' she replied as she walked through the glass foyer doors to the waiting cab outside.

CHAPTER EIGHT

TASMAN WOKE SLOUCHED OVER his desk to the smell of hot coffee. He jolted upright and felt stiff at the sudden movement. It was morning and Tasman knew he had been sleeping far longer than he wanted to admit.

'Shit, what time is it?' he said, rubbing his eyes, before wincing in pain a little. He focused on Zaylee standing above him, offering the drink.

'Yeah, Hill, usually on the night shift you're meant to work, not nap,' Zaylee teased. Tasman looked at the clock, Griffo was long gone.

'Relax, I'm early,' she said as she sat down. 'I've got that piece on the hospital waiting time blowout. I'm trying to finish up before this morning's meeting,' she stopped, looking at Tasman with concern. He strained his eyes. He was barely listening to anything Zaylee was saying, his mind still thinking back to Victoria and Harrison, and then his suspiciously timed promotion.

Zaylee noted Tasman's disinterest.

'Wow, your face. It's getting worse - is that even possible? Have you seen a doctor yet?' she asked, staring directly at his eye and then down at the bruising on his neck.

'Ah. No. Not yet. It's on the to-do list,' lied Tasman. If he told himself he was fine, it might eventually be true. 'How was last night?' Tasman asked, subtly checking his breath and reflection in the glass windows near his desk.

'Oh, you know, it was exactly what we all expected. Harrison Marks this, awards that. Applause. More applause. Yawn,' she summarised. 'Just watching Marks was a whole other form of entertainment. The guy is getting worse. He was plastered by the time his acceptance speech rolled around at the end...

anyway, enough about that. So, I take it that your little nap means you had a rough graveyard shift?'

'Yeah, something like that,' he hesitated for a moment. 'Actually, something did happen,' he continued leaning forward in a hushed tone, aware of the reporters filing into the newsroom. 'Victoria kind of promoted me last night.' He couldn't hide the optimism on his face, despite it being a payoff.

'Wait, what? Hang on. You're still here intentionally? Talk about burying the lead, Hill!' she yelled, struggling to contain her excitement as she whacked him on the back affectionately before instantly apologising - looking at his bruises again.

'Here's the thing though. She tells me this – after I see her and Harrison fighting in the staff kitchen. It's to keep me quiet,' he concluded, his grin fading.

'Wait, so she came back here after the awards? I thought they were all going to the afterparty in town,' said Zaylee, furrowing her brow as she took the chair of the intern right before he could sit down at the spare desk near Tasman.

'I heard them shouting from the other side of the hall, they were mid-fight,' he continued, Zaylee leaning forward as though she had just heard something incredible. She adjusted slightly. Tasman knew he needed to shower.

'So, I'm standing in the hallway, and I see Harrison smash his award, shatters it. He was blind drunk. Harrison and Victoria were arguing over his role here, and something about Harrison not feeling appreciated,' summarised Tasman. He considered revealing that he suspected Victoria and Harrison were having an affair, but thought better of it. No one needed to know, right now anyway.

'Then Victoria asked me to keep it quiet. Next minute Harrison storms out and then that was it. He got in his car and raced off. Victoria acted like it was all nothing, but then on her way out the door told me to be here for the meeting.'

'Oh my God,' gasped Zaylee much too loudly, drawing attention to them in the room's corner. 'Harrison Marks? Not appreciated?' she scoffed in disbelief. 'This guy is just unbelievable.' Zaylee looked at Tasman, she instantly noticed the strained smile across his face. 'So, what's the problem with you then?' she pushed.

Damn, she was good, thought Tasman. It was as though Zaylee could read his mind at times.

'Well, the only reason I'm here is because of what I've seen, and what I've heard. Victoria's clearly just trying to keep me on the side,' said Tasman, as he considered how much he had wanted to be promoted for his work, not for the secrets he had stumbled upon.

Zaylee shrugged and folded her arms. 'Anyone else in your position would jump at this chance – I say you should chalk it up as a win. Victoria would never bring you onto the dayshift unless she knew you were up to it – and you've already proven yourself up on the mountain,' she said glancing at his bruised neck. 'It's also totally possible that the timing is all a coincidence, and you being around the office this week just reminded Victoria that you've served your time on the graveyard shift and...'

Tasman cut her off with a chuckle, snatching the cup from his desk.

'You know I don't believe in coincidences,' said Tasman, taking a long sip of the coffee.

'Well, let's just stop questioning fate and roll with it, shall we?' Zaylee replied, checking her watch. It was time for the morning editorial meeting once more. 'Oh and don't forget to move your car, Hill, remember how you almost died last time you made that mistake,' she teased.

'Lucky, I don't usually make the same mistake twice,' smiled Tasman as he walked to the boardroom.

REPORTERS SAT IN SILENCE around the long oak wooden table, many nursing hangovers from the awards the night before. Tasman looked around, partly anxious at the thought of another showdown with a cranky Harrison Marks, but he never arrived. Instead, Victoria gracefully entered the room and Townsend closed and locked the door behind her.

'Are we all here? No? Well, too bad. You know the drill,' said Victoria as she took her seat at the top of the long boardroom table. Her appearance was immaculate, as though she had enjoyed a complete night's sleep instead of fighting with her lover in the hallways of the Times at night. Tasman's mouth went dry as he relived the memory.

'Good morning, everyone,' said Victoria, formally with a forced-looking, strained smile. 'In case you missed the news – a big congratulations again to Marks for taking out his fourth Golden Quill,' she continued, as Tasman watched her scan the room, before pausing at the empty seat next to Townsend. She carried on.

'Now, despite the joyful news, on a serious note, Head Office has approved security patrols to recommence around the office in light of some new complaints relating to our reporting...' she said, glancing at Tasman's neck and pausing for a moment, as though she had lost her train of thought entirely.

The entire room waited for Victoria to continue when Richard Grayson, a young, general news reporter took the opportunity to interject.

'Before we move on, just quickly, I tried calling Marks this morning, and it went straight to voicemail,' said Grayson excitedly, looking around the room. 'Marks is probably on the other side of the country by now, still partying. He's the only one here who can get away with it,' he said before catching himself, and sinking into his seat a little with embarrassment.

Victoria had snapped out of her daydream and shot Grayson a piercing stare. Zaylee rolled her eyes at Tasman, mouthing "idiot" in response.

'We will congratulate Marks again when we see him next,' said Victoria, regaining control of the meeting before nodding to Townsend to continue. He sat up so enthusiastically it reminded Tasman of an overeager jumping Jack Russell.

As reporters gave updates around the room, the police scanner erupted, allowing a reporter sitting next to Tasman to take a deep breath before it was her turn to pitch. The scanner was intrusively loud, and the room felt silent to listen – something that only ever happened when a truly significant event was unfolding.

'Reporting a suspicious fire in progress at the Ranges National Park. We have three trucks on scene working to contain the fire now,' said the voice.

'Received. Copy that," said another voice, a woman working the dispatch, the urgency undeniable in their tone.

'Confirming crews at Newhaven, Ranges Central, and Ranges City turning out to assist. Standing by for next update over containment status.'

The crackling voice responded. 'Copy. Fire remains out of control, burning across bushland and scrub, teams are evacuating nearby residents. We have also a visual on a car, ignition point. Appears suspicious. We'll need the arson chemist and police to attend.'

'Officer, do we have confirmation over occupants in the vehicle? Is ambulance required?' the woman replied before a long pause.

'We have no visual on occupants, car is fully alight, nil survival possible,' the man eventually confirmed.

The buzzing of the radio continued, and Townsend sprang into action. Everyone in the room could smell the story unfolding. It was what they all lived for.

'Right. Suspicious fire tearing through beloved tourist hotspot the Ranges National Park,' Townsend shouted, clapping his hands together. 'Grayson, I need you to grab a snapper and head off now,' he said, pointing straight at the reporter who had already stood up, self-appointing himself to the story.

'Thanks, Townsend, but Hill will cover this,' said Victoria, intervening coolly, as though the forgotten night reporter was an obvious choice. The entire room, including Tasman, sat speechless. They were stunned.

Townsend's mouth was agape, shaking his head with uncertainty, believing Victoria had misspoken.

'Victoria, Hill has just come off the graveyard shift and I'm sure Grayson can swing this, he's -,' he politely argued, his eyes bulging as he looked to the other stunned faces in the room.

'No. I said Hill, I think that was pretty clear,' said Victoria, irritated and standing from her chair. 'Hill - I'm assuming you're perfectly available to pull a double shift?' she continued, looking directly at him.

Tasman looked at Zaylee in disbelief and she shrugged in response.

'Yes. Absolutely,' Tasman replied quickly, with a rush of excitement flooding through his body.

'Good. Get going,' said Victoria, ignoring Townsend as he sulked, slipping back into his chair while scribbling into his notebook.

Tasman moved quickly from the room, as though the gift of his chance to cover the story could be taken from him, just as quickly as it was given.

An older photographer, Leigh Lindsay, followed, collecting his camera and checking the number of spare batteries in his bag as he struggled to keep pace behind Tasman who headed for the car park.

They climbed into the old news van and Tasman's mind was racing. He knew one thing for certain - that this opportunity was all thanks to one person, Harrison Marks.

CHAPTER NINE

TASMAN WAS SURE he had just run a red light as he sped towards the fire. His hands felt like jelly as he battled the excitement and desperation he felt inside. He navigated the bends to the top of the Ranges National Park as Lindsay sat in the passenger seat, explaining his unsuccessful and tumultuous online dating life. Tasman was not in the state of mind to listen.

Lindsay was mid-forties and had lived in the Ranges his entire life. It was his home, and he adored it. He was the type of person who would stop on the street and talk to anyone in the middle of a story, whether they wanted him to or not.

They followed the sight of the smoke up the mountain, passing through the twists and turns of the freshly wet road. Tasman wondered if the rolling rainfall had actually saved the Ranges National Park from completely burning up altogether. It was the city's treasure, beautiful and irreplaceable.

Tasman's phone rang, the loudspeaker echoing throughout the car, finally breaking Lindsay's rambling as he answered.

Tasman held his breath as he realised it was Townsend.

'Hill. Just so you know, I'm expecting some copy on this as soon as you can, right? I don't really understand why you're on this job, but I'm expecting results. So, you know, don't fuck it up, got it?' he barked.

'Right. Got it. Thanks for that,' Tasman replied sarcastically, rolling his eyes to himself.

'Oh, Townsend, it's Lindsay here,' said Lindsay, yelling into the car's microphone. 'I think the reception is breaking up! OK! Yep. It is. Okay then bye!' Lindsay chimed without waiting for Townsend to respond as he ended the call.

The move took Tasman by surprise. Maybe Lindsay wasn't such a pain after all, thought Tasman.

'That bloke is a dead set dickhead,' concluded Lindsay as he checked the settings on his camera casually.

Lindsay paused for a moment after the comment, pretending to take in the scenery.

'He's a real pleasant bloke. Reminds me of Eric Gleeson. He was a fucking dickhead too,' he scoffed. 'Of course, you're probably too young to know who I'm talking about. I'm showing my age now,' he laughed.

Tasman smiled politely, desperate to maintain his focus on the story he was chasing, but his mind was being pulled sideways into the past.

Tasman, of course, knew of the great Eric Gleeson. He was his father. Tasman wondered what his old man would think to know he was chasing his first big story for the Times. Tasman was only eight years old when he knew he wanted to be a journalist. He had idolised his father for as long as he could remember.

Eric Gleeson had carved out one of the most successful journalism careers in the country. He was bold. Unapologetic. And broke some of the most historic stories not just in the Ranges, but in the country. He was famous for his work and Tasman idolised him for it. Everyone did.

As a young boy, all Tasman had wanted was to make his father proud, but Eric Gleeson would quickly toss his son's imagined news stories he had spent days drafting aside, leaving it in a pile, ignored. Tasman could never make sense of his own father's aversion to him, and he never forgot the day he discovered his latest article stuffed into the bin in his father's study. It had broken his heart. But Tasman gave his father a million chances to be the man he deserved, as only a child can do. His mother had tried to protect Tasman and offer him all the love in the world, but the rejection of his own father was something from which she could not save him.

It was less than a year after his father had left them, abandoning his own family to run off with a younger woman to the other side of the country, when he suddenly died. He never saw his mother cry, both when he left them or when she finally got the phone call from his mistress to tell her he was dead.

It had been just Tasman and his mother ever since, but then, everything changed again, men and marriages came and went from their lives, and now Tasman was more alone than ever before.

Tasman often recalled the last conversation he had with his father before he had left them. Before his death. Just a young boy, Tasman had spent hours sitting and reading over his father's published articles and notebooks, amazed at the shorthand he effortlessly jotted down. Words. Codes. All equating to stories broken, uncovered.

When Tasman failed his pen licence test at primary school, unable to provide the detail and control of the pen required for eloquent and neat writing, Tasman had feared to tell him. When his report card revealed his failure, Tasman would hold on to his last words to him.

'See? How could you be a proper journalist if you can't even write like one?' he had said, his words a searing burn to a child desperate to impress his own father.

Tasman had left the room, trying to hide his tears. Remembering the doubt he placed on himself that he would never be smart enough to take on the code breaking language of a true journalist. It was another slap in the face for his dreams. But things were different now.

Sometimes Tasman wished he could tell his eight-year-old self that he would become one of the few remaining reporters to know how to write in short-hand, a fitting middle finger to his old man. Tasman had taken it as an elective class at university, and even when the class was cancelled due to a lack of student numbers, he managed to find a tutor to learn it himself, just in case. He didn't just want to be a good journalist, he wanted to be exceptional.

Tasman knew he had never really dealt with his grief. The anger Tasman felt about how he and his mother were treated always overshadowed any sadness.

As a teenager, Tasman had wondered if his father's heart attack was the price he had paid for abandoning them. The swirl of emotions of hating and loving a parent was intense and consuming in only a way that a child on the verge of adolescence could really feel.

It was why Tasman had totally abandoned the Gleeson surname, instead only going by Hill, his mother's maiden name. He knew that if he was going to make it as a reporter and truly prove himself, he wanted to do it on his own and not because of who his father was. In fact, he didn't want to be a reporter, anything like him. If he ever had a family, nothing would stop him from being there for them - he would never repeat Eric Gleeson's mistakes.

But all these years later, here he was, still determined to prove to the dead man that he had been wrong. He was wrong for abandoning his family. He was wrong for crushing his child's dreams. Tasman was determined to make it to the top. Now he was driving to the most important story of his career. It was his moment right now.

They pulled up to a winding road of bright green tree ferns and trees, covered in the electric reflection of red and blue flashing lights shining in the smoke. It was a road that appeared out of nowhere, on the way to the top of the Ranges National Park Lookout.

Men and women in brilliant orange coveralls stood around the burnt-out frame of what was once a car with half a dozen fire trucks lining the winding road.

Tasman's chance to become the brilliant reporter he had so desperately wanted to be had finally arrived. And now, more than ever, he was ready for it.

WITHOUT HESITATION, Tasman got out of the news van and took in the scene before him. He was speechless. The fern lined forest, famous for its hundred shades of green and vibrancy, was now reduced to a black and charred, smouldering skeleton. He had expected the light and fresh rainforest air, but there was nothing but the stench of a damp smoke filled haze.

Tasman could taste the bitterness of the smoke. The spitting rain seemed to evoke the smell even stronger.

'Get a load of that,' said Lindsay, breaking the silence beginning to cough. 'I thought I forgot my inhaler for a moment.'

The police scanner crackled in the van, causing the entire vehicle to shake.

'Copy. Confirming at least 10 hectares burnt. Fire is contained and crews on scene. Fire point of origin appears suspicious. Destroyed vehicle is unoccupied. Requesting additional police assistance for boundary control of crime scene please, media has arrived,' said the woman's voice.

'It's a crime scene,' said Tasman to Lindsay, who was busy fiddling with his asthma inhaler. Tasman looked ahead at a woman in uniform hanging outside of a fire truck holding the radio. She was watching him from twenty metres away.

'Received, copy. Thanks,' another voice replied.

As Lindsay examined the burned surroundings and began shooting Tasman hung back, attempting to quickly make himself look presentable brushing his hair through his fingers, while the light rain continued to damper his cheap suit.

Tasman was nervous, and his imposter syndrome was at an all-time high. He reminded himself of a high school student on work experience, it was his first time out on the road, especially during daylight hours. He needed to at least fake some kind of confidence if he was going to get anywhere.

'Well, are you going to just stand there?' asked Lindsay, looking at Tasman up and down.

Tasman swallowed his nerves and approached the police tape positioned at the entrance of a dirt road, easily missed amongst the banners of towering trees across the Ranges National Park. Tasman's notebook open, he began scribbling shorthand of what he could see.

Almost the entire side of the track was burned. While along the other, it was still untouched, filled with dense rainforest that carried on for kilometres, wrapping itself around the large and famous mountain top full of hiking, running, and camping tracks. It was one of those picturesque places of beauty by day, isolated and eerie by night.

As Tasman looked around, he knew it was a miracle the rainfall stopped the entire mountain from going up in flames. He stared at the charred vehicle and wondered how it came to be there. He couldn't place it, but it looked oddly familiar somehow. As though he had seen it in a dream or déjà vu.

A young male police officer stood in uniform blocking the track, he couldn't have been older than 25. Tasman could tell he had been positioned along the tape for some time, with his police-issued heavy-duty raincoat saturated on his shoulders and back.

The officer was speaking politely with two elderly women dressed in bright lycra from head to toe, out for their morning walk clutching umbrellas. It was clear they were much more interested in finding out what had happened at the attraction than their exercise routine.

As Tasman approached, he could hear the officer telling the women that the fire had been brought under control, just in time.

'We evacuated the neighbouring homes on the mountain as a precaution, but we're just lucky the fire didn't take a hold faster. Think this rain helped the firefighters save the day,' Tasman heard the officer say.

'Oh, thank God,' replied one of the grey-haired women.

'Well, that's good news,' said Tasman as he moved closer to them, attempting to find a way into the conversation. The officer barely looked at him and Tasman felt like a pest.

'And that car... just awful. You know, I bet it was those teenagers causing trouble again. They're always coming up here having parties in the bush. We hear them at all hours of the night, echoing across the mountain,' said the other woman.

'Thanks, Ma'am, I will pass that on to the detectives,' said the officer politely.

'Good. We will leave you all to it,' said the first woman, acknowledging Tasman was waiting to speak to them. They continued their walk, keeping a slow pace down an unscathed mountain trail.

The officer turned to Tasman, his waterproof coat beginning to drip from the shoulders.

‘Sir, you’ll need to move along or return to your vehicle,’ said the officer, gesturing for Tasman to move back.

‘I’m actually here for the fire. I’m Tasman Hill, with the... Sapphire Times,’ Tasman began as he searched through his satchel, desperate to locate a business card to prove his credentials.

‘Yes. I gathered that,’ the officer replied light-heartedly for a moment as he looked past Tasman to the decorated Sapphire Times news van.

‘Yes. Exactly,’ replied Tasman, turning back to the officer who had regained his serious, polite-yet-dismissive demeanour. Tasman wondered if his own inexperience was obvious to the officer who was years younger than he was. Tasman looked at his name badge, it read Constable Rohan Ashley.

Before Tasman could continue talking, Constable Ashley leapt from his post alarmed by Lindsay who had walked straight under the police tape, beginning to snap photographs of the burned car wreckage and forest surrounding it.

‘Hey! You can’t go down there! It’s restricted! It’s a crime scene! Get out of there!’ Constable Ashley yelled, shaking his head as he ran towards Lindsay.

The officer marched Lindsay back to the other side of the police tape, Lindsay appeared completely unfazed by the ordeal. It wasn’t the first time he had been frogmarched from a restricted area.

‘So, you mentioned this is a crime scene?’ said Tasman, desperate for the conversation to continue. ‘Is there someone I could speak to about what’s happened here?’ he asked, peering over Constable Ashley’s shoulders at the shell of the destroyed car.

Tasman needed an interview with some hard facts for his story, and he needed it now.

Constable Ashley looked at Tasman’s bruised eye suspiciously.

‘You’re the guy from the truck crash. I knew I had seen your face before,’ he replied with interest, before considering Tasman’s request for a moment. ‘Look, I’ll see who is around to help you out, but I can’t promise anything. You might be waiting a while.’

Constable Ashley walked several steps from where they had been standing and radioed a message, looking back, watching Tasman through his peripheral. He was helping him.

Tasman's face lifted. He would take anything he could get. 'No worries. I've got all day,' Tasman lied as he ignored two consecutive calls from Townsend.

Tasman watched and waited as firefighters continued to work, spraying trees and the charred forest. Tasman's palms began to sweat as he looked at the time. Thirty minutes had passed, and he still needed more information if he was going to have any kind of story to show for his effort. He looked around and Lindsay was leaning against a fern tree chatting with locals who had come to check out the scene. The photographer really could talk to anyone, anywhere, for hours.

Tasman's hopes lifted when he watched eagle-eyed as two plain clothed detectives finally approached the police tape, stepping underneath it to address Constable Ashley. The young officer quickly straightened up in their presence and he nodded towards Tasman.

'Tasman Hill?' asked the female detective as she walked to him confidently. She was middle-aged and wore a navy-blue tailored suit and white collared shirt, her brown hair tied back in a tight bun.

'Yes, that's right, I'm with the Sapphire Times,' said Tasman, reaching his hand out to shake, but the detective let the gesture hang in the air.

She said nothing as she looked Tasman over him and began removing light blue gloves used for examining a crime scene. Her more junior colleague, a man with a dark black beard and thick eyebrows, held an umbrella over her head and clutched a large black leather folder filled with documents. He looked at Tasman, his eyes narrow. Tasman couldn't help but notice that he and Tasman were wearing the same cheap brown suit, both damp from standing in the misted rain.

Tasman had no time to waste and broke the silence.

'I know you're probably used to dealing with Harrison Marks, but I'm covering for him today,' said Tasman, flicking open a fresh page of his notebook while standing as tall as he possibly could to exude confidence in the situation.

The detectives exchanged a glance between them. Tasman wondered if he had stated the obvious, of course he wasn't their usual contact. He looked young, green especially compared to Harrison.

The female detective inhaled sharply before she spoke.

'Right. I'm Detective Inspector Alexandra Watts and this is Detective Sergeant Robert Marshall,' she said in a dry, matter-of-fact manner. 'We've closed the area and all I can tell you right now is that this is a crime scene, so we won't be letting you, or your colleague anywhere near it right now,' she said looking at Lindsay still blindly in conversation with a group of bystanders. 'Get in touch with our media unit for anything further.'

The detectives turned to walk back to the scene.

'Hold on, Detective Inspector Watts, just a moment,' Tasman called after them. 'Is it possible for something on the record? We've got a major fire, a vehicle destroyed, a crime scene, and – what about the owner of the car – has anyone been hurt? It's clearly a highly suspicious incident,' he stated.

Watts stopped and raised her eyebrow in response. Tasman was unsure if she was impressed or completely irritated that she was dealing with an amateur.

'I'm just after anything you can say to help me paint the picture of what's happened and your investigation,' he pushed.

The detective considered his words for a moment and nodded at her partner in a private signal.

'Mr Hill, right now, this is all an active investigation. We have a dumped and burned car. We have a large fire that has broken out that thankfully was doused by the rainfall before it could destroy our iconic national park.'

Tasman furiously wrote down every detail as he looked from his notebook to the detective with intense attention.

'We are asking for anyone who may have witnessed anything suspicious in this area overnight to please come forward. That's all I've got for you right now, okay?' she said as she turned away. The conversation was over.

'And what about the driver? Is it a stolen car?' said Tasman, raising his voice in the hope she could still hear him.

Tasman watched as she pretended to look forward, tempted to ignore him, and despite murmurs from her partner, Watts walked back to him furiously.

'We are still accounting for their whereabouts. We will alert the media when we know more. Now please, let us get on with this investigation. You do your job, and we will do ours,' she said, allowing a forensic team wearing white coveralls to enter under the police tape.

Tasman wasted no time, taking out his phone to call Townsend to confirm the news, rushing his speech knowing that the Ranges Advocate could appear at any time to cover the story too. He was so distracted by the urgency of the task at hand he barely noticed he was standing in the worsening rain, his clothes now sticking to his skin.

'It's Hill – we can stick this one with an exclusive all over it. No one has it and no one knows – we've got an active crime scene up here. A driver is missing, and their car has been abandoned and torched. I've no idea how the Advocate has dropped the ball on this – they're nowhere to be seen.'

'Send me your words asap. Get your snapper to email those photos too. We've got nothing without the photos. We'll add it to the breaking story online,' replied Townsend before ending the call.

Tasman jumped into the news van, startling Lindsay who had taken the opportunity to sleep slumped on the passenger side door.

'What do you look so damn happy about? You interrupted my nap!' Lindsay scoffed grumpily as he sat up and rubbed his cheeks.

'Send the link to those photos to the COS desk now. The story will run asap,' directed Tasman. 'It's our exclusive,' he said proudly as he hit the keys on his laptop while sitting in the driver's seat.

'Righto. You're the boss,' replied Lindsay. Tasman couldn't believe how great it felt to hear that expression.

Tasman's story had been online for over an hour when the Ranges Advocate finally arrived on scene, their police scanner had malfunctioned, and their newsroom didn't catch wind of the fire until the Times' story had broken. And it was Tasman who broke it.

CHAPTER TEN

THE SUN WAS SETTING, and the smell of smoke stained the air across the city. Tasman had sat in the old news van for hours, waiting to see if there was any sign of the driver of the dumped car. He couldn't risk leaving early and miss a crucial development - like the discovery of a body.

Tasman hypothesised what was happening behind the police tape, under the bright portable lights that had been rolled in to help investigators at the scene.

There wasn't a coroner arriving on scene to collect a body, thought Tasman as he calculated the possibilities in his mind. The driver of the dumped car, or a possible arsonist, had to be long gone.

The wind picked up, spraying a fresh light blanket of rain across the mountain, urging the remaining teams to begin the pack up of the area while a tow-truck loaded the melted vehicle.

He watched as the police and fire teams slowly left the scene, but Tasman took a double take at one woman - he had seen her before. The forensics team member was the last to walk back towards an unmarked white police van parked along the winding road and as she passed Tasman was certain - he had seen her in his father's news article scrapbooks – the same ones he had poured over hundreds of times as a child. He recognised the fiery curly red hair anywhere. Her name was Monica Sinn.

Now, desperate to succeed, Tasman's stomach twisted as he realised what he was about to do, how far he would go for the story he suddenly felt so protective over.

'Excuse me,' he said, hurrying towards Dr Sinn as she loaded a black hardcase of equipment into the back of the van. The woman jumped back holding her hands in front of her.

'Wow, good God, you scared me,' she said, standing back and placing her hand over her heart, still startled by Tasman's sudden appearance behind her.

'Sorry, let me introduce myself – my name is Tasman Hill, I'm writing up the story for the Sapphire Times,' he said.

Dr Sinn appeared disinterested and continued loading the van, water pooling on its opened boot door.

'I'm hoping you can spare just a moment to confirm a few details for me,' Tasman continued, ducking into the woman's view again. Again, she said nothing as she manoeuvred around him, lifting and stacking equipment.

And that was the moment Tasman realised he would do anything to succeed at this moment, at least.

'It's Sinn, right? Dr Monica Sinn? I think you might know my father,' said Tasman in desperation, as he began walking alongside her back towards the police tape.

'Excuse me? How do you know my name?' she finally replied, staring at him confused. She rightfully couldn't place Tasman.

'Eric Gleeson. He's my father, well, was my father,' said Tasman correcting himself. It felt so odd to speak his name aloud after so many years, thought Tasman.

'He kept a copy of the article he wrote for the Sherbrooke Serial Killer investigation. Your forensics solved the case, right?' he said hoping the flattery would give him some kind of advantage.

Dr Sinn stopped moving and thought for a moment. 'I haven't heard that name in a long time,' she mused.

Tasman looked around realising the reporter from the Ranges Advocate had been watching him, peering over to see if she was about to miss a scoop or not and weighing up whether to follow and intervene. Tasman moved to obscure her view of his conversation.

'I take it you are his son then, following in his footsteps I see,' as she glanced at Tasman's notebook and pen in hand. 'Well tell him I said hello,' she said attempting to walk away once more before Tasman raced back to her side, narrowly avoiding a massive puddle of mud.

'He actually passed away, a few years back now. Heart attack.'

'I'm so sorry to hear,' she said stopping, suddenly changing her demeanour, as if she had let her walls down a little too easily, and just as quickly decided to correct her mistake.

'Listen, I know you don't know me. I may very well be grasping at straws here, but please, if there's anything you might be able to tell me give me a call,' said Tasman as he handed her his business card.

'I am really sorry about your dad. I owed him for how my career turned out after his article. I never got to thank him,' she paused for a moment, considering her words and looking around them, checking if they would be overheard. 'Can I offer you some advice?' she said looking at Tasman and back at Lindsay who was leaned up against the news van with his camera, streaming a sitcom from Netflix too loudly from his phone.

'This one might be a little bit closer to home than you realise, okay?' she said in a lowered tone.

'What do you mean exactly?' he asked, puzzled by the unusual comment.

'I've got to get back to it. Sorry I couldn't be of more help. Good luck,' she said breaking eye contact. Before Tasman could utter another word, she had walked away, passing through a group of firefighters changing their shift. He looked past the group and realised she had already gotten into the forensics van, and she was gone.

As the beeping tow-truck approached, Tasman called to Lindsay who was barely paying attention to the vehicle reversing out of the scene with the charred remains of the vehicle strapped on board.

'Mate! Get it! Get the shot!' Tasman yelled as the beeping grew louder and louder. Lindsay eventually glanced up from his phone and snapped into action just in time to photograph the melted remains of the car tied to the truck moving past. Tasman also had his phone, filming the scene before his arms shook, the hairs on his neck standing tall and he audibly gasped, although the sound of the truck echoed so loudly no one would have heard it. Tasman knew he wasn't mistaken.

Behind the police tape, Tasman hadn't been close enough to see the charred, twisted and, melted number plate before. But now it was clear. He could see through the black ash the personalised, tacky GOLDN number plates he had scoffed at so many times in the Sapphire Times parking lot.

His stomach leapt as the gravity of the situation hit Tasman hard in the face as he sucked in more smoky air than he wanted.

Tasman finally understood, Dr Sinn had tried to warn him. The story *was* close to home. And the story was about none other than one of their own.

The car belonged to Harrison Marks.

'MATE, IS HARRISON BACK YET?' asked Tasman calling from in the news van on his way back to the office. Tasman had asked Lindsay to drive, as Tasman's stomach leapt at the realisation of what was happening.

Lindsay hummed casually as he drove, completely undeterred by the situation as though he had seen and heard every bad news story there was, and one about someone he knew was of course, par for the course and bound to happen eventually.

'What? Are you serious, mate?' barked Townsend. 'If you think you're going to handball this back to Marks, forget it. Victoria assigned this to you. You can bloody well see it through!'

'No. Not that,' interrupted Tasman. Tasman could feel sweat on his forehead as he waited frustrated for Townsend to listen 'Has anyone seen or heard from, him today?'

'No, Hill! He's still off on another one of his award-win-benders. And lucky you, otherwise you wouldn't be doing this yarn in a million years,' Townsend snapped.

'If you would let me speak - the car – on the mountain – it's Harrison's-,' but it was too late. Townsend had already ended the call.

Tasman sat dumbfounded at the conversation and turned to Lindsay who continued to hum.

'Aren't you at all bothered by this?' said Tasman coldly, judging Lindsay's casual and careless attitude. 'Harrison could be missing. He could be –,' he couldn't say the word before Lindsay happily interrupted.

'Dead?' said Lindsay, looking at Tasman who was speechless at the photographer's crassness. 'What?' he shrugged, noting Tasman's shocked expression. 'We've all got to go sometime. And we're talking about Marks. The guy plays with fire. Eventually, you're going to get burned.'

CHAPTER ELEVEN

TASMAN BURST THROUGH THE DOORS of the Sapphire Times and Townsend appeared, blocking his path to Victoria's office.

'Have you got an update for this car fire story or what?' said Townsend, as Tasman manoeuvred past him without stopping.

'I'm going to need to speak to Victoria,' replied Tasman, ignoring Townsend's fury, moving past him to open the door of Victoria's office when Detective Inspector Watts appeared, opening it for him. Both Victoria and Detective Sergeant Marshall were already inside, Marshall sat at the small meeting table, taking notes.

'Mr Hill - please give us a minute,' said Victoria, her eyes locked on him, furious at the intrusion as he entered, looking at the detectives with wild eyes. Victoria closed the door in Tasman's face.

Tasman sat distracted, impatiently waiting at his desk.

'Are you okay, Hill?' questioned Zaylee, looking over his face with concern.

'Yeah...,' he said, distracted as he stared at Victoria's office door.

Tasman looked around nervously, lowering his voice while his eyes darted to the intern perpetually eavesdropping nearby.

'Okay. Now I'm actually concerned. What the hell is going on with you? You look like you're freaking out,' she said, spinning Tasman's chair around and clicking her fingers in front of his face.

'That car up at the Ranges. I think it's... Harrison's,' said Tasman, desperate to keep his voice down.

'What? You're kidding!' said Zaylee in disbelief.

'It has his personalised plates, well, what's left of them anyway. Think about it. No one has seen or heard from him today either, right?'

Tasman and Zaylee stared at each other in stunned silence before Victoria's office doors sprung open.

'Oh, shit Hill, you're up,' said Zaylee.

Watts stepped outside of the office with Victoria, their eyes searching for a target before locking directly on Tasman as they spoke in hushed tones. Victoria's expression remained steely, calm.

'Hill, come in please,' commanded Victoria. As Tasman moved, the rest of the newsroom watched on.

Townsend followed Tasman into Victoria's office.

'Hill, I understand you have already met Detective Inspector Watts and Detective Sergeant Marshall,' she began, gesturing for Tasman to sit, leaving Townsend to awkwardly stand next to her desk.

'There has been a concerning development with your story. Before we go any further, I want to make clear we will need to keep this information within these four walls... for now.'

'Of course,' said Tasman nervously, already knowing what was about to be said.

'We will cut straight to the point, shall we?' said Marshall, his voice much lower than Tasman had expected. 'The owner of the vehicle is missing. We've spent some time since we first met today confirming their last movements and whereabouts. And that has brought us to this office. Are you following where I'm going with this?'

Tasman paused for a moment and matched the seriousness in the detective's tone.

'It's Harrison's, isn't it?'

'We understand Mr Marks attended the Golden Quill Awards, then you and Ms Stanley can verify you were here with him late that night?' asked Watts.

'Yes, that's right. I usually work the night shift... I saw him here after the awards,' replied Tasman, feeling Victoria's stare.

'Was there anything unusual about Mr Marks' behaviour, or anything we should know?' Watts continued.

'Only that he had a few drinks too many... and then he left in a hurry. The last I saw was he was fishtailing it out of here onto the highway,' said Tasman, deliberately avoiding meeting Victoria's gaze.

'We can, of course, provide CCTV vision from the entrance if that is helpful,' interrupted Victoria.

Tasman wondered if Marshall could tell he was omitting information, as he watched him jot down line after line of notes from the conversation. The fight Tasman witnessed between Harrison and Victoria flashed through his mind. He was willing to dance around the exact, intricate details of the truth, at least for now.

'We're prepared to provide whatever you need,' said Victoria loudly.

The room fell silent, and Tasman watched as the detectives took their time observing them in the discomfort.

'Right well, if you think of anything else... or if anyone has any idea why Harrison might have been up at the Ranges National Park at that time of morning, please let us know. We aren't ruling anything in or out at this stage,' said Marshall, standing slowly, while Watts sat for a moment longer, still watching them all. 'We understand this is a hard situation for you all here. However, we are still trying to contact his wife to let her know he is missing.'

Tasman peered over at Victoria. Her eyes seemed momentarily filled with tears.

'We haven't been able to contact her since this morning,' said Watts, glancing at her watch. 'There's a fair amount of work that needs to take place so we can take our best shot at finding Harrison as soon as possible,' she said, reassuringly.

'Wait. Cressida is also missing?' asked Victoria, her voice breaking into a louder, unexpectedly alarmed tone, contrasting her usual calm exterior.

'No. Gosh no,' said Watts, shaking her head. 'No one said *missing*. We are just having some difficulty reaching her urgently, which is holding up our investigation. You know, check under every rock first. It's standard protocol,

Ms Stanley,' said Watts, smiling gently. 'Look, we know this is your colleague we are talking about,' she said, leaning on Victoria's desk. Townsend moved further along the couch to remain in sight.

'I'm certain that this is something that you're probably wanting to run in the paper as soon as we walk out of this room. But what we are asking is that you give us time to continue our investigation and to rule out that Harrison is missing at all,' said Watts, smiling gently at Tasman and Victoria.

'Publish what you need to, but we just ask that you leave out his identity until we reach his wife. If Harrison is... his family must be told first.'

Victoria and Tasman nodded.

'Well, certainly we will appoint one of our more experienced reporters, given the sensitivities, the scale,' began Townsend, standing awkwardly to the side of Victoria's marble white desk, shunning Tasman.

'That is something we can surely discuss in private in a moment,' hissed Victoria. Townsend sat down immediately, cowering like a naughty puppy.

'Detectives, we will, of course, take your concerns and requests into account,' said Victoria in agreement, warmly standing at her desk to shake their hands.

Tasman swallowed hard. His mind raced back to that night after the awards and whether Victoria had disclosed to the detectives what had happened between her and Harrison in the kitchen before he drove off that night.

'Detectives, given our colleague, our friend is missing, and the favour you're asking of us, is there any room for some information to be ah, shared with us in advance?' said Townsend. He had no shame, thought Tasman, before he quickly recalled how he had used his own father's name to get information from Dr Sinn just hours earlier.

Marshall let out an audible scoff in response.

'We're focused on finding Mr Marks and on this investigation, not cutting deals with reporters on stories,' said Watts bluntly. Marshall silently scolded Townsend in agreement. Townsend's ears turned a deep red as he realised his error in judgement.

Victoria spoke up. 'I can assure you Detectives that our reporter Tasman Hill here will handle the situation delicately. He'll be covering this should it develop any further,' she said, opening the door for Watts and Marshall.

'Call us if you think of anything else we might need to know,' said Watts with a polite nod as they walked out of the office.

Victoria pointed at Tasman. 'Hill, head home and get some rest. We will see you tomorrow morning. I believe Townsend has found someone to cover your night shifts this week,' she said, gesturing towards Kyle the intern leaning on the back of his chair.

Before Tasman could speak, Victoria dismissed him and Townsend, who remained stunned at what had just transpired.

Tasman walked outside at the exact moment the rain picked up again. A rush of water flooded the carpark, including the empty reserved space belonging to Harrison.

As he rushed back to the old news van to avoid the downpour, lightning cracked and lit up the sky in a blanket of purple. And that was when Tasman saw it, the unmarked police car still sitting outside of the Sapphire Times.

Detective Inspector Watts and Detective Sergeant Marshall were there, watching them. And waiting to see what happened next.

CHAPTER TWELVE

ONE DAY GONE

TASMAN BARELY SLEPT THAT NIGHT. The sound of pounding rain on his apartment roof and the force of it hitting the city street below left him tossing and turning for hours. He had finally made it into the day shift, but it was all at the cost of his colleague's disappearance.

Tasman was benefiting from someone else's bad news, someone else's nightmare. But that was what the news was. Every single day, and he knew and understood that irony.

Tasman woke to the sound of his phone ringing just after 6am. He already knew it was his mother, calling again on her way to volunteer at the hospital, delivering tea and coffee to patients.

It was hard to stay mad at a saint, he thought. Sending the call to voicemail, he instantly felt guilty and listened to the message.

'Honey, I've seen the papers - your story is on the front page! I've taken it and started a scrapbook of you,' she said. 'I'm so proud of you. Please call me. I would love to hear all about it. Please, darling. Love you.'

Rolling into the mattress, Tasman couldn't face hearing her voice. He looked at his text chain with Zaylee and Peter. There was still no sign of Harrison. It was as though he was already a ghost, a figure that no one could reach, who may very well be watching on, enjoying the commotion he was causing. Or he could really be dead.

The Detectives had asked for at least 24 hours before the Sapphire Times named Harrison as a missing person, with his car discovered destroyed and the cause of the suspicious blaze up at the iconic Ranges National Park. Tasman wondered how generous Victoria would be with that deal. She would do anything for an exclusive and to beat the Ranges Advocate.

The phone rang again, Tasman lifted his face from the mattress, expecting a second, follow-up call from his mother but instead he jumped, realising it was Jet Townsend.

'Hill, get yourself to the Sapphire Ranges Police Headquarters right now. There's a press conference on the missing... person. Right, get down there now, got it?' said Townsend, barking down the phone.

'Got it, of course. I'll be there,' Tasman said, scrambling to get dressed. 'Is there any word on... Harrison?' he asked slowly, holding his breath and waiting as his name hung in the air.

Seconds passed in silence. Tasman looked at his phone, expecting Townsend had just ended the call in his usual fury, but he was still there.

'No. Still nothing. He's... just disappeared. All I've been told is that the police are moving with the case fast... and they've called the press conference. Victoria wants you there so, just get there.'

Tasman knew what Townsend was thinking. With every hour that passed, the chances of finding Harrison were becoming less likely.

He pulled on his jacket, looking outside the apartment window to see the rain hit the streets below. The big wet had settled in.

'Ever since the rain arrived, my entire world has been turned upside down,' thought Tasman.

He stood outside the Sapphire Ranges Police Headquarters with his branded news umbrella, positioning himself with the small but growing media pack. Journalists he recognised from across the city stood waiting, clueless of the real, hidden story beneath it all - that one of their own was missing.

'The Times did alright breaking the fire yarn,' said Rick Tancred, a reporter from the Ranges Advocate. He had the same thick British accent and smug, confident smile as Harrison. For a moment, he thought it was actually him.

'I've never seen you before. Are you new? Didn't think they sent the interns to these jobs on their own,' Tancred quipped, looking over Tasman like a bouncer at a nightclub.

'I guess it's my lucky day,' Tasman replied sarcastically.

Tasman turned back to the front doors of the building as television news crews continued to set up their cameras under the only shred of cover outside the steps of the old white brick police headquarters. The group waited waiting for the press conference to begin, grateful to be sheltered by the rain surrounding them.

Tasman knew the reporter's reputation. Rick Tancred was completely free of any morals or ethics - he was a perfect fit for the Ranges Advocate. Eric Gleeson would've like him, thought Tasman.

'I guess there's a vacancy coming up soon anyway,' the same reporter said in a low, hushed tone behind Tasman.

Tasman froze. Tancred knew.

'What did you just say?' said Tasman, turning immediately to face Tancred, his eyes wide, as though a switch had been flicked inside of him.

The reporter smiled knowingly at the reaction. He was enjoying himself.

'Don't look at me! I didn't say a word,' shrugged Tancred. 'Wow, mate. Are you alright? You look like you've been through hell and back,' he said, faking sincerity while pointing at Tasman's fading black eye and bruised neck. 'Lucky you're not on camera for those interviews the Times has been doing online. More of a face for radio, right?'

Tasman knew Tancred was deliberately provoking him.

Before they could exchange another word, Detective Inspector Watts opened the glass reflective doors wide, followed by Detective Sergeant Marshall, fronting the cameras. She paused a moment to allow the cameras to roll, before confidently beginning to speak to the media pack.

'Good morning. I'm Detective Inspector Alexandra Watts. I am leading the investigation into the suspicious blaze that caused a significant fire at the Ranges National Park in the early hours of yesterday morning,' she began, addressing the cameras and the journalists surrounding her.

'We can now confirm that the car that was found at the scene was the ignition point and source of the fire that destroyed at least ten hectares of the forest.

'Nearby homes were evacuated. And luckily none came under fire thanks to the work of the fast-acting firefighters who responded. Unfortunately, the owner of the vehicle, a local man aged in his late 30s, was not located at the scene and -,' she continued.

'The missing man - do you believe he is dead?' Tancred suddenly interjected with a look of pure arrogance that made Tasman want to knock him out.

Watts took a moment before continuing, staring straight ahead at the cameras, she had done this before thought Tasman.

'Our forensic teams have confirmed that no human remains were located inside the vehicle,' replied Watts, slightly irritated at the interruption.

Tasman let out a sigh of relief at hearing those words. Harrison wasn't inside the car, there was still a chance he was out there alive, somewhere.

'Our investigation remains in its early stages, however overnight we spoke with family members of the missing man and subsequently gained permission to access his phone records.'

Reporters watched on, holding phones recording every word, while Tasman continued to jot quotes down in shorthand.

'We can now confirm the man is indeed missing in what appears to be under suspicious circumstances.'

The media pack shifted slightly at the revelation. Although dealing with such serious and bad news was not itself something that shocked this crowd, reporters were used to bad news - they sought it out.

'And that missing man is journalist Harrison Marks - is that correct?' said Tancred loudly, staring straight at Watts before turning to Tasman with a slight smirk.

Watts' mouth was slightly agape as she lost her focus and turned to look at Tasman. She was stunned.

Watts believed we leaked Harrison's name, thought Tasman as he stared back at the detective.

Tasman could feel his arms and legs turn numb; he was furious. How did the Ranges Advocate already know about Harrison? Who had leaked his name? And here Tancred was, rubbing it in his face.

As the reporter repeated the question, Marshall stepped forward, nodding to Watts.

'We can confirm the 38-year-old Ranges City man involved is... journalist Harrison Marks,' said Marshall.

The change in atmosphere amongst the journalists at the press conference was immediate.

'We are urging anyone who may have seen or heard from Mr Marks on Thursday or the early hours of Friday morning to please come forward. We will today be launching a wide scale search of one section of the mountain near where his vehicle was located. That is all we have for now. Thank you, no further questions,' said Marshall, before both detectives turned and walked back inside the police station.

Within moments, the phones of those standing in the scrum buzzed and jumped to life, each with updates from the Ranges Advocate, somehow already breaking the story: one of the Sapphire Times' own star journalists was missing, feared dead.

Tasman looked up from his phone and realised almost all the reporters were watching him like hawks, as though he had more detailed information to share with them.

With disgust Tasman shook his head, walking with his notebook and pen in hand as he shoved past Tancred to make his way out the scrum and into the rain, sucking in the smoky air hard.

Tasman took his phone and dialled. For a moment he was utterly speechless but continued when Victoria finally answered.

'They know. They know it's Harrison,' he said.

CHAPTER THIRTEEN

TWO DAYS GONE

THE NEXT MORNING Tasman watched as dozens of search and rescue teams pulled on fluorescent coveralls under pop-up canopies, preparing to scour the dense bushland for any sign of Harrison. The rain was already pooling on the tarpaulin, spilling over the sides. The sense of urgency was clear. If Harrison was somewhere nearby and alive, he needed to be found, and it needed to be now.

Police officers stood directing teams to maps of the Ranges National Park. Some were already placing precautionary body harnesses around their waists to protect them from the unexpected cliffs covered in bushland below. A helicopter circled above briefly before continuing, scouring above the thick terrain.

Detective Inspector Watts and Detective Sergeant Marshall appeared to give their orders before leaving the scene, their eyes meeting Tasman's accusingly as they passed by.

'We only want to be performing one rescue today,' said the Officer in Charge, gesturing towards the crews placing the guide ropes through their harnesses.

It was not uncommon for hikers to simply fall from the unexpected fern-covered cliffs, and the authorities could not risk another tragedy to one of their own.

'Teams need to be aware of the abrupt cliffs covered in trees. Some drops are hundreds of metres, so we will need only the most experienced crews in this section. Volunteers should stay in this green zone, closest to where we discovered the vehicle,' the man in a fluorescent yellow vest labelled OIC continued, pointing at the map.

'This rainfall has also put the mountain on alert for landslides - let your members know that they're notorious for blocking the tracks. And bringing down the 100-metre-tall gums with them. It's like it's the bloody wet season already.'

Members of the community arrived in dozens, waiting in the rain to sign up to assist with the search. Now that Harrison's name had been leaked, it was as though his disappearance had united the community to help. Even a community church group set up a BBQ tent to feed the police, search crews, and volunteers.

Tasman stood alongside the growing number of journalists and television crews, waiting to see if the star reporter had met his end. They did not have the sense of hope that the community was holding onto. The waiting media, Harrison's own colleagues, were visualising the bigger story. It was a habit hard to break, even when it was personal, thought Tasman.

Zaylee texted Tasman, urging him to call her.

'Edwards, what's going on?' he asked after she answered on the first ring.

'You haven't heard, have you?' she asked in disbelief.

'Oh my god, Hill! The leak - the one who gave Harrison's name to the Ranges Advocate - it was Townsend!' she squealed. 'He tried to use it as leverage for a top job at the Advocate. I always knew he had zero morals. He would be a perfect fit over there. Can you believe it? Absolute shithead. Victoria had him marched out of the newsroom by security just now. She made a beautiful scene of it and told him he would never work in this city again,' she said, speaking so quickly she had to gasp to catch her breath.

'How did she find out?' said Tasman in disbelief. He knew that Townsend would do anything to succeed but was still shocked Victoria's second-in-charge would risk his career just to get to a promotion.

'The Ranges Advocate editor called Victoria. Turns out they have a mutual code of conduct between them. He owed her a favour from way back when, apparently, but who cares? No one thinks it was us at all, so that's a relief,' she said.

'Well, I'm not so sure about that.' Tasman said. 'The Detectives running this thing down here aren't our biggest fans. You should've seen the look they gave me; they definitely think I leaked it.'

'It will work out. These things always do. I believe in Karma,' said Zaylee reassuringly.

Zaylee was a brilliant journalist and an even better pep-talker, thought Tasman.

Peter was the more relaxed and sarcastic opposite to Zaylee. Maybe that was why they were so perfect together, a good balance, and it made Tasman wish he had someone like that to go home to.

'Well, I'm relieved,' said Tasman. 'I hadn't heard shit all morning, and the silence was getting to me. It felt like I was suspect number one for a minute. But Townsend getting fired is up there with that intern who was blackmailing the local nightclub bouncers and bars into giving him free drinks in exchange for good reviews in the paper,' he joked.

'Man, I hate interns,' Zaylee scoffed. 'They are just sooooo ungrateful. Except for us, of course, we were perfection,' she laughed. 'How is everything up there on the mountain?' Zaylee's tone changed, as the conversation inevitably returned to the serious task Tasman was undertaking.

'I'm standing out here in the rain, under a spare canopy, watching good people search for Harrison. Being out here in the cold and seeing the constant heavy rain, I just don't know how he could survive being out here,' Tasman sighed. 'The volunteers are full of hope and determination. But I can tell the media here are secretly hoping for the worst. It's knowing the guy we are out here to find; you know? Usually when we have a story, the person means nothing to us. Now I'm borrowing his desk.'

Zaylee said nothing as she listened.

'There's also something about being out here because of him, because of Marks. I'm benefiting from his suspicious disappearance,' Tasman admitted.

'I know this is hard, Hill,' she replied. 'I don't envy you having to cover this. But I'm telling you, you can't wig out now. You have to keep it together. This is your shot. Look, let's meet tonight after your shift, okay? Debrief over drinks, you know the place.'

Time with Zaylee and Peter at The Lonely Squire was exactly what he needed, he thought.

Tasman turned and noticed a young brunette woman lined up in the community search and rescue information section of the tent.

She seemed to watch the media pack intently, interested in their work as they filmed and reported the scene. Wearing bright pink and orange runners, now covered in mud from the rainfall, she stood there with perfectly applied makeup, looking out of place compared to the other members of the community joining the search.

For a moment, Tasman felt certain the woman was looking directly at him. He turned around to see if he was mistaken, that someone that attractive was perhaps looking at someone standing right behind him. But as soon as he looked back, she was gone.

'Hill? Hello - are you still there? I swear for a mobile tower to be right up on that fucking mountain, your reception sucks,' Zaylee continued. She had been talking the entire time.

'Sorry. Yeah, I'm here,' said Tasman, momentarily confused at where the woman could have gone so quickly.

'And by the way - Harrison's disappearance has broken national news. It's all over the major networks and papers online. I'd say the heat is about to turn up on this tenfold,' said Zaylee, sounding concerned.

After everything that's gone on with Townsend this morning, Victoria's determined to claw back the story, given it's about our own bloody reporter. No pressure, though. I'm here to help, okay? Anyway, we'll see you tonight. Stay dry,' she said before they ended the call.

It had been four hours and search teams continued to step out section after section of bushland, braving the relentless rain. The bellowing voices of the search and rescue group leaders rang out around the mountain, with only the sound of the rushing creeks and water moving downhill filling the air.

As the rain intensified further, the crowds of spectators watching the search dispersed. Tasman stood closely to the decision makers in the main tent, hoping to hear something of value for his next story update.

'We're going to have to call it for the day,' said the Officer in Charge. 'These conditions are becoming dangerous, we don't want to put anyone out here at risk of falling down these cliffs, even with the harnesses on. This rain is making it impossible to see anything beyond a few metres,' he told the group sitting under the rest canopies, drinking tea to warm up in the cold.

'Also, the weather bureau has just called in a big lightning storm. It's coming from the west in around an hour. We're going to have to call time on the search for today. We will recommence again at first light,' said the officer.

Tasman climbed into the old news van and grabbed the steering wheel as he exhaled. Looking out of the driver's window, he saw snappers taking photographs of the van he was in – recalling it still displayed Harrison's huge, smiling face.

CHAPTER FOURTEEN

IT WAS AROUND DUSK when Tasman hesitated for a moment outside the large metal doors of The Lonely Squire, setting his phone to silent before walking through the dimly lit bar. It was the third time he had silenced a call from his mother that day. Tasman weighed up the decision, knowing that placing the phone on silent meant that he risked missing a crucial development in Harrison's search. He switched it back to loud and walked inside.

He was relieved to see Zaylee sitting in her usual spot, the stool closest to the far wall, with Peter leaning over the middle of the bar as he topped up Zaylee's glass. They were in a serious, hushed, conversation that stopped immediately when they spotted Tasman and they silently greeted him with forced, exhausted smiles of acknowledgement. To see friendly faces who understood and shared the pressures of the situation was a comfort he needed right now. Tasman sat up alongside Zaylee and Peter pushed a freshly poured beer towards him.

Peter's bar had become a favourite haunt for the city's media and trendy enough in its own right to be popular on any night of the week.

As Tasman drank, he glanced at the wall that featured a framed signed autograph of Harrison Marks.

When Peter had first hung it on the wall, it had served as an inside joke, but when the region's media took ownership of The Lonely Squire night after night, he had decided to leave it up.

Tasman lingered staring at the photograph; Harrison's eyes were watching them. He truly was everywhere and nowhere at the same time.

'The police were in the office searching Marks' desk,' said Zaylee, after a moment, noting Tasman's stare at the portraits along the wall. 'They were photographing his desk and boxing up his computer and notebooks, even his engraved fancy silver pens he's always carrying around,' she said, sounding deflated.

A journalist's notebooks were sacred, thought Tasman.

The one thing Tasman admired about Harrison was his use of shorthand. He was one of the few reporters still using it, just like Tasman. Harrison was old school. And Tasman hated that he liked that about him.

'At first, when he disappeared, I honestly thought he had just pissed off on one of his epic week-long benders. But now, it's sinking in that he may not actually be coming back,' said Peter, brushing a long blonde dreadlock from his face.

'I mean, let's imagine for just a second that there's someone else responsible for all of this. Harrison had plenty of enemies. He didn't shy away from pissing people off - especially if it led to a great story,' said Zaylee. 'The guy had sources across the country and people just swarmed to him to give him sensitive information. I mean, it could be anyone.'

'Let's not forget you just had an angry trucking company boss standing in the newsroom threatening him. Isn't that surely where the police would start?' said Peter, who looked as though he was mapping out his own investigative strategy on one of his bar napkins.

'But would anyone be that obvious? I mean, we all saw him there, standing off with Harrison. But if I was going to bump someone off or make them disappear, would I do it literally after threatening them in front of a crowd?' argued Zaylee.

'Who knows what anyone would do when they're pushed to their limit,' said Tasman. They all paused and drank in agreement.

'That's the scary thing,' said Tasman, breaking the silence. He held his neck as though he could still feel the truck driver's grip around his own neck, just days before.

'I can't believe seeing him win at the Golden Quills might've been the last time we saw him... alive,' said Zaylee, staring down.

'Except me,' said Tasman quietly, the scene between Victoria and Harrison weighing on him. As soon as he said the words, the memory shot back into the front of his mind. Days later, it still didn't sit right with him.

'Zaylee mentioned that,' said Peter. Zaylee sculled her glass, there were no secrets between Peter and Zaylee. 'Why were they both back at the office, anyway?' asked Peter.

'I mean - Marks smashed his award up,' Tasman replied. 'He was angry, like I've never seen before. And then Victoria completely disregarded it. She played it down and said that he'd just had too much to drink and celebrated too hard.'

'Then minutes later the Editor asks you to not ruin Marks' night with office gossip, keeping you quiet,' said Peter, tapping the bar with his finger.

'And then you're her new favourite reporter,' said Zaylee, winking.

They took a collective awkward sip of their drinks.

'What about his poor wife?' said Zaylee, breaking the silence again. 'What she must be going through right now. It must be torture not knowing where he's gone. If her husband is dead or alive. I wouldn't wish that on my worst enemy.'

Tasman looked at the stack of daily newspapers Peter kept at the bar on display, the Ranges Advocate displayed a large colourful image of Harrison.

'Speaking of enemies, - Did you see the Ranges Advocate?' said Peter, nodding towards the display. 'They're practically running an obituary already.'

'Yes. That would be Tancred's story. He's the one who leaked Harrison's name at the press conference,' said Tasman, taking a large sip of his glass. 'He was actually enjoying it, the spectacle of it all.'

'Right, that's enough of that. It's time to have a drink and finally welcome our dear friend the great Tasman Hill who has finally made it through his graveyard shift days,' said Zaylee, shaking off the depressing mood by raising her glass high in a toast to Tasman.

'Looks like tonight's not all bad news,' said Peter, gesturing at a woman sitting at the bar, watching them.

'I think I know that look,' smirked Zaylee. 'Let us start by shouting you another round and quietly acknowledging there's a beautiful woman watching you at the bar, just over there,' she said, gesturing again to a brunette woman in her early thirties wearing a bright red dress with long sleeves and white gloves. 'Gloves are an interesting choice,' teased Zaylee.

Tasman turned with a smile, believing no one would actually be there. But she was. It was the same woman from the search from earlier that day.

She had worn bright pink and orange, fluorescent runners that were covered in mud from the rainfall at the search site – she had been strikingly beautiful, and together with the bright and muddy shoes, she had been impossible to miss.

The woman smiled at him warmly, giving him a small wave to acknowledge that they had seen each other before, before turning back to her drink.

'Oh, my god Tasman. If you don't go over there and talk to her, I'll bloody have to do it for you! Just like the old uni days, and you know I'll do it,' teased Zaylee.

She would too, thought Tasman.

Tasman felt his stomach flip. The last thing he wanted was for Zaylee to force an uncomfortable and awkward high school introduction to a stranger at a bar. But she wasn't just a random woman, she was there at the scene of the search and could potentially give him a few quotes for his next article as a volunteer.

'She was at the search site. I'll be right back,' he nodded as he moved from the bar stool to the woman's seat, moving with careful, slow steps as though not to intrude on her evening if the last thing she wanted was to be approached for an interview.

'Uh... Hi, I think we've met before,' smiled Tasman, as he leaned on the bar, unsure if taking a seat beside her was too presumptuous.

'You were at the search up on the mountain, right?' said Tasman delicately. 'Hard to miss, with the bright runners I mean,' he said, unsure of what the woman's reaction would be. He felt a wave of relief when she finally offered a small smile in response.

'I hope you don't mind, but I was wondering if I could ask you a few questions about the search and –,' he continued before she finally interjected.

'Excuse me, can I get another please?' asked the woman, signalling to the nervous waitress with her empty wine glass. The new bartender had just been hired; in fact, it was her first night on. 'Actually, make it two. I think my friend is staying,' she said coolly, nodding towards Tasman.

The young bartender spun around, looking completely bewildered at the request while nodding in response. Tasman sat down alongside the woman, taking out his notebook and pen from his satchel, assuming the interview was about to commence.

'I'm Alison,' she smiled, shaking his hand.

Tasman began to ask Alison how she felt about Harrison's disappearance and why she joined the search, but she quickly changed the conversation back to Tasman and his work covering the story.

'Well, how about you have a drink with me first, help me calm my nerves and then I'll give you your interview,' she said cheekily in response to Tasman's third polite attempt to ask her about how the community felt a sense of shock since learning of the city's favourite reporter's suspicious disappearance.

Alison was more interested in getting to know Tasman. She asked question after question about his life, while he took sip after sip of his drink hoping to finally get something usable for his next story.

There were dozens of awkward moments between Alison and Tasman, her eye contact with him was intense, as though she was flirting with him. Tasman was flattered, but wondered if the interview was a bad idea.

Before he could politely call time on their conversation a loud smashing of glasses broke another uncomfortable pause. Tasman was relieved by the intrusion. He peered over the bar to see the new waitress had dropped a tray of glasses, with Peter rushing over to help her clean it up. Tasman looked at the door and saw Zaylee give him a small wave to signal she was leaving, just as a large crowd of university students flooded the bar.

'Come over here so we can talk properly, I can barely hear you with this noise,' said Alison as she gestured to Tasman.

Moving from the bar stool and taking a step towards the door Tasman's legs felt like jelly, wobbling as though he had been drinking for hours. He felt inebriated, like his hands had detached from his body, wanting to speak but unable to recall how to move his mouth. Then a sudden feeling of panic as he wondered if his drink had been spiked. But it was too late.

And that was the last thing Tasman remembered before he found himself in Alison's bed the next morning.

CHAPTER FIFTEEN

THREE DAYS GONE

THE SUN STREAMED THROUGH the stranger's room the next morning and woke Tasman from a deep sleep, like a spotlight in the face. He rubbed his head and looked around the unknown apartment, his vision cloudy and out of focus.

Tasman knew he hadn't drunk enough to feel this bad, and his mind finally recalled the panic he had felt the moment he lost control of his wits, and everything became a blur before... nothing. His drink had been spiked, he thought as he quickly sat up in panic, desperately assessing where he was, and what had happened to him last night.

Before he could speak, a large, golden-brown dog pinned him back down on the bed. Tasman's muscles felt sore and weak, like a boxer trying to get up after they had just been knocked out.

'Down Barkley!' a woman's voice commanded, growing louder as she entered the dark blue painted room.

The large dog licked Tasman's head before jumping off the bed and sitting down beside him, its tail wagging furiously.

Tasman stared at the woman and his mind finally clicked and connected to the memory - he was with Alison, the search volunteer he had been trying to interview at the bar.

'Wow. Thanks for the wake-up call,' said Tasman hiding his discomfort, as he tried to make sense of how he had ended up in Alison's bed. The quilt was silk and decorated with embroidered flowers.

'I'm so sorry,' Alison said. 'He does that every morning like clockwork. It's the one bad thing about him. That and the hair,' she said, rubbing a clump of dog hairs off her long sleeve pyjamas.

'Ah, no, it's fine. I love dogs,' said Tasman, his voice croaky and deep.

He looked at Alison standing before him, appearing as though the entire situation was completely normal. He was safe. There was no danger here, he told himself, calming down. Surely Alison would offer some answers as to what happened last night.

Tasman couldn't believe how perfect Alison looked first thing in the morning. She was wearing a thick charcoal dressing gown, already wearing makeup with her long brown hair perfectly styled.

'I wasn't sure if you were going to stay over. But here we are,' she smiled, shrugging off the awkwardness of the situation. 'I didn't want to disturb you,' she said as she sat down on the edge of the bed. 'Tea?' she said, offering him a cup.

'Oh. Thanks,' he said, as he brushed his matted hair out of his eyes to make himself presentable. His head seemed to ache harder the more he moved. 'I'm sorry but I have no idea what happened last night. The last thing I remember was talking about the interview and then – nothing,' Tasman continued as Alison watched him intently. 'I think my drink was spiked with Rohypnol or something. I just... we didn't have sex... did we?' he said alarmed as he walked through the possibilities in his mind.

Alison just laughed warmly in response before sipping her tea as though this kind of encounter was part of a regular morning routine. Nothing strange to see here.

'Do you remember what happened to me?' Tasman pushed again, remembering how coy Alison had been last night, perhaps she simply wanted to appear mysterious.

Before Alison could respond again, Barkley nuzzled Tasman's hand, spilling the tea on the bed.

'Oh, I'm so sorry,' he said, searching for anything to clean the mess. Tasman looked to Alison's bedside table but there was nothing but dozens of framed photographs of herself, centred around other beautiful women. Tasman stared for a moment, all of the images looked as though they had been heavily photoshopped.

'It's fine. Spills happen a lot around here with this guy. He's so massive, but he doesn't even know it,' she said, wiping the mess away with the sleeve of her robe as the dog tried to lick it from the bed.

Alison began talking to Barkley like a baby and it made Tasman's stomach twist. He looked at his watch and was desperate to find a polite excuse to leave.

'He's a bit of a beast. I've never seen a dog like that before,' Tasman eventually said interrupting the baby talk, as he looked over the dog's coat. The polite conversation was excruciating to him.

'Well, I should hope you haven't seen one like him,' she scoffed. 'He's an Otterhound. They're a rare breed. There's basically none in Australia and something like only a few hundred in the world,' she said proudly, folding her arms to hug herself. 'Dad imported him over from the UK for me. He's a goooood boy, except he sheds like crazy,' she said, pushing more hair off her top.

Tasman glanced around the room, searching for his phone and satchel. The bedroom was pristine, like a room you would see in a magazine or display home, it even smelled of burning coconut and caramel soy candles. The furniture and decor in the bedroom alone probably cost more than he would make in five years at the Sapphire Times.

'Wow. What a gift. I think I got a goldfish when I was four. That's about all the pet experience I've had,' he replied as the dog buried its face in Tasman's hands again.

'Yes, well, that's my dad. He's pretty much M-I-A, but makes up for it with lots of gifts,' she said as she raised her eyebrows. 'But I don't need to tell you about shitty fathers, right?' she said tongue-in-cheek.

Tasman was surprised. He never spoke of his father, and he wondered what exactly they had discussed last night. What secrets had he told this stranger? And why would she want an inebriated journalist to stay the night anyway, he wondered.

Tasman's mind flashed back to the bar, the drinks the young bar tender had served them and then there was nothing but blank space.

Tasman sat in silence in the stress of confusion, while Alison seemed oblivious to his discomfort. She continued talking.

'Barkley is a great running partner. He can actually keep up,' she laughed as she nodded towards the wall full of photographs, an impressive private shrine of self-promotion - each image was of Alison wearing a medal around her neck, posing with triumph to the camera.

'Wow, you're a professional runner?' he said, faking interest in the conversation by acknowledging the blue ribbons hanging from the bookcase. All he could think about was how to get out of the house, and the entire situation, without causing offence.

'Yeah, I used to be in the national under 18 elite squad. It was a lifetime ago now, though. Now I just run for fun,' she said, looking over her display of mementos.

Alison looked back at Tasman to take in his reaction. She focused intensely on him, and her stare made him feel even more exposed than realising that he had woken in nothing but his underwear.

'Don't worry, I didn't forget your name. I know who you are, Tasman Hill,' she said, edging closer to him in bed, making Tasman squirm inside. 'You told me all about your big promotion last night too,' she smiled knowingly.

Tasman's phone rang, and he felt instant gratitude and relief to hear the call. Alison passed his phone to him, and he could see it was Zaylee calling him. He looked down at the phone apologetically and saw his chance to make his excuse to leave.

'I forgot to mention your phone was going off for a little while there,' said Alison. 'I wasn't sure if I should wake you or if that would make this whole thing, you know. Awkward.'

Tasman realised the missed calls were from Victoria and Zaylee. He looked at the time, he was already running late.

'Oh shit. Sorry. I've really got to go. It's work. They'll kill me if I'm not contactable,' he said, checking the time again and then his maps app, trying to figure out where he was.

'Another big story then?' asked Alison, touching his arm with sincere interest. Tasman moved away, reaching for his clothes.

'Yeah, something like that,' he said as he buttoned up his shirt in a rush, spinning, searching for his things strewn across the room while trying to dodge the massive teddy-bear of a dog.

There could be a breakthrough in Harrison's case, and here he was sipping tea and chatting, thought Tasman. He couldn't help but feel furious with himself - was he sabotaging his one shot to prove himself as a serious journalist? How could he have let last night happen?

'It was great meeting you. I've got to get this,' he said, gesturing again to the phone as Zaylee called again.

As he answered, Tasman apologetically mouthed a silent goodbye, unsure whether to kiss Alison on the cheek or to simply just leave. He couldn't shake the sincere feeling of relief that he was leaving her company.

'Wait, one second,' said Alison, gesturing for Tasman to stop.

Alison took out a silver pen and wrote out her phone number on a post-it note, handing to him as he searched the room for his bag, but it was nowhere to be seen. It must still be at the bar. Abandoning the search, he again nodded apologetically at Alison and rushed out the door.

'Zaylee - hello,' he said as reached the stairwell, relieved the apartment door had closed behind him.

'Hill! What the hell happened last night?' she demanded.

'That's an excellent question,' he replied, staring up at the apartment window, noticing Alison watching from above. 'I have absolutely no bloody idea.'

TASMAN TEXTED PETER as he rushed from Alison's apartment to make it to the morning editorial meeting.

'Mate — what on earth happened last night? I think someone tried to spike my drink... the woman I was sitting with ended up letting me crash at her place. And I think I left my bag at the Squire. Get back to me when you're up,' Tasman texted, knowing Peter would still be sleeping off a long shift at the bar.

Without his bag and his notebooks filled with notes, he would have to fly blind.

Tasman rushed through the doors of the Sapphire Times, making it to the meeting room to take his seat just as Victoria checked the clock on the wall and closed the glass doors.

Tasman exhaled. He looked to the back of the room and immediately recognised the two figures leaning against the wall. It was Detective Inspector Watts and Detective Sergeant Marshall.

Victoria's demeanour was unchanged – she was business as usual - as though it was any other day in the news cycle, and it was perfectly normal to be plotting the coverage of their missing friend and colleague, overseen by detectives in the room.

'Team. As you can see, we are joined by some guests this morning. Before we begin, they would like to take a moment to speak with us. The floor is yours, detectives,' she said, gesturing to the back of the room.

'Thanks, Ms Stanley,' said Watts, stepping forward.

'I'm Detective Inspector Alexandra Watts and this is Detective Sergeant Aaron Marshall. You may be aware that we are investigating the disappearance of Harrison Marks. We have already spoken with some of you. Some we are yet to speak with,' she said, looking directly at Tasman.

'We know that Harrison's reporting may have caused some issues with members of the community. Before his disappearance there appear to have been some recent threats to his safety, but also to this newspaper,' Watts continued, moving slowly and confidently behind the reporters sitting at the boardroom table. 'We are currently speaking with Harrison's loved ones and following up on several leads.'

Tasman's heart raced as he looked at Zaylee. The number of people Harrison had targeted in his reporting was endless. And that meant so was the suspect list too.

'If you have any information about what happened to your friend, your colleague, we're asking you to come forward,' said Watts, again scanning the faces in the room.

Watts stopped right behind Tasman; he felt his pulse quicken.

'Any detail, big or small, could lead to a breakthrough,' said Marshall interjecting. 'We know you all want to find him, and so do we.'

Tasman looked directly at Victoria. He could feel her avoiding his eye line. She sat in her leather chair at the head of the boardroom table, unaffected and motionless.

'Thank you, Detectives,' said Victoria. 'Team, we have also secured some additional security that will patrol the property from time to time, until all of this is... resolved. Please try to go about your day as you would any other,' she said reassuringly. 'Oh, and one more thing,' said Victoria, standing and leaning forward on the table. 'Anyone caught leaking stories or information about Harrison that is not destined for print in our paper, will face serious consequences. Come to me. Not the Ranges Advocate, got it?' she said sharply, as she moved towards the glass doors, unlocking them to allow the visitors to leave.

The newsroom rumbled as reporters discussed Townsend's betrayal in hushed voices around the room. As the detectives moved towards the doors, McAllister stood up from the back of the room.

'You'll be stopping by that trucking and logistics group then?' he yelled, suddenly red faced with anger, his concern for Harrison boiling over.

Tasman watched as Watts stopped and turned to look at Marshall in a way that only those who had worked together for years could. They instantly understood each other in a telepathic conversation held in just a single moment.

Watts cautiously stepped back into the room as though she was about to fight a lion in a cage.

'Marks pissed off most of the city but wasn't it just a week ago that another one of our reporters got socked in the face over one of Harry's stories?' said McAllister, refusing to wait another moment for Watts to respond.

'Strangled,' said Zaylee, correcting McAllister. 'They strangled Hill.'

'Whatever. Beaten. Strangled. Threatened. They tried to kill the guy. You get the picture,' said McAllister, nodding briefly at Tasman.

McAllister was standing now, presenting to the newsroom.

'Now, our star reporter goes missing the same night he wins an award for his story exposing the same company. I mean. What are you lot doing? Go out there and fucking get them!' he yelled.

The entire room felt a second wave of embarrassment from the scene McAllister had caused.

'Right mate, just cool off, okay?' said Tasman, rising from his seat and attempting to take charge before McAllister gave himself a heart attack from stress.

Tasman placed his arm on McAllister's back, but it did nothing but fuel his rage as he shook him off.

'And extra security? So, if there's some kind of vendetta against the paper, what then? We just sit here and wait to be bumped off, do we?' demanded McAllister.

The intern in the room's corner suddenly looked up from scrolling his phone upon hearing the outburst.

'Okay, Sir. I think that's quite enough. You need to calm down,' said Watts, ready to defuse the situation. It was nothing she hadn't handled before.

'I can see that you're feeling distressed about your missing colleague. We can assure you that we are looking at every avenue of inquiry as part of our investigation, including anyone who may have wanted to harm him. Teams will also continue the search for Mr Marks up at the Ranges today.'

McAllister looked to his colleagues who sat stunned before him. He placed his hands on his hips, still unsatisfied with the detectives' response.

'And have you even bothered to speak to anyone over at the truckies? Or is that also on the to-do list for today?' scoffed McAllister.

Watts raised a hand gently to Marshall, signalling she would take this question.

'We've actually spoken with an individual and all *you* need to know is that we have now ruled them out as having any involvement in Mr Marks' disappearance,' Watts said, holding McAllister's stare.

The old journalist silently slinked back into his chair, folding his arms and Tasman leaned back on the wall, feeling relieved the situation was diffused.

'Oh, Mr McAllister, some free advice before we go. How about you let us do our job - and we will let you do yours,' she said, looking at Tasman, knowing the next news update on their investigation was about to be written up and posted online.

'Ms Stanley, thank you for your time. We will be in touch,' said Watts, snatching her waiting coffee from Marshall's hands on the way out.

Victoria spent the next hour laying out the news plan for the Sapphire Times and its coverage of Harrison's disappearance in the foreseeable future.

The city had never been a bigger story and Tasman knew there were only two possible outcomes for their news coverage. The newsroom was holding their breaths, waiting to see if Marks' disappearance would end in tragedy or triumph.

At the end of the meeting, Tasman rushed past Zaylee, adrenaline still pumping through his body following McAllister's scene, he knew he needed to speak to Victoria, to confront her about that night.

'Victoria, can I have a minute?' he asked, standing in her path to her office just metres away. The editor was immediately irritated by Tasman's delay.

'Hill, what are you still doing here? The search is resuming any minute, and we need you to chase Cressida Marks. She hasn't spoken to media yet and I'll die if she goes to the Advocate before us. Don't screw this up, got it?' she said, pulling her hair tightly behind her ear.

'Yes, of course. But I was hoping we could speak... privately for just a moment,' Tasman pushed.

Victoria looked at Tasman uncomfortably, dropping her professional façade for just long enough, as though she was considering the request.

Before she could reply three other journalists surrounded the editor, desperate to speak with her, each demanding direction on their stories as part of the Harrison Marks coverage.

Raising her hands in the air, overwhelmed and irritated at the swarm around her Victoria cried, 'If anyone else would like to speak with me, please go through… McAllister,' she said after a long pause before walking into her office.

She had clearly looked around the room and made a snap decision, thought Tasman.

'What is going on in this place?' asked Zaylee as she strode up to Tasman, witnessing the spectacle. Tasman didn't understand either.

A few minutes passed before Victoria looked through the blinds of her office staring outside. The entire newsroom had fallen silent.

Outside, in the pouring rain, dozens of television news vans were parked on the nature strip of the Sapphire Times.

The media frenzy had begun. Tasman knew the disappearance of the great Harrison Marks was the story. And so was the Sapphire Times.

CHAPTER SIXTEEN

THE RAIN LIGHTLY SPRAYED the scrum of reporters gathered around the search tent, listening to police directing the volunteers at the Ranges Lookout. The heavy rainfall had forced another suspension to the search, with only a fraction of ground covered. Tasman couldn't help but note the tone of voice of the officers, still hopeful and optimistic that Harrison could be located alive, even after the severe weather overnight.

'There has been a landslip overnight on the far-right side of the mountain,' one officer announced. 'Teams on the ground must be mindful of every step they take. If we've seen one landslip already, there's a good chance we will see more in the coming hours, days and weeks. We can't have anyone getting injured or falling down these tree-covered cliffs,' he said as the group wearing bright fluorescent vests and coveralls listened intently. 'Without knowing the bush tracks around here, finding your way back up will be a whole other challenge, so keep your harnesses on. And remember, whistle if you see or locate anything... or anyone.'

The teams nodded as they moved off into groups for separate briefings when Tasman saw her standing there. Alison was amongst the crowd of volunteers, just hours after Tasman had left her apartment.

She slowly approached the media tent holding Tasman's satchel and two cups of coffee. He felt the wave of relief to see it. The entire morning had felt fuzzy, even now but at least some things were finally falling into place.

'I think this might be yours,' she smiled confidently as she handed him the bag. 'I went with a plain latte. I hope that's okay.'

Alison looked directly into his brown-green eyes before Tasman broke the stare, checking the search underway behind him.

'Wow. Alison,' Tasman replied, still surprised to see her. 'Thank you, you didn't need to do that... or go to the trouble.' He must have missed the bag in his haste to get out of Alison's house, and the entire situation.

'I was starting to worry I had lost it or left it at the bar,' he said, looking away again as she gazed into his eyes.

It was her trademark, thought Tasman.

'Thanks so much. I really would be lost without my notebooks in here,' he said patting the bag. 'I was about to call you to check if I had left them.'

'Is that the only reason you would've called me,' replied Alison, poking Tasman's arm in fun.

'Oh, of course - I mean I would've called you, regardless,' he stumbled regretting every word as he spoke.

'Well, it was an easy guess where you were... following the news,' she gestured around the search site with more volunteers pulling on orange coveralls and checking over maps in the drizzling rain.

'Yeah, it feels like we are in some kind of nightmare, but we're hoping we can find him soon...' said Tasman, his voice trailing off.

'I know. You told me all about it, last night,' confirmed Alison. 'We spoke about, well, everything,' she said, her intense stare returning, making Tasman so uncomfortable he couldn't muster a proper response.

The awkward silences didn't seem to bother Alison at all. Tasman let her comment hang in the air as he considered her words. It irritated him that she seemed to be playing a strange game. She already knew Tasman had no idea about what had happened last night. What was she playing at?

'I haven't yet got the call yet to help volunteer – turns out the whole city wants to help with the search – you know – everyone loves Harrison Marks, so I'm not sure I'm needed yet. I thought I'd come here and let them know I'm free just in case, you know, do my bit for the community,' she said, qualifying her reason for being there.

It was the first time Tasman had seen Alison at all uncomfortable, as though she had just realised Tasman was there working a story. He thought back to his attempt to interview Alison the night before, and instantly felt grateful it had never gone ahead.

'My dad has been at me for months to do some community service. He's all about it, helping others, helping the city as a Councillor.'

The penny finally dropped for Tasman, there was only one man serving on Council that fit the description Alison had briefly painted of her cashed-up father. 'Wait, your father isn't Glenn Mosca? Is he?'

As soon as he spoke the words Tasman recalled the last encounter with Mosca, standing inside the Sapphire Times newsroom as the Emerald Trucking & Logistics company boss threatened Harrison.

'Yeah. That's the one,' she said, brushing the detail aside. 'We still barely see each other, even though he convinced me to move back here. He offered me a job in his Council Office. Anyway, this all counts towards community service so... here I am.'

Tasman looked around and realised the other reporters were watching their awkward exchange. Tancred smirked as he enjoyed the entertainment. The spotlight made Tasman instantly uncomfortable. It was time to wrap this sideshow up he thought.

'Well, thank you again. I appreciate you coming up here, even in the rain. And maybe we will end up doing that interview later on or something. I'll keep you in mind,' said Tasman light-heartedly, hoping to wind up the conversation. Alison seemed to want to linger, to stay.

'Oh yes, actually, let's put that on ice – there's plenty of other volunteers here I'm sure that would be a better fit. Thank you though,' she said, shaking her hands in the air as though the idea now offended her.

It surprised Tasman she would refuse a shot at the limelight. She seemed like an extrovert.

'It *is* awful though,' she continued, skating over the gap in conversation as though it had never occurred. 'I've never seen so many cameras in this city before. I know Harrison Marks was a big deal. Sorry, *is* a big deal.'

Tasman let the comment hang in the air for a moment. 'Well, I've never covered a story like this one. About one of our own,' said Tasman, looking around at the search underway as cameras moved towards another location abruptly.

'They've found something!' said one of the camera operators as they thrust past Alison and Tasman. He wanted to move with the pack but stood still out of politeness.

'I better crack on,' said Tasman, lifting the coffee in gratitude as he stepped backwards outside of the tent. 'But maybe we could finish this conversation soon, over drinks or something,' he lied, looking back again at the search teams.

'That would be amazing,' Alison said, her eyes lighting up.

'Oh, and the tent is over there,' he said, pointing back to the volunteer tent as the rain fell even harder.

'Oh yes, of course. Thanks,' she said as she kissed him on the cheek goodbye and walked away.

'False alarm. It's nothing!' Tasman heard echoing back towards them from the search group.

'Just an old shoe, nothing in it,' another yelled.

Tasman scrambled through the journalists and television crews that had retreated to the media tent, taking cover from the rain.

He rifled through his satchel, his laptop was thankfully still inside. He continued to search for his notebooks, but they were nowhere to be found. Tasman tipped the bag upside down, his phone, wallet and old newspapers fell to the wet ground. His notebooks were gone and he didn't have any more time to waste.

Feeling frustrated, Tasman opened his laptop to make a start on his story. Hitting the keyboard, a black and white error message displayed across the screen. It was locked and somehow out of battery.

Becoming desperate, Tasman cursed under his breath. He hated to rely on his phone, but he would have to make it work - everyone else did.

Tasman chewed his lip as he considered where his notebooks could be and what had happened to his computer.

He looked up in search for Alison, a fleeting thought that perhaps she recalled seeing his notebook on the floor of her room or the bag hit the floor. Then in a hot sweat his mind jumped back to last night at the bar. Tasman was instantly suspicious. Someone had spiked his drink and now his notebooks, filled with every detail of his work, were gone. His computer, mysteriously offline. And that was the thing, Tasman didn't believe in coincidences.

Tasman's panic was interrupted as he saw the media pack look up at once.

Police vehicles arrived at the search site, causing journalists and cameras to move again. Cameras were following each step of Detective Inspector Watts and Detective Sergeant Marshall.

Watts strode into the nearby coordination tent and was greeted by officers leading the search and rescue. After a few minutes of hushed discussion, she walked to face the waiting media, huddled under their shelter.

The rain pummelled the media tent, forcing Watts to strain her voice as she spoke.

'We would like to provide a quick update on our investigation and search for missing journalist Harrison Marks,' she began. 'Police have launched a new search in this immediate area, in hopes of locating Mr Marks. Over the past 48 hours, our detectives have created a timeline of his last movements and interactions with loved ones before his disappearance and the discovery of his vehicle. We are working alongside several specialist teams including Missing Persons.'

The reporters stood quietly, hanging on every word of the detective, with nothing but the rain falling on the canopy and the smell of the rainforest filling the air.

'We can confirm that Mr Marks' mobile phone last pinged at the Ranges National Park mobile tower transmitter at around 3am on Thursday morning. He has not accessed his bank accounts and credit cards since.'

'How can you be certain Marks isn't drunk in a ditch somewhere?' Tancred from the Advocate interjected. The interruption did not deter Watts who remained focused and calm.

'We are aware of reports that Mr Marks has been known to take extended breaks of leave where he is not in contact with family and colleagues for long periods of time. However, our initial investigation suggests that, on this occasion, that is extremely unlikely, and his disappearance remains suspicious. Our concerns are now that Mr Marks has met with foul play, possibly on this mountain,' she stated.

Tasman desperately bashed notes into his phone, listening intently as he considered Marks' death.

'Where did Marks' go on the night he disappeared?' shouted one journalist from the pack.

'Our officers have accounted for Mr Marks' movements after his attendance at an award ceremony in the city and a short period after this,' responded Watts. 'We have CCTV cameras capturing Mr Marks' driving his vehicle towards the Ranges National Park area. Given the time since his disappearance, the significant rainfall hampering our search and rescue efforts, along with the circumstances of the fire, we hold serious concerns for his safety,' she said seriously.

The crowd of reporters murmured at the point and Tasman turned around to see volunteers gathered nearby, listening. Alison stood at the back, watching with concern, clutching an umbrella.

'How long are you anticipating this search of the Ranges to go on for?' another reporter yelled, competing with the sound of the rain.

Watts nodded and replied, 'In relation to the ground search we will keep going for as long as it is safe to do so. We recognise the ongoing rainfall and risk of landslides remains a significant hindrance for our search teams. We would like to thank the community volunteers who are also lending a hand during this effort.'

It was no longer a search and rescue operation; it was a recovery mission, thought Tasman, the reality of the situation finally hitting him hard in the stomach.

'Before I conclude, we would like to appeal again to the public,' said Watts. 'I urge anyone who may have any information in relation to the disappearance of Mr Marks to come forward. There's an anonymous tip-line and we have a dedicated team of detectives who are working this case, day and night. Thank you.'

'No further questions,' said another officer standing in front of the cameras as reporters began yelling excitedly, as Watts shook the hand of the officer in charge before walking with Marshall back through the rain to the waiting car.

Journalists were busily typing at their phones and laptops, writing up the stories, while others were on their phones, urgently relaying the breaking news.

Tasman held his phone to his ear to make the dreaded call to report back the news to the Times, and specifically to Victoria.

She needed to be the one to hear this first, he thought, thinking of what he had secretly witnessed between Harrison and her that night.

Tasman shivered as he felt the air around him turn cold.

He turned around, and Alison was gone.

CHAPTER SEVENTEEN

TASMAN FOLLOWED THE STORY, driving to one of the nicest upmarket and tree-lined streets in the city. He lingered outside the perfectly curated home of Harrison Marks, sitting in the news van longer than he would for any other story, thinking over Victoria's reaction on the phone when he told her that the odds of finding Marks were almost impossible.

'I'm here at his place now, just outside, you know to see if his wife wants to comment,' Tasman assured Victoria, filling the silence as he waited for her to react.

After several moments she eventually snapped back into editor mode, urging him to continue to keep the newsroom updated on any further developments.

Tasman eventually summoned the courage to begin walking up the footpath of Harrison's home. He paused again, his hand hesitating over the shining antique brass doorbell.

Tasman loathed this part of the news chase. It was unnatural. Here he was, standing outside Harrison's own home, preparing to ask his wife for an interview, all while her husband was missing, feared murdered. Yet as a journalist, Tasman needed something from her, for himself, during her moment of pain.

He shook himself, knowing that if it were reversed, Harrison Marks would have no hesitation. Marks could do a death knock with his eyes closed.

Harrison had married into the wealth. Cressida, a known Sapphire Ranges artist, had largely retreated from the art scene, her gallery, once the epitome of Ranges society and social events was now empty.

Tasman had planned to convince Cressida that the story could actually help with the search for her husband, that it could help to jog the memories of possible witnesses who may have seen him in his final moments before he disappeared. It could even find him, or at least what had happened to him.

Tasman finally rang the doorbell and was surprised by how quickly the white glossed wooden door swung open.

'Yes?' asked a woman in her early twenties wearing a blue nursing uniform. The sound of voices from the hallway spilled outside.

'Hello, I'm Tasman Hill,' he said, hesitating as he presented his media pass.

'We're not speaking with media. Please leave,' said the young woman, beginning to close the door.

'Wait! Please,' Tasman cried, stepping forward to prevent the door from slamming in his face. 'I take it you're not Cressida Marks. I actually work with Harrison at the Times,' he said as the woman's eyes narrowed. She looked at Tasman suspiciously.

'Look, I can't help you. The family doesn't need people poking around the house, okay? You need to please leave,' the nurse said again.

'Please, wait a second,' Tasman pleaded, as the woman sighed. The voices in the hallway calling her louder.

'You obviously work for the family... and for Harrison, right? Please, just hear me out before you close the door,' Tasman pleaded.

Tasman couldn't leave without something. Anything was better than returning to the newsroom without a shred of news, he thought.

'Look, I can't say anything. I'll lose my job,' she said, poking her head outside the door, surveying who was around, as though she was already being filmed or snapped by photographers.

She was right to be concerned about that, thought Tasman. They would surely arrive at any moment.

'I can assure you, it's just me out here. Right now, anyway. Could I speak with Cressida? Is she here?' he asked, attempting to hide his desperation.

'No. She's not here. She hasn't been... for a while,' she replied.

'Okay. Well, if you can let her know I stopped by, I would be really grateful. And if you think of anything that might be important, get in touch with me, okay?' he said, handing over his bent and worn-out business card.

'I'll think about it,' said the nurse as she closed the door.

Tasman walked down the driveway and watched as half a dozen cars appeared at once, filling the street in pursuit of a vehicle turning into the property. News vans, filled with reporters, cameras, and photographers, followed behind.

A thin, bohemian styled woman wearing a long flowing skirt and singlet with long wavy blonde hair got out of the back of the car. It was Cressida Marks.

Watts and Marshall escorted her to her front door, followed by more police officers in a marked car.

He watched on as photographers snapped Cressida as she shunned herself from view with her long beige cardigan. The same nurse Tasman had spoken to opened the front door to allow Cressida and the officers to quickly enter inside.

Tasman knew he had lost his chance at any exclusive with Cressida. The flood gates had opened, and the media were camped outside both the Sapphire Times and Harrison's home.

The national networks would probably offer her four figures just to give them updates on how she was feeling as the search for her husband continued.

Tasman saw his own photographer Lindsay appear.

'Heard it on the scanner,' he said as he smoked standing next to him, watching back his shots on his camera.

'Search warrant in play. Sounds like it was all voluntary. Good, you got here first before these bastards,' Lindsay said, gesturing to the camera crews setting up tripods on the grass.

'Yeah, I didn't get anywhere, though,' Tasman replied.

'I'm not surprised she's not talking,' said Lindsay as he put his cigarette out on a tree nearby.

'What do you mean?' asked Tasman, Lindsay seemed to know something more. 'Surely Cressida gets it, married to a reporter herself. There's a chance it could help piece this whole thing together and...'

'Harrison and Cressida... are a whole other story on their own. Not my place to say, though, naturally. Of course, given the circumstances...' said Lindsay, raising his eyebrows cheekily as he inhaled a new freshly lit cigarette.

Lindsay wanted Tasman to beg him for information, it reminded him of the way Alison had been playing coy, minus the intense eye contact. Tasman knew Lindsay was enjoying knowing something Tasman didn't.

'Thought you said you wanted to be an investigative journalist - better brush up on that, Hill,' Lindsay said condescendingly.

'Sounds like it,' said Tasman rolling his eyes as he ignored the baiting of the photographer.

Tasman was grateful to see Zaylee calling, breaking the conversation.

'His wife, Cressida Marks, has just released a statement, well, via her lawyers at least,' she said immediately when Tasman answered.

Zaylee always spoke quickly when she was upset or excited. 'It's the usual lines,' she said, disappointed. 'She is assisting police with their inquiries, but that's about it. You know blah blah blah, thanking the community for their support, blah blah blah. And then the usual please respect her privacy during this difficult time,' she summarised.

'Shit. She won't be speaking to media or even us then. Doesn't Victoria know her personally? Surely, she could make a call?' said Tasman.

'Well, she is grieving her possibly dead husband right now Hill, what do you expect from her?' snapped Zaylee.

'Well, I'm wondering if it's worth me standing out here for much longer,' said Tasman, the force of his body resting on his lowered head leaning against the tree. He still didn't feel right after his possible drink-spiking ordeal.

'I'm sorry for snapping. It's just so close to home, isn't it? I mean, we're writing about the potential murder of Marks right now. My head is spinning. I was happy believing he had gone off on some epic bender. But now...'

'I know. The whole situation is... surreal,' Tasman offered. 'I don't think there's a handbook for how to think or feel about something like this.'

Tasman let the silence hang in the air for a moment before Zaylee eventually replied.

'I'll update your story from this morning with Cressida's statement. Let me know how you go out there, okay?' she said, sounding more like her calm and cheery self.

As he ended the call, he heard a commotion as the media pack pushed towards the driveway again.

Watts and Marshall had left the house, while uniformed officers carried clear plastic bags of evidence from the home to the waiting cars. The cameras parted sides of the driveway as the police cars pushed through.

Lindsay returned to Tasman triumphantly, showing his camera. He had photographed the contents of the bags - some of Harrison's notebooks and expensive silver designer pens, clothing and toiletries.

Tasman desperately wanted to leave, longing to return home and rest, but he felt compelled to stay, to wait it out for the chance to speak to Cressida. If he could get an interview with her, it could selfishly make his career.

He couldn't allow one of their competitors, the Ranges Advocate or even one of these metropolitan competitors, the chance to steal the story that rightfully belonged to the Times. It wouldn't be right. It wouldn't be what Harrison Marks wanted, he thought, as he slid down the tree and sat in the gutter of the beautiful street.

Another hour had passed and Lindsay had long gone, the man never stayed a minute longer than his rostered shift. Tasman was left to rely on his phone's camera should there be any developments in the neat and tidy street. It had turned dark. Steel streetlamps lined the road, and he could only a dim light inside the home.

Tasman couldn't shake the feeling of being almost a stalker, an unwanted person standing outside, watching, waiting for a grieving woman. He told himself it was all in the name of journalism. In the public interest. But he cringed at the thought.

And that's when he saw it, the large automatic garage doors opening and Cressida in her expensive SUV packed with suitcases in its boot, speeding out of her driveway and just like her husband, within a second, she was gone.

CHAPTER EIGHTEEN

ONE WEEK GONE

THE DARK RAIN CLOUDS had been hovering over the Sapphire Ranges ever since Harrison had disappeared. There had been days of silence from the police and the search constantly hampered by rain and fog, it was clear they were no closer to finding the missing journalist.

Tasman's imposter syndrome reared its head as he sat at Harrison's desk, in the centre of the newsroom. It had the best view of the city and beyond through the Sapphire Times' floor to ceiling glass windows. The same windows that Tasman had looked through as he watched Harrison speed away in his car that night, the last time he or possibly anyone had seen him alive before his likely death.

The desk had been disturbed by the police and forensics team, who had already seized all of Harrison's possessions as part of the investigation. They had taken it all, except an old, framed photograph of Cressida and him. Tasman picked it up and traced the wooden frame, examining the image. They looked young and happy smiling to the camera, both unaware of what would one day follow.

The Times had already run this image on the front page, as part of its rolling coverage of his disappearance-turned-possible-murder.

Outside, a steady flow of people gathered on the grass, placing flowers and cards at the steps of the Times, all for the famous journalist.

As the hours passed, the vigil for Harrison grew larger and had even spilled out onto the grounds, even encroaching around the space where Tasman's old broken-down car still sat. Standing in the rain and under the cover of the Times' foyer, the mourners stood and waited, lighting candle after candle for a man they really didn't know.

Tasman watched as Victoria shook hands with Councillor Mosca outside on the lawn under two umbrellas. The editor accepting flowers on behalf of the city, as cameras flashed, capturing their staged hugs and handshakes.

When Victoria returned to the newsroom, Tasman could tell she too was fighting hard to hold back emotion. Her usual calm and controlled exterior was crumbling. And he didn't blame her.

Tasman walked by Victoria's office dozens of times, unable to gather the courage to confront her about what he had heard and seen that night. Every time he approached, her office door was locked, the blinds closed.

With the rain expected to ease mid-morning, Tasman packed his satchel, ready to return to the search site. As he moved towards the foyer, Christine stood in front of him, blocking his path. Every time he saw her bright pink over-applied eyeshadow, he could not help of think of his mother, then the dozens of calls he was still yet to return.

'There's someone here to see you,' Christine said seriously.

'Oh, thanks, Christine,' said Tasman, itching to continue on his way. 'Is it okay I leave them with McAllister? I'm about to run up to the search. It's hopefully resuming once the rain eases off.' Tasman looked towards McAllister who was leaning back in his chair scrolling YouTube in a zombie-like state.

Christine tugged at Tasman's arm, still standing in his path.

'No. It has to be you. She asked for you specifically,' she said, her eyes darting behind her. 'She's sitting in the foyer. I told her you wouldn't be long.'

'Thank you,' said Tasman calling after her, but Christine had already returned to her desk to answer the ringing phone. He hurried to the foyer.

Tasman's eyes widened as he recognised the woman standing in the foyer. It was the in-home nurse from Harrison and Cressida's house. The young woman was frantically biting her brightly painted red fingernails as she looked at the television screens displaying the Sapphire Times news headlines.

Tasman had heard rumours that Cressida had given up her career to help care for Harrison's elderly parents, housing them in their sprawling home.

'Tasman Hill,' the young woman began, as she hid her hands up the sleeve of her cardigan, stretching it. 'We met the other day and, you know, you asked me to let you know if there's anything else. You know, about Harrison Marks.'

'Yes… of course,' said Tasman as he invited her to sit down, but she declined.

He glanced down at her name tag fixed to her blue uniform's pocket, realising he did not know the woman's name.

'It's Amanda… Mandy Adams,' she confirmed. Mandy looked tired, her face pale.

'Thanks for coming in. I wasn't really expecting you to get in touch,' said Tasman, loosely folding his arms before abandoning the idea altogether. He wanted to appear approachable.

'If I'm honest, I'm not even sure what I'm doing here, I mean, I could lose my job. I just want people to know that Harry isn't this complete hero that he's being made out to be,' she said as her eyes dotted around the foyer. 'I just thought maybe it was the right thing to do, you know to come forward and give you the whole story,' she said slowly, choosing her words carefully.

Tasman nodded encouragingly, wondering what she was about to reveal while battling the surge of excitement he felt inside his stomach that he was about to find his next big story. He couldn't appear desperate.

Mandy pulled her cardigan tight around her waist. 'People should know that there were *other* women in his life, if you know what I mean. There were plenty. He told me about it, like all the time,' she began.

Tasman remained silent, hoping Mandy would continue to talk out of obligation to fill the awkward silence. It was a classic journalistic tactic. And it was working.

'He had affairs, like, all the time. And I should know!' she cried. Mandy used her index fingers to hold back tears to avoid ruining her makeup.

'Okay,' replied Tasman. 'So, you and Harrison were together?' he asked delicately.

Mandy glared at Christine as though she was about to accuse the receptionist of eavesdropping on their conversation.

'Not like a proper relationship or anything. It was just a few times,' said Mandy, looking down at the shining white floor. 'He didn't want to take it any further. He used me to get what he wanted and, well then, he didn't really give a shit about me after that, or what I wanted. Mandy closed her eyes tightly to stop her tears.

Tasman paused. His mind flashed back once more to Harrison and Victoria and how he had inadvertently discovered their relationship the same night the journalist had disappeared. He had more than one affair; the man was busy, thought Tasman.

He turned his attention quickly back to Mandy as she stood before him, waiting for his response. Tasman knew he needed to play this just right. 'It sounds like you've been through a lot,' he offered, still assessing what the young woman's motives for telling him this information were.

'The thing that really got me was that after it was over, he treated me like I was invisible. It was hard to take,' Mandy said loudly, as her cheeks turned bright red. 'Like, I think his wife should know the truth. He was unfaithful to her. Anyway, I've got plenty more to say, that is, if you're interested,' she said pointedly.

Mandy's tears were suddenly gone, and she was standing taller.

'So, you're fine to talk about all of this on the record?' asked Tasman.

Mandy stepped back slightly; her eyes were wide with surprise.

'What do you mean? Put my name to it? Couldn't it be anonymous? I could lose my job if the agency finds out, I've heard about them blacklisting people for fraternising with clients,' she said appearing panicked.

Tasman looked at Mandy, considering her request.

'So, you're thinking you will still want to work for Cressida Marks after it's in the paper?' queried Tasman.

'I thought I would come to you first. I mean, he worked here, didn't he? And you know, you're kind of cute. I probably wouldn't have said anything if you hadn't of knocked on the door first,' she smiled, looking optimistic.

Tasman was speechless. Finally, she spoke the words that made it all make sense.

'Okay, so how much is it worth, then?' she said, raising her eyebrows. Mandy folded her arms impatiently. She was ready to negotiate.

'What do you mean?' Tasman questioned.

Mandy rolled her eyes. 'So how much will you pay me if I go on the record, you know name and all? If it's the right price, I don't even have to worry about going back to work,' she shrugged, smiling. 'I'll tell you whatever you want. All the details,' she gloated.

Tasman's stunned reaction visibly irritated Mandy, as she chewed on her nails again, her confident negotiator façade diminishing for a moment.

'Yeah. Like I said. Those are my conditions.'

Tasman knew the Sapphire Times had never paid for a story. And beside that point, he needed more than Mandy's word that she had an affair with Harrison. He needed actual proof before he unleashed another story like this, just when the entire country was desperate to cover the search for Harrison Marks.

'And before we go any further - do you have any proof of your affair, or the other affairs?' asked Tasman, matter-of-factly, suspicious if Mandy could verify the claims.

Mandy shook her head and stepped backwards a little.

'Like I said, I'll tell you whatever you want. All the details,' she said. Tasman could tell she was insulted at the request for evidence.

'Look, Mandy. I appreciate you coming to me. But I'm sorry, we don't pay for stories or information,' he said, watching her carefully to gauge her reaction. 'If you want to sit down with me and tell me your story and offer insights into your relationship with Harrison in the lead up to his disappearance, I absolutely want to speak with you. However, we can't pay you for it. That's the bottom line. We never have, never will,' he shrugged.

'Right. Well, whatever then,' said Mandy, struggling to hide her anger and embarrassment as her ears turned a deep red.

Mandy ignored Tasman's outstretched hand as she walked towards the doors, almost shouting.

'Whatever, mate. This is your loss. Don't say I didn't come to you first. I know that lot outside would love to chat with me,' she said loudly, nodding towards the scrum of television cameras outside filming the growing memorial of flowers for Harrison.

Tasman knew she wasn't wrong.

'I'm sure there'll be plenty who want to hear my truth. Probably at the right price too,' she said, clicking her fingers together as though money was pouring through her hands.

Tasman wondered if he had made a serious error of judgement. Was this his decision to make? He looked at Christine who had heard the entire exchange, she looked away quickly, as though embarrassed she had eavesdropped on the conversation. Had he made the wrong call?

Christine's raised eyebrows seemed to be hinting that he had. How could he have stood so firmly on his own morals without even asking Victoria, he thought in panic. The stakes had never been higher for the Sapphire Times to break and cover every angle of the biggest story in its history. And he had just sent the only new shred of information he had out the door.

Tasman watched on as Mandy walked directly into the scrum of television cameras and sighed, knowing he just handed the latest angle of the Harrison Marks' story directly to the competition.

CHAPTER NINETEEN

EIGHT DAYS GONE

TASMAN HAD PLANNED to go to bed early, but he lay awake staring at the ceiling. His body clock remained on night shift time, and he still hadn't adjusted to life working during daylight hours.

Harrison's story was consuming almost every waking thought, and he couldn't switch off from the pressure of delivering the next Harrison-related headline.

Tasman had watched on as search teams spent another fruitless day scouring the Ranges National Park. The search zone had expanded past the Lookout and broadened to the dirt roads and tracks surrounding it, but the rainfall had already caused much of the bushland to turn to mud. The once hopeful and optimistic faces of the volunteers had now faded, and Tasman didn't blame them. The constant rain delays did nothing to raise their spirits.

There had been rumours swirling that the search was about to be suspended altogether. The big wet was too much to compete with. But no one wanted to make that call just yet, despite hourly questioning from the media.

Tasman gave up trying to sleep, rolled out of bed and opened the only window in his small apartment, smelling the rain and the fresh air as he looked at the street below. The sun was only just setting, and he knew there was no way he would sleep yet. All he wanted was a distraction, to think about anything other than Harrison or the never-ending task before him.

Without another thought and within seconds, he dialled Alison's number.

'Hi Alison, it's Tasman... Hill. From the other night. And day, I guess,' he began, almost shocked she answered the phone on the second ring.

'I was wondering when you were going to call me. I thought you might have forgotten about me,' said Alison.

Tasman couldn't tell if she was joking or offended. 'Listen, I know it's getting late, but do you want to meet for a drink tonight?'

'See you in twenty minutes,' replied Alison instantly. 'Same place as last time,' she said with no hesitation before hanging up.

And just like that, Tasman had a date with his one-night stand.

TASMAN ARRIVED at the doors of The Lonely Squire at exactly the same time as Alison. He stood back and opened the door for her, as he wondered why he had orchestrated a date with a woman he really didn't feel connected to. All he knew was that Alison's company would be better than sitting at home alone, thinking about Harrison Marks and the wake of destruction one man had left behind him.

They sat down at a booth towards the back, and Tasman's mind instantly wondered around the room, tracing back to where they had sat at the bar the night they met, before his drink had been spiked. The waitress that had served them, the same one who had dropped the tray of glasses was no longer there. Peter had mentioned she'd been let go after a couple of trial shifts.

Tasman offered to take Alison's jacket, and she vehemently declined as she wanted to stay warm, her over-the-top reaction setting an awkward tone in the air that Tasman was desperate to ignore.

Alison placed a napkin on the table before carefully positioning her designer handbag on top of it.

'Wow, that must be quite a special bag,' noted Tasman stifling a laugh.

Alison stroked the large black leather bag covered in metal buckles like a pet. 'Oh yes, it sure is. This one is straight from Milan. I hope you don't mind. I think it deserves its own seat at the table, don't you?' she said with a laugh. 'It's probably worth the entire bottle collection behind the bar here,' she said smugly looking over the expensive alcohol bottles presented on sparkling dark green glass shelves. Those upmarket bottles were Peter's pride and joy.

Tasman sat opposite Alison and wondered how to handle her comments, after all, she didn't appear to be joking, in fact she appeared to enjoy flaunting her father's money. There was an awkwardness between them, an energy that felt forced. He wondered if he was judging her wrong, but she certainly was undeniably as superficial as she seemed.

Tasman couldn't begin to wonder what life would be like having personal wealth like Alison. He had watched his mother struggle to pay his school tuition year after year on her single wage. He really should call his mother back, he had punished her enough, he thought.

After the waiter returned with their wine, Tasman noticed the staff watching them, discussing them, before Peter quickly ushered them back to work.

Tasman couldn't deny it. He knew they were an unlikely match. Tasman had tried to brush through his tangled brown hair and showered, but he still looked as though he had rolled out of bed.

'Do you know when you'll be joining the search?' asked Tasman reluctantly. He was irritated with himself for turning the conversation to Harrison when that was the exact topic he wanted to avoid.

'What do you mean?' asked Alison, confused at the question.

'The search for Harrison?' he continued, desperate to find a conversation that flowed, to find any common ground.

Alison sipped her wine. 'Oh. No, they told me all the volunteer places were already filled. There is a waitlist or something, so fingers crossed I get called up,' she shrugged.

Tasman frowned. He had spent hours at the search site and did not know the teams had created a waitlist just to deal with the demand to help find Harrison. It was the first he had heard of it.

'Wow, a waitlist. It's kind of... grim, isn't it?' he said as he took a mouthful of more wine than he wanted.

He knew he was doing all the heavy lifting for the conversation as Alison sat back, watching him with her trademark intense eye contact. He wondered how long it had been since she had blinked. It had been a mistake seeing her.

Tasman's phone broke the silence, and he felt a wave of gratitude sweep over him before he realised it was his mother calling. Alison's eyes darted to the screen and the displayed photograph of Tasman hugging his mother during happier times.

'Sorry, it's my mother...,' Tasman apologised. He considered using the call to make his escape, but he thought better of it.

'You're still not speaking to her?' asked Alison, suddenly reaching across the bench to hold his hand in comfort.

Tasman froze. How did she know this about him? He must have told Alison the night they met.

Alison laughed. 'You don't remember, do you?' she said, enjoying Tasman's surprise. 'You ran me through the whole deal. And yes, you're right to be pissed off with her, moving on with another husband. No wonder you've felt so out of sorts,' she said, patting his hand again as though she knew every inch of Tasman's life.

'Yeah. Well, she's happy. She's got a new start with a new life,' he said, trying to hide his surprise. 'It's good for her. I'm happy for her,' he lied.

'That seems like something someone in denial would say,' said Alison, her eyes fixated on Tasman's again. She smiled at him. Like someone about to play the winning hand in poker, she was enjoying holding all the cards.

'Well, anyway, let's talk about something else. Here I was thinking I was the journalist asking all the questions and here you are getting all the details from me!' he said, desperate to change the subject.

'Don't worry. We've all got our family dramas,' shrugged Alison. 'We're all perfectly imperfect as they say, right?'

'I think that deserves a toast - to being perfectly imperfect - whatever that means,' said Tasman as he raised his glass and drank.

Alison continued to talk but Tasman was staring past her.

'Hello, Tasman - are you in there?' she said, clicking her fingers in front of his face abruptly.

'Sorry. It's just something for work,' he said, his eyes again fixated on the television screen above the bar. Alison turned to see what he was looking at and her mouth fell open.

It was a preview for the following morning's television news, showing a sit down, tell-all interview exclusive with none other than Mandy Adams, detailing her affair with Harrison Marks before his disappearance. It looked like she found a TV network willing to pay her the right price, after all.

Tasman shook his head and looked back at Alison. A look of disgust and anger crossed her face.

'I need to go. Thanks for the drink,' she snapped as she collected her handbag without another word, practically running out the door.

Tasman sank back into the booth and pushed his fingers through his hair, the promo of Mandy seemed to have pissed Alison off. Was it that he had been rude, while on a date? Or was it something else altogether?

Tasman signalled to Peter that he would be back in a moment as he sped outside the bar and looked in both directions - Alison was nowhere to be seen. She had truly made a quick getaway, even in the rain. His calls to her phone were unanswered.

Tasman walked back inside the bar and ordered another round. Taking a deep breath, he couldn't deny that he felt relief the date was over. He felt guilty for both going on a date with a woman he had no real intention of pursuing, and also for letting his work run into his personal life, but that wasn't a choice when someone was a journalist, you were always alert and on the hunt for a story or following one at least. Perhaps he was more like his father after all.

CHAPTER TWENTY

NINE DAYS GONE

TASMAN TAPPED HIS KNUCKLES on the wooden boardroom table anxiously. He was the first to arrive at the editorial meeting that morning. Tasman was certain Victoria had seen the Network 360 News promotions featuring the interview with Mandy – it was being hailed the Harrison Marks' secret affair exclusive.

Zaylee had tried to reassure Tasman that he made the right call, knocking back Mandy's interview and demand for cash. But with Victoria under pressure from headquarters to deliver, it would be impossible to gauge how the editor would react if she knew Tasman had the story first, and let it slip through their fingers.

Had Christine told Victoria that Tasman had turned down the interview with the young mistress? Or had Christine again saved him from another embarrassing moment. The receptionist owed Tasman nothing. In fact, he owed her, he thought as he squeezed the keys to the old news van in his pocket.

Tasman adjusted his shirt collar as his stomach flipped as he watched Victoria move around her office, speaking angrily on the phone. It was not a good sign.

'They paid her twenty thousand or something insane like that,' said Zaylee, texting with a friend at Network 360. 'This Mandy girl even had a bidding war happening, apparently.'

Tasman held his breath as Victoria jolted her office door open and breezed into the newsroom. He waited, about to wince, but the scolding never came. Victoria looked downcast, her dirty black bob pulled back tightly and her eyes bloodshot. She looked at Tasman and asked about the missed opportunity. She knew. Christine had ratted him out after all, but Tasman didn't blame her. He couldn't.

'Hill, did she offer you any proof of a genuine affair?' asked Victoria in front of the room, still busy with chatter from reporters.

Tasman braced himself and quickly replied 'No, nothing, only her account that it happened.'

Victoria nodded satisfactorily and turned to the room.

'Excuse me. Just a quick announcement, right,' Victoria shouted across the room.

McAllister whistled loudly and the room fell silent.

Victoria continued, 'In case anyone is confused let me reiterate to you all, the Sapphire Times has a strict 'no cash for comment' policy. And no matter how desperate things get, that's not about to change, at least not on my watch,' she said, glancing at her office and then the growing memorial for Harrison outside of the large glass windows.

Tasman looked around the boardroom in amazement, the entire newsroom's faces all reflected the same surprise at the editor's calm and poised reaction.

'I think we can safely assume that there's potential for more... allegations to come out of the woodwork. Especially if it's clear there's money on the table for stories about our friend and colleague. We need to stick to our guns. Let's actually run something from a source that's credible,' she concluded, turning back to Tasman. 'Please tell me we have something locked in, something with Cressida Marks by now?' she said sternly, her tone quiet so only Tasman could hear. 'Securing an exclusive with the family is essential. What on earth is the holdup?' asked Victoria, her trademark irritation returning.

Tasman hesitated as he searched for the words, 'She's disappeared. Cressida Marks hasn't returned home since the search warrant at her house,' he said.

Zaylee stepped into the conversation, standing alongside Tasman.

'We've been rotating shifts, cold calling, and nothing more has come from the police on her,' said Zaylee, backing him up.

Victoria tilted her neck, her jaw clenched.

'I would say it's time to ask again. Get me something by tomorrow, surely between you all, you can manage that,' she said to Tasman and Zaylee.

Tasman swallowed hard at the thought of what was an impossible task. Find the woman who doesn't want to be found and make her talk.

'That will be all. We've got nothing else right now and if anything this story is *ours*. Make it happen, Hill, especially if you don't want to fly back to the nightshift,' said Victoria looking at Tasman. 'Tick, tock.'

THE NATIONAL MEDIA COVERAGE featuring Mandy's interview rolled on throughout the day. The affair revelation added significant fuel to the fire that was the media frenzy surrounding Harrison. And it wasn't showing any sign of slowing down. The narrative surrounding Cressida Marks was quickly changing from a sad victim's wife to a scorned, vengeful woman. Some media outlets televised pseudo criminal experts, speculating Cressida Marks had known about the affair and was behind his disappearance, behind Harrison's murder. On social media, armchair detectives were quick to point to the fact that Mrs Marks had not once attended the search site, a truth that only supported the speculation. And after the police had searched their home, Cressida had not shown her face in the Sapphire Ranges since.

Grayson had joined the media pack staking out Cressida Marks' home while Tasman and Zaylee cold-called Cressida's extended family and friends on her social media pages and contacts from Cressida's work at the art gallery. The pair were digging for anyone who could point them to her whereabouts to chase her for an interview.

'She has gone completely dark,' Tasman said to Zaylee while sitting at Harrison's desk. He slapped his phone down, it was the third time he had tried calling Cressida's mobile that day, only to hear the same voicemail message. The phone was off.

'Well, they have a point, don't they?' said Zaylee, looking up at the wall of screens showing replays of Mandy crying on camera and zoomed in images of Harrison and Cressida posing happily in photographs together at an upmarket art show.

'If Peter disappeared, nothing would stop me from being out there on that bloody mountain, day and night, searching. I don't think I could eat or sleep, but where's Cressida? She's gone M-I-A instead,' said Zaylee.

'We can't assume we know the ins and outs of it all, though. I don't even know what it would feel like. People do crazy things when they're in shock... or in grief,' Tasman replied, pondering the thought of Harrison's murder and who could possibly be behind it. 'But the sense of suspicion, it's growing, isn't it?' he agreed.

Tasman could tell Zaylee wasn't listening to him, her face instead scrolling her phone's screen.

'Wait, shut up. Look at all of this,' said Zaylee, showing Tasman a social media news feed on her phone.

'It's blowing up. They're picking Cressida apart. They're saying she's actually fled town because she's killed him. Her disappearing right after the search warrant definitely makes her look...' Zaylee paused. 'Guilty.'

'I don't get it, why would you leave town if your husband was missing... or presumed dead,' asked Tasman staring into the space on Harrison's desk.

'Well you wouldn't. Not unless you had a good reason. Or needed a good place to hide,' said Zaylee.

It was in that moment that Tasman had a breakthrough. He suddenly knew where Cressida Marks was. He picked up the framed photograph on Harrison's desk, the single item spared by police aside from a collection of journalism awards. He had taken the photo of a younger Cressida and Harrison on the deck of a beach house, a lighthouse visible in the background.

Zaylee looked at Tasman bewildered as she tried to understand.

'I know where she is!' said Tasman, rising to his feet with no hesitation. 'I think I do, at least. Zaylee, just hold Victoria off for me as long as you can, alright?' he said as he grabbed his satchel and keys, practically jogging from the newsroom to the carpark.

Tasman could hear Zaylee calling after him, but he didn't stop. There was no time. Tasman turned the key on the old news van and was ready for the long drive. He was leaving the mountainous and rain-soaked Sapphire Ranges and headed hours down the highway.

Tasman knew Cressida Marks was a woman who desperately did not want to be found. But he had a feeling he would find her, and that lighthouse, at Hideaway Beach.

CHAPTER TWENTY-ONE

TASMAN HAD BEEN DRIVING for almost four hours when he reached the freeway exit that would lead him to Hideaway Beach. He looked at the setting sun, he was quickly losing daylight.

Tasman had known where to look for Cressida, only because he had been there before. Driving through the quaint touristy seaside town brought back a flood of memories. He passed the same landmarks that he had marvelled at as a child on camping holidays with his mother down at the coast. The area had changed since then, but only slightly. It was still the charming beachside village built around a historic old, decommissioned lighthouse. The same lighthouse in the background of Harrison and Cressida's photograph that now lay on the front passenger seat of the old news van.

There were only a handful of houses that the stunning lighthouse view could have been from - and they were all from old money – holiday homes that never went up for sale and were instead passed down to each generation. No one wanted to give up the view of the Hideaway Beach lighthouse.

Tasman avoided staring at the lighthouse as he drove within its view. The memories of it stung him. He recalled spending hours sitting on its steps as a young boy just watching the waves, passing the time after his father had left. Being in its orbit again felt bittersweet. The past was always catching up with him like that, forcing him to deal with his pain, with his feelings.

His mother had never let Tasman see how much being abandoned by the man she loved hurt her. After all, she didn't see it coming either. One minute Eric Gleeson was there. The next, he was gone. He had disappeared in the middle of the night, leaving behind only a note explaining that he had met someone else, a younger woman, and was never coming back. Less than a year later, he had a fatal heart attack. Tasman and his mother had sat in the front row at his funeral, with his mistress sobbing behind them. It was a memory Tasman did all he could to avoid. It still made his jaw clench.

'Your father's getaway car seemed to run out of gas, right before he hit the highway,' his mother had tried to joke to a young Tasman as they walked from the cemetery after the burial. 'Although, the spare tyre didn't go the miles he expected, honey, he should've stuck with us, right?' she continued, rhetorically, embracing Tasman's small shoulders. 'Sometimes it's better just to be alone, isn't it honey. Avoid all the trouble. But at least we've got each other, don't we? We can stick together, just you and me,' she said as she kissed him on the head. Tasman never said a word in response. And they never spoke of that day again.

The scars of abandonment never truly left Tasman, even as a grown man. And now his mother had found yet another new husband, another new life and even a new family, albeit with older children. For Tasman, it felt like lightning had struck twice in the same part of his heart, reopening the old wound again. He wondered if it was simply easier to be alone, without family, without the pain altogether. But he knew deep down, he didn't want to be.

Tasman sighed, and finally played aloud the stack of voicemails he had ignored from his mother. Being in this place again with that damn lighthouse had made him miss her, he thought.

'It's Mum… again. Sweetheart, I don't know how much longer you're willing to ignore me. But I just want you to know, nothing changes for you and me. We are still a family. I want you to be there, darling. David wants you there too. I think if you just gave him a chance… anyway, call me back, okay?'

He shook his head and let the phone fall to the passenger's seat, hitting the picture frame.

Tasman parked the van at the end of the main street set against the beachfront with a view of the lighthouse. He knocked on the front door of every house within its view, expecting Cressida to appear behind each one. No one knew who she was, or where to find her, and after the ninth house, Tasman wondered if his plan was about to fail spectacularly.

Then he saw it. A beach house set upon a perfect coastal block that had a near identical view of the lighthouse to the one in Harrison's photo.

Tasman sucked in the cold dusk air and knocked on the front door. The lights were on, but no one answered. Taking out his phone, he again tried to call Cressida, before realising his own phone was out of service out here. Perhaps it was a good sign, he wondered. It could mean he was in the right place.

He jumped back, startled by the sound of a rustle of leaves at the driveway's entrance. Spinning around, paranoid, Tasman was certain he was being followed, or watched. But no one was there.

Tasman stood in the driveway of the beach house, considering his next move. A man opened the door of a neighbouring house, and stood on its veranda smoking a cigarette, watching him intently. Tasman realised he looked like he was about to break in and moved on with haste back towards the main street.

The beach town shops were the heart and soul of the tiny village. There would be no way someone like Cressida Marks would go unnoticed in a place like this, thought Tasman.

'Excuse me, I'm a reporter with the Sapphire Times. I'm looking for this woman. Have you seen her in town?' he asked, showing her social media account photographs to shopkeepers and the few people left walking on the footpath at that time of day. Most avoided him, shaking their heads, desperate to get away from him before he could finish his sentence.

Tasman looked at the boutique bottle shop on the corner and decided to give it one last try. The shop looked as though it could be a 1920s film set. Each piece of wooden furniture was perfectly restored with a deep red shining varnish. As Tasman entered, an old doorbell rang to announce his arrival.

A shopkeeper obscured by a newspaper sat at the refurbished old wooden counter. He was reading the Ranges Advocate, and Harrison's face was splashed across the front page, along with shots of Mandy crying on camera, just like every other paper in the country.

Tasman approached the distracted shop attendant, becoming more doubtful by the minute of finding the woman who did not want to be found.

'Excuse me, have you seen this woman?' Tasman asked politely.

He didn't move an inch. Tasman spoke louder, wondering if he simply didn't hear him approach over the sound of classical music playing.

'Hi, I'm a reporter from the Sapphire Times. I'm wondering if you've seen this woman, Cressida Marks?' he repeated, unsure if he should actually move around the counter to step into the shopkeeper's view.

But the shopkeeper remained silent as he adjusted the paper in his grip.

Tasman scoffed, 'Right. Well, thanks for nothing, mate,' said Tasman, unable to hide his irritation any longer.

As Tasman moved towards the door to leave, the shopkeeper shuffled the papers again, moving them slightly away from his face.

'Didn't see anything you like then?' said the man, his voice low and deep. 'I can recommend one or two new spirits we've just shipped in from Europe. I highly recommend them,' the odd man said, his Irish accent now clear and loud, projecting from behind the newspaper.

Tasman looked back at the shopkeeper in disbelief.

'No. Thanks. I'm all set,' replied Tasman, incensed by his rudeness.

'Perhaps a nice bottle of red. We have a bold Shiraz that —,' the shopkeeper continued, sounding more interested in the potential sale.

'Have you seen this woman? Her name is Cressida Marks. I think she might've come through here,' said Tasman once more, perplexed by the quirky shop attendant.

'Right,' said the shopkeeper, folding the paper slowly before throwing the paper down to reveal his boyish face and bright red cheeks. His grey beard was intertwined with tiny decorative baubles that distracted Tasman for a moment.

The shopkeeper wore a dark green knitted Christmas jumper, despite it being June. He turned to the shelving behind him and selected a bottle of wine, its label written in French, presenting it to Tasman.

'I think she might appreciate this one,' the shopkeeper insisted, sliding it towards the cash register as he watched Tasman awaiting a response. And that was when the penny dropped. Tasman realised he would not get any information about Cressida Marks without making a sale first.

'Okay. Fine. How much is it?' asked Tasman hastily. He wondered whether this counted as cash for comment and if he was about to become a total hypocrite after the Mandy Adams fiasco.

'That will be $198.99,' he replied, hitting buttons on the cash register.

'Look, I think you know I'm not interested in the wine,' replied Tasman. 'Do you actually know who I am looking for or not?'

'Listen, ah, Mr Hill, isn't it?' the shopkeeper replied, surprising Tasman by the recognition. 'I'm sure you can understand I'm running a small business. And we don't see a lot of trade around here during the cooler months. If you want to know who may have come past my shop or not, I might need some help jogging my memory,' he smiled.

Tasman resisted the temptation to walk out of the store altogether. He couldn't face returning to the Sapphire Times empty-handed again. If he didn't find Cressida, the media pack eventually would and Victoria could easily send him packing back to the night shift.

'Right. I'll take this one then... thank you,' said Tasman, admitting defeat.

'That's an excellent choice, Mr Hill,' he replied, smiling as he bagged the wine handing it to him.

As Tasman paid, he felt like he was about to explode, knowing he would eat tuna out of a can to pay for this absurd wine for the next month and a half. Yet he clung to the hope he was about to find her.

'I think you might find what you're looking for on the front beach,' said the shopkeeper casually.

'Cressida Marks? On the beach just here?' said Tasman, pointing behind the shopping strip.

'Yes. She stopped by here just a few minutes before you walked in,' he said with a chuckle.

'Ah. Thank you,' said Tasman as hastily made his way out of the shop. He was half grateful, half completely irritated by the entire exchange.

'Oh, and one more thing, Mr Hill. I can't let you leave without knowing this is basically toilet roll compared to your fine publication,' he said, raising the Ranges Advocate in the air. 'Have a good night, Mr Hill and please, call again soon,' the man smiled, flapping the paper back open across his face.

CHAPTER TWENTY-TWO

TASMAN MADE IT TO THE SAND dunes as the daylight faded. It was a beautiful scene, the sun setting with a purple, pink and orange glow across the horizon. He paused as he took in the sky. The rain had fallen for so long he had almost forgotten what it was like to see the sun. And that's when he saw her.

Clutching the overpriced bottle of imported wine in a brown paper bag, Tasman hesitated as he stood only metres away from Cressida Marks, unsure of how to announce himself. As he took a step, his foot sinking deeper into the sand, he realised Cressida was also drinking from a bottle of wine, the same one he held in his hands, watching the waves in view of the lighthouse. Another empty bottle sat beside her, dug into the sand.

'Ah, Cressida?' he began, walking slowly in fear he would startle her. 'It's Tasman Hill... from the Sapphire Times.'

Cressida stared ahead silently, taking another sip from the bottle.

Tasman followed her gaze out at the glistening ocean.

'I think we have the same taste,' he said, presenting his bottle from the paper bag. 'Do you mind if I join you?'

Cressida looked up at Tasman for a moment, expressionless. 'So, you found me,' she eventually said, shrugging. 'Sit wherever you want. It's not my beach.' She wiped her mouth and eyes. She had been crying.

'I'm sorry. I know you're going through something... unimaginable. They asked me to see if I could speak to you about Harrison,' asked Tasman reluctantly. 'I thought I might find you here because of this.' Tasman handed the framed photograph to Cressida and she flinched before throwing it across the sand.

'Well done. Quite the investigative reporter then, aren't you? Congratulations,' Cressida slurred as she took another sip. She was drunk.

'Are you doing okay there? Here, take this,' he said, offering her his jacket as the cold set in, the sky now a deep dark navy blue. 'People are looking for you. They're worried.'

Cressida cackled sarcastically. 'Please - you mean journalists like *you* are looking for me,' she cried. 'Little carbon copies of *him* are looking for me. They want to parade me around to be part of the great Harrison Marks show, right?'

She wasn't wrong, thought Tasman.

'What has that awful wife done to the wonderful Harrison Marks? She must've murdered him if she isn't out searching the mountain peaks for him,' said Cressida. 'Do you know what it's like to be suspected of something like that? You know, all I have ever done is to be that man's supporting act. All I have ever done is love him. Dedicate myself to help him, his career and his family. All at my expense,' she scoffed.

Tasman settled into the sand nearby, listening, forgetting what his purpose was entirely.

'I was grateful to be with him,' she continued. 'Life was exhilarating. At least it was for the first few years. I should have known what to expect - people like him are bright stars that eventually burn out.'

'Did you see the interview... with Mandy Adams?' asked Tasman, selecting his words carefully.

'Yes. I knew about the cheating. I mean, I'm not a total moron,' she replied, wiping tears away before taking another sip from the bottle. 'The first time it was heartbreaking. The second, third and fourth time... well, it was utterly humiliating. He was always out working. Most of the time, I never knew where he was. And I stopped questioning it. He would always spin a story. Putting the job first, his sources first. Harry wanted to be the best, but even being the best isn't enough for him,' she said, digging her heels into the sand.

A loud crashing of bottles from a nearby bin startled them both, and they turned back towards the Main Street, towards the sound. They waited a moment, but no one appeared.

'Why am I telling you all of this, anyway?' sobbed Cressida. 'You're here to use all of this against me. That's exactly what Harrison would've done.'

'No one is being interviewed right now,' offered Tasman.

Tasman recognised Cressida was in a state of grief. He again offered her his jacket, which she eventually pulled on as the breeze off the ocean picked up.

'If I am honest with myself... the Harry I loved actually died years ago. And now... even after everything he's put me through, I still would give the world to at least see his face one more time. Even now, it's still all about him,' she sobbed, wiping more tears from her face. She finally turned to look at Tasman.

'I haven't drunk for years until now. I stopped out of protest when Harrison was plastered around the clock. It was enough to make anyone turn sober. Maybe it was his way of coping in our marriage. I don't know.'

'I don't think you're the problem,' interrupted Tasman, to comfort the woman. 'Maybe we should get you home?'

'Here, cheers to you. To Harrison. Oh, and your wonderful boss, Vicki. My dearest friend,' she added sarcastically. 'Yeah. That one I actually didn't see coming. When I found out Victoria and Harrison were basically a couple. Well, I just shut down. That was it for me.'

Tasman listened intently, hanging on every word.

'She turned up on my doorstep soon after to apologise, to confess,' said Cressida. 'Victoria said she wanted to make it right. But I know she kept going back to him the moment he rang,' she said as she stood up, swaying. 'So, you'll have to forgive me if I don't want to search for my often-missing husband or to plead for him to come back to me in the media, when there's every chance he just ran off with another woman,' she admitted.

Tasman was lost for words. 'I'm going to need a drink,' he said, cracking open the wine he had brought.

'Welcome to the club,' said Cressida. She stared at Tasman, perplexed for a moment, before her face softened, as though Tasman had earned her respect on some level.

'Did you tell the police? About the women? The affairs? It could be of help to the investigation,' he said.

'Of course, I told them! They have the whole bloody list. That was a charming exercise, writing it all out before they searched my house. Another truly humiliating moment. And so, I take some time out here for myself. Here I am, hiding from the world, drowning my feelings but you have found me, ready to do your story,' she said sarcastically. 'Good job. Go home and collect your Golden Quill.'

'Cressida, all of this was off the record - I hope you know that,' said Tasman.

Tasman searched for the right words. He felt torn between both his obligation to his job and the poor human sitting beside him, clearly in need of support.

'I'm not here to humiliate you. What you've been through, no one can even try to understand,' he said, taking another drink. 'You don't have to feel this way, you don't have to hide. If you decide you want to, let me tell your side of the story, what you've told me tonight. Let people see he isn't a perfect person, and that you had nothing to do with his disappearance.'

'What? That I didn't murder my husband?' she yelled, as a couple walking along the beach together turned their heads to look at them. 'What are you looking at?' she yelled at them. And within seconds, she vomited onto the sand.

'Okay. I think it's time I dropped you home. It's dark and you're drunk. You shouldn't be out here as the tide comes in,' Tasman offered.

Cressida reluctantly clung to his extended arm. 'You can't be serious?' she said to Tasman, looking at Harrison's smiling face printed over the news van as she got in.

IN THE SHORT DRIVE TO HER HOME, Cressida stared out of the passenger's window, gesturing silently with her hand to direct Tasman back to the same house he had knocked at earlier.

The gravel cracked as the old news van's tyres rolled over the driveway. Cressida's neighbour was still sitting outside, observing as he smoked another cigarette, the plume of smoke visible in the hazy winter night that had set in.

Cressida got out of the car and swayed a little. She leant on the door and leaned down to look at Tasman still sitting in the driver's seat.

'I had nothing to do with Harry's disappearance. But I am glad he's gone,' she said, and she slammed the door behind her.

CHAPTER TWENTY-THREE

TASMAN REPLAYED HIS CONVERSATION with Cressida on the beach over and over in his mind on the drive home. She was all he could think about. The moment he reached the city limit, the rain sprinkled his windscreen, as though the black rain cloud lingering over the Ranges was welcoming him home.

Tasman was exhausted. He had been riding the constant highs of adrenaline for days, and the rollercoaster of his new life was finally beginning to take its toll.

The rain intensified, washing over the car and the road ahead. The pounding surge of water drowned out the music he played. The rain pounded like a drum hitting the windscreen, forcing Tasman to pull over onto the side of the road to wait for it to ease.

Tasman slumped forward onto the steering wheel, knowing he could easily fall asleep, even with the storm outside. But he needed to get home so he took his chance in the deluge.

Twenty minutes later Tasman finally arrived home to his apartment. Running through the wet carpark and up the stairs to his front door, he felt instant relief, and that's when he saw it. A parcel sitting on his doorstep.

Tasman picked up the long white box wrapped in red ribbon and turned it over in his hands, looking around as though a neighbour would appear to collect it at any moment. He examined it. There were no postage markings, it had been hand delivered, thought Tasman as he looked around the entryway again, as though he was being watched.

A small card revealed the initials 'T. H'. He turned it over; 'Saw this and thought of you. Every good journo needs one. Love A x.'

Alison had been here, realised Tasman as he unwrapped the gift to reveal a beautiful silver pen. It felt heavy and expensive, and he knew if it had come from Alison - it probably was. It was the exact same style of pen Harrison had used; it was always on display resting in his blazer front pocket.

Tasman quickly placed it back into the box. The last thing Tasman wanted was for his colleagues to think he was not only trying to become Harrison's replacement but trying to replicate him too.

Perhaps it was Alison's way of breaking the ice after their train wreck date the other night, he wondered as he turned the key into his apartment door, shaking off his soaked jacket.

Tasman placed the box on the counter and looked back at the front door, the hairs on his arms stood tall. He stared at the box and wondered how Alison had known where he lived. He opened the door again and looked out at the rain sprayed carpark, as though he was expecting Alison to appear. An icy wind swept through the outdoor foyer, making the lights flicker. There was no one there. Tasman concluded his paranoia was the product of his complete exhaustion.

'Thank you for the pen, you really shouldn't have,' he messaged Alison. Even when he felt uneasy, his compulsion to be polite always prevailed.

'Apparently all the best journos have this one. I'm sorry about the other night. Let's try that date again soon,' Alison replied instantly.

Tasman threw his phone aside and placed his frozen microwave meal, the same old chicken kiev and vegetables he ate each week into his microwave and waited. He took the gift box containing the pen and placed it into a kitchen drawer, slamming it shut. How had Alison known where he lived? He felt like Alison's strong and sudden interest was like a force of nature, pushing towards him rapidly. It didn't feel organic, although Tasman never had a long-term serious relationship with a woman. He didn't know what it was holding him back from Alison. He just simply couldn't connect or communicate with this beautiful, successful woman who seemed to want something with him, or from him.

Tasman let the thought go as he waited for his meal, looking out of the window at the flooding streets below as the water receded down the storm water drains. The night reporter would need to cover this for the paper, he thought, unable to switch off from the news.

He stared at the glow of the streetlamps, reflecting on the wet bitumen. Looking outside his little apartment window gave him a sense of calm amongst all the chaos in his world. Gripping the windowpane, Tasman leaned forward, squinting as though his eyes needed to focus. He could see a figure standing with an umbrella on the street below. It looked as though the figure were directly facing him, watching him from afar. The stalker didn't move, a statue in the rainfall. Unable to look away, he continued to watch.

Why would anyone stand on that part of the street at this hour, in the pouring rain? He thought as he swallowed hard. It was probably nothing.

He moved from the window to check on his meal and slammed the microwave door shut. It was still frozen. He scrolled his phone, scanning the news for any updates on Harrison before the device started ringing, the call from an unlisted number.

'Hello?' he asked, scrambling to answer the unexpected call.

There was nothing but silence on the line.

Perhaps it was a source. Calling to break another big story or to reveal new information about Harrison's disappearance, he wondered. No one ever responded, so he hung up.

'Bloody prank calls at this hour,' he said, reminding himself of a grumpy old man.

The phone flashed again, with another call from a private number. He answered, and again there was silence. All he could make out was the sound of rain and static blast through the phone before it suddenly disconnected.

Tasman uncomfortably laughed to himself. Some high school kids had probably found one of his business cards and were sitting back enjoying themselves pranking a journalist. It had to be nothing.

Tasman strode towards the microwave, passing the window when he saw it again. The same figure with the black umbrella was still there, standing in the rain. The water rushed past its feet, streaming into the drain beside them.

'He must be out of their mind,' said Tasman aloud. He opened the window, the sound of rushing water on the street filling his apartment as he leaned out to get a closer look. 'Hey! Are you right?' he shouted. He wanted the figure to know he had seen it. But so did the figure. In their hand Tasman could see an illuminated phone, glowing.

Tasman felt the jolt of fear as he considered the figure was the culprit calling him from the street below. Why would anyone want to watch him? Why would it want to stand in the rain, to intimidate him? To scare him?

Locked in the silent standoff, Tasman hung out of his window, becoming drenched as he contemplated what could happen next. The figure waited a few moments and, without acknowledgement, slowly turned and walked away.

The microwave beeped, causing Tasman to jump, hitting his head on the windowpane. He ran his hands through his hair and no longer felt tired. A fresh shot of adrenaline was coursing through his veins.

Tasman checked his door, ensuring it was locked, jolting it to make sure. He climbed back into bed and stared up at the ceiling once more, knowing he would check the street twice more before he would make it to sleep.

CHAPTER TWENTY-FOUR

TEN DAYS GONE

THE NEXT MORNING, Tasman stood under the makeshift search headquarters at the Ranges Lookout. The once frenzied media pack had now dwindled to just a few local reporters waiting for the promised police update.

'Alright then, Hill?' asked Rick Tancred, the same reporter from the Ranges Advocate who Tasman had wanted to punch in the face when he revealed Harrison as the missing man.

'Tancred,' replied Tasman, his lips pursed.

'Sorry to hear about Townsend. That's got to be rough. First Marks, then him. Tough times at the Times,' Tancred smirked.

Tasman's cheeks tightened. Tancred reminded him of how arrogant and needlessly cruel his father would have been as a competitive journalist back when he was king at the Advocate.

'There's rumours that this thing is going to be called off any minute,' Tancred continued, leaning closer to Tasman as though he had shared secret information with him.

Tasman rolled his eyes.

'I think anyone might've guess that, given the conditions,' Tasman replied, staring straight up at the tent as a large pool of water gathered in its centre while the heavy rain continued to fall.

The energy of the police and volunteers had shifted, and from the look on their expressionless faces, the sense of urgency had disappeared. It was time to call it quits on the search.

'Good morning. I'll aim to keep this short,' began Detective Inspector Watts, who stood in front of the waiting cameras. 'It will not surprise you all why we have called this press conference this morning in relation to the search for Harrison Marks. We can confirm our search and rescue teams, along with droves of volunteers, have found no trace of Mr Marks. The increasing rainfall over the Ranges has hampered our efforts considerably.'

Tasman furiously jotted down the speech in shorthand in his new notebook, each time he turned a fresh page he wondered after his missing notebooks, the same ones that contained the original information about Harrison's disappearance. As he looked up, he caught Watts' passing stare.

'I am sad to say that the conditions have now become far too dangerous due to the significant risk of landslips, the movement of heavy rock, trees and mud on the mountain. Therefore, the search is suspended, effective immediately,' said Watts.

The detective paused as an audible murmur came from the group of dozens of reporters, some out of confirmation of suspicions, others out of surprise.

'In the meantime, our investigation will continue. I again ask that anyone who has information about Mr Marks or his movements before his disappearance to please come forward. I won't be taking any further questions, thank you,' Watts concluded, stepping away from the simultaneous flash of cameras.

Television crews filmed the search teams packing up tents and installing temporary fencing around the scene. The police tape remained strewn across the water-logged site where Harrison's car had been discovered. The burnt smell of the fire had been long washed away and the mountain air returned to its original state.

'WOW, YOU LOOK LIKE SHIT,' said Zaylee to Tasman as they sat in their favourite spot at The Lonely Squire later that night. It was true, Tasman looked dishevelled. He couldn't deny that. The pressure of covering the disappearance of their own colleague and his probable murder was getting the best of him, along with the stalker watching his apartment.

'Are you okay?' Zaylee asked patting him on the back in comfort. She looked down at Tasman's phone flashing beside them. 'Jesus, someone's popular,' she said, noting the barrage of texts appearing on the screen.

'Yeah. It's, ah Alison,' Tasman replied, sliding the phone back towards him to hide in his pocket.

'Wait a minute, someone's buried the lead, are all of those messages from her?' asked Zaylee, snapping her hand on top of the phone.

She was like a schoolteacher about to confiscate a note being passed between students.

'I've got to see this! I thought you weren't keen on seeing her again?' she asked as she began scrolling through the messages – almost all had not yet been responded to.

'I wasn't... and then I was. And now, I don't know to be honest. Maybe the lack of sleep is just getting to me,' replied Tasman as he awkwardly sipped his beer hoping to change the conversation. 'I'm becoming a bit paranoid and started seeing things, like I thought someone was standing outside my apartment watching me the last night,' he laughed.

Zaylee almost spat out her drink in surprise.

Peter stopped shaking a cocktail and moved closer to them to join the conversation.

'Sorry, you think someone was standing outside of your apartment watching you? You've got someone stalking you?' asked Peter.

Tasman hesitated before answering. Peter's tone worried him and Peter wasn't someone who ever took anything too seriously.

'It was someone dressed in black, under an umbrella, just standing there facing my window. It would've been a few minutes at least. It was the strangest thing. As soon as I yelled out to the figure, it didn't run, it said nothing and just slowly turned and walked away. I think it might've been calling me.'

'Are you sure it wasn't Alison?' asked Zaylee cheekily as she handed Tasman back his phone. 'What did the calls say?'

'No one was on the line; it was just silence. At first, I thought it might've been just Mum. And I had just spoken to Alison after she left me a gift and...' said Tasman, his stomach feeling tight with worry.

Zaylee was leaning across the entire bar now, as though she was piecing together a puzzle.

'Hang on, rewind,' she interrupted, hitting the bar. 'Alison left you a gift last night. At your house? How did she even know where you live?

Tasman shrugged. 'That's crossed my mind too,' he said.

'So, what was the gift? Let me guess: a heart-shaped locket with your initials inscribed on the inside,' said Peter, trying to lighten the mood.

'It was an expensive silver pen,' Tasman grimaced.

'Wow. That's a fair amount to spend on a one-night stand,' said Zaylee. 'She's done her homework, though. I only know of one other journalist who has a pen like that.'

'And he's missing... ' said Tasman in agreement. Tasman knew something was off and speaking with Peter and Zaylee had only confirmed his suspicions.

'So, you think... Harrison possibly knew Alison?' asked Zaylee.

'Well, there's no such thing as a coincidence, is there?' replied Tasman.

CHAPTER TWENTY-FIVE

TWO WEEKS GONE

TASMAN COULDN'T HELP BUT CHECK the street below each time he walked past the window of his apartment, expecting to see the dark figure standing there watching him. But there was always nothing.

He sat down to watch the late news. Councillor Mosca, Alison's father, led the coverage slamming the local police for suspending the search for Harrison, demanding it continue despite the rainfall and dangerous conditions.

'The family of this man, along with the community, this great city, needs answers and we must bring this man home,' the politician demanded on-camera.

Mosca was a true showman, thought Tasman.

He mindlessly scrolled his phone's news feed and paused, realising he had not heard from his mother in days. She had finally stopped calling, stopped chasing him. And he felt relief to be permitted to sit with his feelings and make the next move when he was ready.

Within seconds, Tasman's phone rang loudly. The intrusion surprising him and he hesitated. It was yet another late-night private call.

He answered, but said nothing, waiting for their move while desperately listening to any defining noises in the background to place who they were.

'Hello? Is anyone there?' said a strange, yet familiar woman's voice.

'Oh hello, yes hello. Who is this?' asked Tasman, sitting straight as he realised it was not likely to be another prank call at all.

'It's Cressida... Marks,' she said, slowly. The rocky start to the call had clearly unsettled her. Tasman was embarrassed, but Cressida continued.

'I'm sorry it's late. I wanted to let you know that I've thought about it and... I'll do it, I'll do the interview.'

Tasman moved to the edge of his tiny couch, wanting to jump for joy.

'Cressida, are you sure?' he asked, hoping his enthusiasm wasn't too obvious.

'Yes. I'll do the exclusive, or whatever you want to call it. But I'll do it on one condition: that it's you I'm sitting down with, right? No one else.'

'Yes. Of course,' stammered Tasman in shock over his own personal professional victory. 'When can you do it?' he asked.

'I'll come in first thing tomorrow. Any later, and I might change my mind again. See you then,' she replied before ending the call.

In an instant, Tasman had secured one of the biggest interviews of his career. He couldn't help but clench his fists and punch the air in elation. He was about to deliver, to prove that he had what it took to be great. To be a worthy journalist, after all.

THE NEXT MORNING, Tasman walked into the newsroom with a certain confidence that he had been missing ever since he joined the Sapphire Times on the night shift – he had the exclusive Cressida Marks interview. Tasman stood at the doorway of Victoria's office, interrupting her discussion with McAllister about the Harrison Marks coverage numbers.

'Hill, are you right?' questioned McAllister, irritated at his intrusion.

Tasman looked past McAllister ignoring him entirely as he turned to Victoria.

'I've got her,' said Tasman triumphantly.

'Who?' McAllister demanded.

'Cressida Marks. I found her. She's coming in now,' said Tasman, checking his watch. 'She's agreed to let me interview her. It's an exclusive.'

Victoria looked stunned. She rose from her leather chair and leaned on her desk for support in disbelief.

'Victoria, this is surely one for one of our more experienced reporters -,' interjected McAllister.

'Nope. I'll be doing it,' said Tasman, cutting him off. 'It's her only condition – unless you want to let someone else snap up the interview, mate,' said Tasman, beaming with confidence that was almost Marks-like. 'So, no need to reassign, thanks mate.'

'Well done, Hill,' said Victoria, holding her stare on Tasman for a few moments. 'McAllister, get the team to prepare the studio. This needs maximum exposure. It must be our lead across every platform.'

McAllister looked shocked as he moved towards the door, before Victoria continued.

'Also call Network 360 News. Let them know we will sign over the rights for them to air the story right after our copy breaks. We need to lead this across the country.'

'Right, Boss. Good work, Hill,' said McAllister sarcastically as he left the room.

Tasman knew this may be his only opportunity to speak with Victoria alone.

'Victoria, there's just one more thing,' he said, lingering in the doorway.

'Don't you have plenty to prepare, Hill?' she looked at him suspiciously as she adjusted her laptop screen.

'I just want to say that you never had to give me this role... to keep quiet,' said Tasman, searching for the right words to explain.

Victoria took off her glasses, looking up at Tasman from her screen.

'What I saw that night, what I heard, I know it wasn't any of my business,' he continued, his newfound confidence quickly deteriorating.

Victoria shut the laptop and looked up at Tasman, her lips pursed.

'Hill, I gave you a role that I thought you were entitled to,' she replied, taking Tasman by complete surprise. 'And whatever it is you think you witnessed, can only be described as regrettable and unprofessional. Did you consider that perhaps me being at the office at that late hour may have, in fact, reminded me you had been on the night shift for far longer than most? Perhaps it was just as innocent as that,' she said, looking back at her work. 'And before you ask... yes, they know. I told the police everything.'

Tasman nodded and turned to leave before looking back at Victoria.

'Including about the affair?' said Tasman. He could tell his forwardness had caught her equally off guard.

Victoria paused for a moment. His words had struck a nerve.

'Yes. Including the affair,' she said, hesitating as though in pain, as she put her pen down to look at Tasman. 'Well, all you need to do right now is get the story, Hill. Okay? Think of it as just another chance to show us what you're made of. You know, show us you've got that same edge as... the great Eric Gleeson,' she said slowly, her trademark business tone returning.

Tasman froze. Victoria knew his secret. She knew about his father. She must have known all along.

The phone rang at her desk, 'This is head office. I need to tell them the good news,' she said. 'Thank you, Hill, that will be all,' she said as she directed him to the door.

CHAPTER TWENTY-SIX

TASMAN SAT in the small storage cupboard that the Sapphire Times had converted into a mini television studio. He adjusted the barely used microphone fixed to his blazer again, it was the fifth time he had touched it in just a matter of minutes.

The Head Office had ordered all its major publications to include broadcasting and social media content, including the Sapphire Times. The news team had been expected to multitask and record their best interviews in the studio, an additional pressure to their deadline driven days.

The studio door opened, and McAllister showed Cressida Marks inside. Cressida was dressed in a pale blue skirt and knitted top, her blonde hair perfectly styled, her makeup highlighting just how naturally beautiful she was. But Tasman could see the tension she felt written across her face. Her lips pursed, and her eyes were bloodshot.

The atmosphere felt fragile. Tasman wondered if she may just change her mind and walk out altogether, and he wouldn't blame her. He admired her grace in the face of grief, by choosing to be interviewed in a newsroom overseen by her husband's mistress, or one of them at least.

Tasman stood to shake Cressida's hand, forgetting the connected microphone cord pulling him back into place. He slowly sat down, as though any sudden movement may spook Cressida, causing her to abandon the whole thing altogether.

'Cressida, thank you so much for being here,' said Tasman softly, desperate to put her at ease.

Cressida nodded without looking at Tasman, staring ahead, her mind somewhere else altogether. 'If it will stop these people chasing me down the street, then it's worth it,' she said sarcastically.

'I know it couldn't be easy being here. But we appreciate what you're doing,' Tasman replied, looking at the time to check how long they had before the livestream began.

'I need to put these accusations to rest,' said Cressida reluctantly. 'Besides, we have plenty of history here. It's what Harrison would want,' she said. She seemed to still be struggling with what she was about to do, thought Tasman. Before Tasman could say another word, a camera operator from 360 Network News and McAllister appeared, adjusting the lighting setup and instantly wrangling another microphone to place onto her.

'Right, Cressida - there's water just over here and tissues, anything you need just here,' said McAllister, being as hospitable as he could, holding his hands together in a light clap. The ex-television veteran was at least at home in the studio, thought Tasman.

'Hill, uh, I mean Tasman, will wrap you up when we're running short on time and, of course, if you need a minute, just let him know. Jase, here on the camera will count you in when we're about to go live on our social platforms.'

Cressida nodded in response, taking a sip of water to steady her nerves as though she were bracing before undergoing an intrusive medical procedure.

Reporters gathered near the two-way reflective glass along the side of the studio, behind Cressida. Tasman was fine with an audience. He had never been more focused on anything or anyone.

The camera operator looked at Tasman and counted them in.

'Five. Four. Three,' he shouted, before silently counting the final two beats. They were recording and streaming live.

'This is Tasman Hill with the Sapphire Times. I'm here with Cressida Marks, the wife of missing reporter Harrison Marks, who disappeared under suspicious circumstances more than two weeks ago,' he began, effortlessly, as though he had done this dozens of times before. 'Authorities have just called off the search, with heavy rainfall lashing the region set to continue days, possibly even weeks. Cressida, thank you for speaking with us today.'

Cressida nodded confidently in response, as though she knew what was about to come next.

'Cressida, no one could try to imagine how you're feeling right now, but you've agreed to join us today to give us some insight. Your husband has disappeared under suspicious circumstances somewhere, presumably at the Ranges National Park. Can you walk us back to the last time you saw him?'

Cressida carefully contemplated her words before she answered. Tasman and all watching were already hanging on the moment, anticipating her response.

'I saw Harry the day of the Golden Quill Awards. There was nothing unusual about the day. He left for work, he walked out the door and that was the last time I saw him,' she said.

'Do you remember anything usual about Harrison that day?' asked Tasman casually.

'No. Harrison wasn't a traditional husband. He wasn't a homebody, he often worked around the clock. It's common for him to not be home. We were often just ships passing in the night, so to speak,' she explained.

'Did you attend the Golden Quill Awards with Harrison that night he disappeared? It was another big moment for him. Another win,' Tasman continued.

Cressida looked mildly irritated, but adjusted in her seat.

'No, I did not attend,' she replied, pausing for a moment. 'We haven't attended that event together in quite a few years.'

'So, when did you raise the alarm? When did you realise that Harrison hadn't returned home?' he asked.

Cressida looked directly into Tasman's eyes.

'I didn't raise the alarm. I never called the police. He just... never came home.'

Tasman paused for a moment, swallowing so hard, expecting the microphones to pick up the sound. 'For the average viewer watching this, you can see that would strike most people as extremely odd. Your husband of what, fifteen years or more, has disappeared and you do nothing?' he continued.

'Well, I can see why you would think that way,' she said. 'My husband often disappeared at a moment's notice. He would frequently go missing from our life together. He was – is – a heavy drinker. And he's someone who is married to his work. You might not understand this, but eventually I learned to stop waiting for Harrison to come home,' she said, her eyes brimming with tears. 'It is an incredibly lonely existence to always be someone's second option in life,' she said, looking him dead in the eyes, holding her composure.

Tasman paused. He knew this was extremely difficult for Cressida to open up this way. But he had to remain impartial, he had to continue.

'So, it was a regular occurrence for Harrison to disappear and not be in touch with you at all?'

'Yes, exactly. There would be days on end that Harry would be gone. He would sometimes be so drunk he would just turn his phone off and pick up and leave at a moment's notice. And I've understood that was the deal to be with him. Warts and all.'

'So, your marriage has been under strain for quite some time?' he asked, glancing at the two-way windows, noticing Victoria hovering at the back of the group, observing. 'Were you aware of the affair, the allegation raised by the young woman employed by you?'

'Yes. I knew Harrison was no longer faithful to me. I never really knew whose bed he was spending the night in. Our marriage was a train wreck,' replied Cressida, becoming more comfortable and candid.

'Some people might believe that such a thankless marriage might be a motivation for revenge, especially when someone had treated them so badly...' pushed Tasman.

Cressida knew where he was going with the questioning and suddenly raised her hands, interjecting.

'I've dedicated my fortune, my life, to Harrison. I loved him then and I still do now. But yes, I would be lying if I didn't agree that the affairs, and yes there were more than just one, killed me,' she said, her cheeks flushed. 'He had told me he wanted to try again, to work things out. I really wanted to believe him. And then... he disappeared,' she said as she finally wiped tears from her eyes, snatching a tissue from the box nearby.

'You have spoken with the police. How do you believe the investigation into his potential murder is going? There have been no arrests. What do you make of that?' Tasman asked.

'I have to keep faith that they are doing all they can to find him and whoever is responsible for his disappearance. It was the detectives who told me he had vanished, after they found the car,' she admitted. 'And from that moment on, I have done anything they have asked of me. I have nothing to hide. I want to find Harry and I want him to come home, regardless of what has happened in the past.'

'Why didn't you help search for Harrison?' said Tasman quickly, sweeping past her heartfelt plea.

'It was too much for me to take in. To know it was real. That it was more than just another one of his disappearing acts,' she replied, dabbing at her eyes with the tissue she gripped tightly in her hands.

'And then when the young woman came forward to discuss the affair. What happened then?' Tasman pushed, ignoring his instinct to stop the interview, but he knew he had to ask the questions the public had been waiting for.

'I ran. I couldn't face the media circus or the public humiliation. People have been camped outside of my house for goodness' sake! Picking apart my life and calling me a murderer. Tell me how any human deals with that kind of pressure? You would run too,' she said, anger building in her tone.

Tasman took a moment before asking the question he had been building up to, praying Cressida understood he had no choice but to ask.

'What do you say to those media commentators, people on social media who are accusing you of being involved in Harrison's disappearance?'

She stared back at Tasman, insulted. She was hurt, he thought.

'What exactly do I stand to gain in hurting my husband? What could he possibly do to me, that he hadn't already done, that would suddenly make me want to hurt him? I have dedicated my life, my career, everything to Harrison and his family.'

Tasman looked to Jason, and nodded that he was done. He had put her through enough.

'And finally, Cressida,' he said. 'What do you have to say to the person, or anyone out there who may know what happened to Harrison – what's your message to them?'

Cressida took a deep breath in and exhaled slowly, as though she were in pain.

'The truth always comes out,' she replied as she looked down the barrel of the camera.

CHAPTER TWENTY-SEVEN

CRESSIDA WASTED NO TIME ripping her microphone off and making her way towards the studio door as soon as the interview was over.

'I hope you understand I had to ask,' said Tasman as he rushed to keep up with Cressida, searching to meet her eyes to know she was okay. But she didn't look at him.

Opening the door, Cressida was face-to-face with her large audience. Some of them were the same journalists and staff she had once known years ago when she would stop by the Sapphire Times to visit Harrison. But now it was different. Irreversibly so.

Cressida stopped and looked directly at Victoria, who stood arms folded against the wall towards the back of the room.

'I hope you got what you're after,' Cressida finally said to Tasman. She shook her coat on, while maintaining her stare at Victoria.

'Let me show you out,' offered McAllister, gesturing to the door and Cressida followed.

Tasman watched her leave and immediately felt deflated. He knew he should feel proud, or even successful after his exclusive with Cressida. But he wondered what his interview had done to his subject, what impact it had on Cressida, a woman grieving her husband.

Tasman threw himself into his seat at Harrison's old desk. Zaylee grinned as she walked towards him ready to congratulate him.

'Seriously, Tasman Hill - a legend already in the making,' said Zaylee, squeezing his shoulders proudly as she sat on the edge of the desk. 'This is already blowing up,' she said looking at the Sapphire Time's social media feed on her phone. 'They love Cressida. They've completely changed their tune about her now.'

'Do you think I was too hard on her?' asked Tasman, his eyes wandering to the Harrison Marks flower memorial outside. Before Zaylee could respond, his friend quickly stood up, practically jumping off the desk, like a soldier standing to attention. Tasman looked back and Victoria had appeared behind him.

'Hill, can I have a word with you, in private?' said Victoria. 'Perhaps in my office,' she suggested, walking ahead.

'Yes, of course,' Tasman replied, quickly following behind the editor as she closed the door and offered him a seat on the lounge in front of her desk.

'I think congratulations are in order,' Victoria began. 'Your interview with Cressida Marks was exactly what we needed. I'm told the online views via our website and social platforms alone have already broken records,' she said, smiling lightly.

Tasman wondered where the conversation was headed, Victoria rarely dished out praise, something felt off, he thought.

'It's really the shot in the arm we needed. Especially with the pressure on us, given the circumstances...,' her elegant voice beginning to trail off. 'And the romantic affairs element. You handled delicately... thank you,' she continued, looking relieved.

Tasman said nothing in response. As Victoria poured a drink, Tasman felt compelled to fill the silence, but fought the urge and instead sat and waited.

'Head Office have said they would like to see a lot more of you, especially on the crime and investigations round,' she said, taking a sip of her drink slowly. 'However, this role does comes at a price, of sorts. They'll be expecting big things from you. And I hope you understand we need more from you, from the entire news team, than ever before.'

'Yes, of course, I understand,' agreed Tasman as he considered her words.

'They're already tempted to cut back on the cost of Marks' replacement, so let's make sure they know that you're indispensable. That they can't sell another paper without you, right?' she said, looking him dead in the eye.

Tasman felt exasperated. It had only been an hour since he had delivered one of the biggest interviews of the year and yet his success was already short-lived, and the next goal was in sight. No wonder Marks drank so much, he thought.

'Put in the time and the effort. If you want to get to the top, or not - it's your choice,' Victoria continued, looking over his face.

Tasman could feel the pinch of pain as his jaw locked from the tension of the conversation. He wondered if Victoria could tell.

Victoria moved to her desk, signalling the conversation was over as she started sifting through the draft outline for the following day's paper.

'Thanks Victoria, I won't let you down,' Tasman replied, standing to leave.

'Oh, one more thing before you head out,' she said looking up at him. 'You've got three months.'

'Sorry, what do you mean?' asked Tasman, confused by the comment.

'A probation period, of sorts, to secure Marks' role permanently. After all, you mentioned you were concerned about your promotion not being merit-based, you wanted things to all be above board – so that's what we're doing,' she snapped. 'So, you might need to bring us a great Tasman Hill investigative story soon, otherwise, well, who knows, you might just end up back on the nightshift' she shrugged, throwing the papers back down on the desk.

Tasman's cheeks burned, he had been caught off guard. His success was already a punishment of sorts. Tasman accusing Victoria of not being upfront with the police had come back to bite him. Now, Tasman was on notice.

It was in that moment that Tasman understood how Harrison and Victoria clicked. They were both brutal, and both comfortable in chaos, in fact, they thrived in it.

'That's all. Thank you. Please close the door on your way out,' she said politely dismissing him.

Tasman closed the door behind him and waited a moment, still shocked at what had just happened. He stared across the room, the vision of his interview with Cressida replayed across every television screen. His interview was everywhere, yet he had barely a moment of celebration, instead he now had no time to waste. He had a time limit. An expiration date. And the pressure to deliver clouded in his thoughts.

'So, what was that all about?' asked Zaylee as Tasman collected his things at his desk. 'You don't look okay,' she said suspiciously.

'Oh, ah nothing much. I just need to deliver another hard-hitting investigative story and need to have delivered it by yesterday,' he said, deflated.

'Wait – what? But you just -,' began Zaylee before Christine the receptionist appeared, interrupting their conversation.

'Excuse me Hill, the police department just called for you. They asked for you specifically,' she said. 'They need you to get down there... right now,' she Christine, passing him a contact number on a post-it note.

'See? Things are looking up for you, my friend,' said Zaylee. 'Think of it like this: you can repair some of the damage Townsend caused by leaking Harrison's name to the media and maybe get your next story, see? Easy,' she offered enthusiastically.

'Nothing in journalism is ever that easy,' huffed Tasman.

CHAPTER TWENTY-EIGHT

DUSK WAS QUICKLY CREEPING in, casting shades of blue and grey over the city that afternoon. Tasman walked under the entrance, where the media pack had once gathered, sent into a frenzy over the search for Harrison Marks. Now, no one was there huddled under the small section of cover to avoid the drizzle. It was just Tasman.

He entered the lobby and immediately was caught by his own reflection, looking directly into his own eyes in the mirrored glass wall with a plastic protective barrier in front of it. Tasman could hear loud muffled voices but could see no one. Staring up above to the corners of the ceiling, he peered at the CCTV cameras monitoring him. He looked for a bell to ring, but as soon as he moved, a man's voice startled him.

'Tasman Hill?' asked an officer who appeared seemingly out of nowhere from a door within the glass wall.

'Yes, ah, I'm here to see Detective Sergeant Marshall.' he hesitated while the officer punched a code into a keypad and quickly opened another door from the room to his left.

'This way please,' said the officer, holding the heavy door open for him.

Tasman felt as though he was being ushered through to another portal. He followed through a long passageway with cubicles and interview rooms scattered throughout. Officers passed him, watched him silently. It was clear outsiders were not meant to pass beyond the glass walls, at least not without handcuffs on.

The officer he had followed eventually led him into an interview room, swiping him through the door and inviting him to sit at an empty silver metal table, with a large industrial light, its globe covered in a protective cage, hanging above.

It was less than a minute later when the escorting officer appeared again, this time holding the door open for Detective Inspector Watts who strode into the room holding a coffee, followed by Detective Sergeant Marshall, who held a large plastic tub filled with notebooks that he placed onto the table. Tasman suspected they had been waiting for his arrival from behind the two-way reflective glass window in the interview room.

'Mr Hill, we appreciate you coming down,' said Watts, shaking his hand. 'As you know, we've been asking some of your colleagues to come in to ensure we've checked under every rock, so to speak.'

Tasman knew why he had been called in. The investigation had stalled, and now Watts was tracing back over every statement, every explanation anyone had given about what they knew about Harrison's disappearance.

'Of course, whatever you need,' Tasman replied earnestly.

Marshall folded his arms. 'Obviously, we ask that this conversation is strictly off the record,' said Marshall.

'Absolutely,' said Tasman, feeling the same sinking feeling he had experienced when the same detectives thought he had leaked Harrison's name.

Watts flicked open a manila folder containing photographs and typed documents relating to the case. She appeared to read over one piece of paper for a moment, taking a sip of her coffee before eventually closing the folder again to address Tasman. She leaned forward on the table.

'Mr Hill, I was hoping we could revisit your statement about the night Harrison Marks disappeared. You were one of the final people to see him, is that correct?' she asked.

'Yes. That's right,' confirmed Tasman. 'I saw him in his car late at night at work. He had been drinking and I went to call him a cab, but he drove away before I had a chance.'

Watts considered Tasman's words, he could tell she had the Harrison Marks' timeline memorised.

'And, looking over your statement here, it doesn't seem to mention anything about Mr Marks before that part of the evening,' Watts said pointing at the manila folder. 'Did you see or speak to him before he got into the car at the Times?'

Tasman clenched his teeth and his jaw locked at the question. Victoria had said she had told them everything, so he had nothing to hide, he thought. Despite this, his stomach felt like he was on board a rollercoaster.

'Well, yeah, Harrison was at work late with Victoria. I was on night shift and heard some noise, I went to check it out and realised that they were fighting. Obviously, Victoria has already mentioned that to you,' said Tasman. He felt like he was over explaining what was already known.

Watts tilted her head and looked at Marshall, who quickly reopened the manila folder and made a note on the margin of a page in red pen. Surely, they knew this information, Victoria had scoffed at Tasman when he asked her directly if she had told the police about the last time they had seen Harrison alive.

'Right,' agreed Watts slowly. 'And in your words, what was your understanding of what the fight was about?' she said calmly, taking another drink from her coffee.

'It sounded like it was about their relationship, and also about Harrison's work. He was threatening to leave the Times,' said Tasman. 'Harrison was upset, he was angry, he smashed his award he'd just won.'

'And Victoria, how did she seem?' said Watts, revealing nothing like an expert poker player.

Tasman shrugged. 'She was calm, she was trying to deescalate the whole thing. That was it. I went back to my desk and then Harrison left, not long after she did too,' he said.

'And then you got a promotion?' said Watts quickly, watching his reaction like a hawk. Tasman adjusted on his cold metal seat. The light swung above slightly and the spotlight irritated his eyes for a moment.

'Yes,' Tasman replied. 'Victoria asked me to start on the day shift and then –,' he said before Watts quickly interjected.

'Then you took over Harrison's job. Pretty sweet role, isn't it? The new star reporter in the city. Your parents must be proud,' she tilted her head to the side again, watching Tasman carefully. She was testing him.

Tasman could feel his hands beginning to sweat. Of course, he had benefited from his own colleague's disappearance, but now he was being accused of it. Tasman took a sip of water from the glass in front of him on the table.

'I've taken the opportunity, yes,' he said, his voice clear and strong. He had to remind himself he had done nothing wrong, and most importantly, he had nothing to hide. 'Now, is there anything else I can help you with? You know, off the record?'

Watts and Marshall looked at each other and nodded in agreement.

'No, thank you Mr Hill. Unless there's anything else you would like to take this opportunity to discuss with us?' asked Watts.

Tasman shook his head in response.

Marshall pulled the tub of notebooks towards him and stood lifting the lid off.

'These were seized from Harrison's desk at the Sapphire Times. We've had them copied and can return them. Given you've taken over for Harrison, we will sign them over to you, Mr Hill,' said Marshall, his expression deadpan.

'We've been having a hell of a time trying to crack these shorthand notes and codes. There are literally thousands and thousands of pages of notes here,' said Watts, suddenly speaking in a lighter, more conversational tone. 'So far, we have only been able to identify about a quarter of it while we wait on a handwriting expert.'

As Marshall pushed the tub towards Tasman, a notebook fell to the floor. Tasman reached down to pick it up and looked at the pages. Harrison had been meticulous with each page of his notebook filled with shorthand, codes, and random scribbled notes.

'See anything interesting?' asked Watts, watching as Tasman scanned page after page before stopping at the final page at the back of a half-filled book.

Tasman looked up at the detectives. 'You're going to need to see this. This bit here, in shorthand, it's about corruption at the City Council. I think this could be Harrison's final story.'

CHAPTER TWENTY-NINE

THREE WEEKS GONE

TASMAN WOKE HIMSELF with a vicious sneeze. His nose was running and he shivered with chills. Lying in bed, his head ached. He coughed and spluttered as he pulled himself up from his pillow just in time to shut his window as the rain picked up again.

In the reflection on the glass, he could see the colour had drained from his face. Tasman had never called in sick. His father had never taken a day off from work in his life. It was considered weakness in Eric Gleeson's book; a sign that you weren't cut-out for the demanding world of news.

It was the single trait Tasman knew he had inherited from his father. Convinced he could somehow overcome his illnesses, that he could somehow force himself to keep going, to carry on if he simply ignored the issue.

But with Townsend long gone, and McAllister at the helm, Tasman didn't fear the public shaming or email blasts. Instead, it was Victoria's looming deadline. He imagined a countdown clock, ticking down, minute by minute. How could he find the next story when he was sick and confined to his bed?

Tasman thought of Harrison's notebook, the shorthand, the notes, all leading to what could have been the final piece the star reporter had been working on, yet Tasman couldn't make sense of any of it without more information, more context and more time. He needed to dig, and he needed to start now. Tasman knew that if he didn't deliver, Victoria meant it when she said she would send him back to the night shift, and he simply couldn't go back, not now. Not after everything he had achieved.

'Hill, what is it?' snapped McAllister on the phone. He had answered Tasman's call immediately. 'I'm in the middle of breakfast. This better be good.'

Tasman could tell McAllister was enjoying the power. The old television reporter had really transitioned into the perfect copy of Townsend, thought Tasman.

'I've woken up sick and -,' Tasman began slowly before McAllister abruptly cut him off.

'Right, so you're not coming in then?' McAllister said loudly, sighing into the phone to relay his frustration at Tasman. 'This is going to put a lot of pressure on us today. You know that don't you?'

A few seconds of silence passed, and Tasman wondered if McAllister actually thought he might change his mind.

'I can't come in like this,' said Tasman, barely making out the sentence as he coughed.

'Right. When will you be back? Tomorrow? Or do I need to cover that shift too?' said McAllister, as though Tasman could see his eye roll through the call.

Tasman felt rage bubbling inside of him. He was so unwell that his level of tolerance for McAllister unexpectedly disintegrated.

'Listen mate,' Tasman shot back loudly in frustration, surprising himself, his voice hoarse. 'I think you can tell that I'm not well. And you? Covering work? You haven't bloody worked in years so you can get back in your box, okay? I'll be back on deck when I'm back on deck, right?'

Tasman heard nothing on the other end of the call for a moment before McAllister quietly replied. 'Fine. You'll need a sick certificate.' And McAllister hung up.

Tasman threw the phone down and unscrewed the lid of his cough mixture syrup, desperate to sleep. He may have felt terrible, but he couldn't help but think he had finally put one of the newsroom bullies back in their place. And that, at the very least, felt very good.

CHAPTER THIRTY

TASMAN FELL INTO A DEEP cough syrup-induced sleep. He dreamed of notebooks, a pile growing so large that it towered above him, like an impossible ladder he was desperately trying to climb. His dreams felt lucid, in one moment he was sitting in the driver's seat of Harrison's burned car, desperately trying to find a way out, the door handle burning up as a ball of flames in his hands.

Then, he was again sitting next to Cressida on the beach, watching the sunset. Cressida handed him the silver pen; the same one Alison had gifted to him, the red ribbon still attached, blowing in the wind. Cressida pushed the pen towards him, as though encouraging him to sign a contract, forcing it on him.

There was a sudden rush, like a vacuum sucking away the scene. Tasman clung to the sand, but it was no use, he was being pulled back into the water, catapulted into a portal that dropped him into Alison's bedroom. Her designer dog barked aggressively at him. Tasman shielded his face as the animal launched towards him.

Tasman tried to speak, to call for help, but no words would come. And that's when he realised, he was somewhere else, surrounded by lush green tree ferns, and he was being strangled by the same truck driver all over again.

Covered in sweat Tasman woke with a loud gasp, as though he was taking his first breath, clasping his throat. He felt his neck, expected fresh bruising, but there was nothing at all. It had all just been a terrible dream.

IT WAS HOURS LATER when Tasman woke to his ringing phone. His head ached and he felt groggy and disorientated.

Tasman lifted his head from his pillow to see the call was from another unlisted number. He was tempted to ignore it, but knew he couldn't risk missing a lead, even when he felt so unwell.

'Thank God. You're alive!' said Alison, sounding relieved. 'You know, just because you're a big celebrity now doing your tell-all interviews doesn't mean you can just stop answering my calls and messages!'

Tasman sat up in bed, running his hands through his hair as he wondered if he could possibly still be dreaming. 'Alison? Is that you?' he asked. 'You're calling on a private number?'

Alison paused for a moment. 'Oh, is it? That's so strange, I didn't realise it was,' she said, laughing a little. 'Well, I hadn't heard from you in a while so I thought I would check-in and see if you wanted to get together tonight?' she said enthusiastically.

Tasman felt relieved to tell Alison he was unwell, and a perfectly timed cough was his proof when he asked for a raincheck.

'You know, I'm an exceptional nurse,' replied Alison. She was not someone who accepted being told 'no', thought Tasman. 'I could come over and take care of you,' Alison offered.

Tasman was stunned. He didn't need looking after, he could look after himself, as he had always done. Tasman was fine being a lone wolf. He was comfortable this way.

'Come on, let me look after you. I can be there straight after work!' Alison pushed; her mind set on the plan.

Becoming frustrated at Alison's lack of boundaries, Tasman's fuse shortened.

'I'm sorry I've got to go. I'll talk to you soon,' he said, abruptly ending the call. Tasman exhaled; he was relieved it was over.

As he climbed back into bed with his head throbbing again, Tasman was grateful to be alone in his apartment. As he fell asleep, there was one clear thought on his mind - he wished the call had been from Cressida Marks.

CHAPTER THIRTY-ONE

HOURS PASSED BY and Tasman woke to a loud knocking at his door. He stumbled out of bed, opening the peephole cover on his door. He rubbed his eyes in disbelief, but within a second he knew that he was not mistaken. This was real. Alison stood, waiting outside, staring back at him through the door, impatiently. She leaned forward and knocked again, adjusting her colour coordinated suit.

Was it too late to pretend he had never heard a sound? He wondered, unable to think of how to lie his way out of the intrusion. He was desperate to avoid Alison, but it was becoming impossible to pretend he had slept through the banging on the door as it grew louder and louder. Seconds passed, and Tasman knew he had to decide.

'Tas! It's me. Open up!' Alison yelled loudly. Hearing her give him a nickname made him cringe. No one called Tasman, Tas.

'Come on, don't make me stand out here all night,' she half laughed, as neighbours passed his door looking at the unwanted visitor.

Tasman opened the door slowly, standing between it and the hallway, protective of his space. 'Alison. What are you doing here?' he asked, undecided if he would entertain letting her inside.

Alison looked Tasman up and down. He was dressed in only his shorts and a dressing gown filled with used tissues in its pockets.

'Hello to you too!' she said sweetly. 'I know you said not to come... but I've come with supplies for you,' she said holding up grocery bags. 'You're going to let me in, right? It's freezing out here.'

Tasman reluctantly held open the door and Alison strode into his apartment confidently, as though she had been there hundreds of times. Tasman faked a grin but couldn't shake the feeling of irritation from Alison's blatant disregard at his request to be left alone.

'Sorry, the place is a mess. I wasn't expecting company,' he began, wondering how he could get her out of the house.

'Don't you worry about a thing,' she said, unpacking the shopping bags in his tiny kitchen, making herself at home.

'I can make you dinner,' she said, holding up two different containers of soup. The visit had turned into a dinner date. Alison began taking bowls out of his cupboard, somehow naturally knowing where they were placed.

Tasman couldn't help but frown, yet Alison remained unfazed. He had reached his limit and he wanted her gone. Tasman couldn't understand why she was forcing their connection so desperately, but he was too sick to care anymore.

'Alison, I'm sorry but I really can't hang out tonight. I can't do dinner. I just really need to go back to bed and sleep this thing off, okay?' he said bluntly.

Alison's smile dropped; she was heartbroken.

'I'm sorry if I wasn't clear when we spoke before, but I'm just not good company when I'm like this,' he said, moving towards the door.

Before Alison could speak, Tasman's phone rang, breaking the tension in the air. When Tasman saw it was Zaylee, he answered quickly. 'I've got to take this,' he said apologetically, hoping Alison would take the opportunity to leave. But she didn't.

'Hill, how are you feeling? I'm surprised you answered the phone,' said Zaylee, the sound of her voice from the phone loud in the small apartment. Alison moved from the kitchen towards Tasman, slowly lingering.

'Edwards, can I call you back?,' said Tasman to Zaylee, turning away from Alison. 'I've just had someone, ah, stop by,' he said, aware Alison could probably make out every word Zaylee was saying.

'Oh wow, has your mum come down to look after you? Shit, you must be sick,' continued Zaylee. Tasman had said nothing in response hoping his friend would pick up on his cue.

'Okay, let me guess, you asked Nurse Alison to come and look after you?' she joked. 'Are you there? Hill, if you've been taken hostage, cough twice!' she said, acknowledging the awkward silence.

Tasman watched Alison pretend to read the instructions on the box of cold tablets she had brought for him. But he knew she was listening.

Tasman coughed. 'Yes, Alison has just stopped by, she's brought me soup,' he replied politely.

'Hill, are you serious? Do you want me to call the police?' joked Zaylee. 'Next minute she will be boiling your bunny rabbit and stealing strands of hair as a souvenir before she murders you,' she said laughing in disbelief that Tasman had let this woman into his apartment.

'Thanks Edwards, it's all fine. I'll see you at work,' said Tasman winding up the conversation while watching Alison through his peripheral.

Tasman hung up the phone and scanned Alison's face to see if she had registered any of the conversation. He barely knew her, but even he could tell she was forcing a faked smile.

'Thanks for stopping by, I better get some sleep,' he said, touching the doorhandle to open it.

'Right, well I guess this nurse is off duty then,' she said seriously. 'Let me know when you're feeling better, Tas,' she said, squeezing his arm and kissing his cheek.

Tasman stood in the doorway and watched Alison walk down the stairs and cross the carpark in the rain. The breeze brought sprinkles of rain that hit him in the face.

As soon as Tasman closed the door, he left out a sigh of relief. He walked two steps, before turning back to wiggle the handle, just to make certain it was definitely locked.

CHAPTER THIRTY-TWO

THE NEXT MORNING Tasman walked down to the carpark to reluctantly drive to work. He could have easily spent another day in bed recovering, but with Victoria's looming deadline, threatening to make or break his career, he had no more time to lose.

Tasman looked at Harrison's smiling face still plastered on the old news van as he got in, a reminder of the story left unfinished, one of their own still out there somewhere, missing.

He felt like his senses were slower, and he sat in traffic watching the old, worn-out windscreen wipers struggle to move the rain washing across his windscreen.

Cars lined the streets leading towards the Sapphire Times, its carpark overflowing into the neighbourhood around it. As Tasman passed the cars, he felt grateful the old news van had its own permanent space.

Moving closer he suddenly stopped in the street, pulling over to the side with the box van rear-end hanging out into the street. He was surprised to see Peter standing with Zaylee, holding an umbrella over her while she spoke on the phone, she looked panicked. Pulling over, the van slightly encroaching the road, Tasman jumped out holding his coat over his head.

'What's happened?' asked Tasman, rushing over to his friends standing alongside Zaylee's Suzuki Swift. He stood on crushed glass that crunched on the ground below his feet.

'Someone smashed the back window of Zaylee's car right after she got to work,' said Peter, as he rubbed her back. 'She's called the police, she's pretty shaken up,' he said.

'They're sending someone over now to take a look,' Zaylee sobbed, as she put her phone away.

'How did it happen? Are you okay?' asked Tasman in disbelief.

'With the traffic from Harrison's bloody memorial there isn't any parking anywhere so I parked down here,' she explained, wiping away more tears. 'I got out and started walking, the rain was so crazy I had the umbrella and didn't see anyone around. Then next minute all I hear is glass smashing and I turn around, its someone in a black hoodie running away!' she sobbed. 'Maybe I cut someone off on the road or something? I thought there was meant to be extra security around work after everything that's gone on!'

'Probably not on the streets outside, love,' offered Peter, with the comment met with a scowl from Zaylee.

'They just jumped out of nowhere, smashed it and ran away, like, literally they came out of nowhere!' said Zaylee as she looked over the broken windows, the rain beginning to drench the inside of the car.

Tasman looked around the street and the neighbouring houses. 'Is there any CCTV down that street or around the corner?' asked Tasman hoping to help.

Before anyone could answer Leigh Lindsay the photographer drove up stopping alongside Tasman, Zaylee and Peter in his small grey hatchback.

He observed the broken glass and tutted.

'Maybe whoever went after Marks is back for more. You never know,' said the photographer loudly.

'Alright mate, what are you trying to do, freak her out completely? Keep moving why don't you,' shouted Peter, stepping towards Lindsay's car in the pouring rain. Peter was one of the calmest and considerate people Tasman knew, but even he couldn't hide his fear and anger at the situation. No one was safe anymore.

'Wow. Easy Tiger,' said Lindsay, laughing in response to the outburst. The guy couldn't help but stir the pot. Peter leaned up over Lindsay's window, delivering a furious stare. Tasman thought the bartender might just knock him out.

'Look, all I'm saying is, the old Sapphire Times might still be a target,' said Lindsay, raising his hands in the air in defence.

'Keep driving,' said Peter sternly, whacking the top of the small car. The entire display distracted Zaylee long enough for her to stop crying and look at Tasman in bewilderment.

'Don't say I didn't warn you,' shrugged Lindsay. 'Be careful, you might turn the car on and bang! It explodes! You know, just like in the movies,' he said, as he rolled forward to drive away, with Peter running after him.

CHAPTER THIRTY-THREE

FOUR WEEKS GONE

TASMAN WAS ALONE in the newsroom, but he couldn't shake the feeling he was being watched. He had been sitting in the office for hours, looking over Harrison's old notebooks, searching for answers. Victoria had been clear that Tasman's time in Harrison's chair was on shaky ground, unless he could prove he had what it takes. The pressure was mounting and the stories he had dug up just weren't cutting it. The doubt was sinking in. And so was his imposter syndrome.

With the national media frenzy over Harrison all but over, the missing journalist was now only mentioned in the news briefly. Without a body and without a killer - there was only speculation left and the commercial TV commentators were becoming bored. One TV anchor had resorted to interviewing distant family members of the Marks Family. Then occasionally his interview with Cressida would be replayed. She had been all he could think about for days. Replaying the last time he saw her, the way she rushed out of the newsroom the day of the interview, he had wondered how she was doing and if she would forgive him for how it had all played out.

Tasman felt there was something there, a connection back at that beach that night, something that made her trust him. It was something that he had never felt before. Without hesitating, he picked up his phone and called her.

His heart was in his throat, his arms becoming numb as he waited for Cressida to answer. When she didn't, the wave of disappointment hit hard, catching even Tasman by surprise.

CHAPTER THIRTY-FOUR

SIX WEEKS GONE

TASMAN STOOD IN LINE at the new café just around the corner from his apartment. As soon as he left his house each morning the wind carried a smell of freshly brewed coffee. Of course, Tasman never drank coffee until he became a journalist, now he was a complete addict. The entire café, aptly named Pinkies, was of course painted a variety of shades of pink, complete with matching furniture and neon lights, the wave of colour enough to wake any customer up first thing in the morning.

Tasman ordered his coffee, always a full cream latte with an extra shot, and stood to the side to wait for his order, along with six other customers. He stared at his phone, scanning news sites and checking social media feeds when he heard a familiar voice.

'Is that muesli slice gluten free?' the woman's voice asked.

It was unmistakeable. It was Alison. Tasman looked up from the counter and his palms began to sweat. Out of all of the cafes, the one woman he wanted to avoid was right there in front of him. Tasman felt trapped, as though the walls of the too brightly coloured coffee shop were closing in on him and pushing Alison even closer towards him.

'Oh, no. It's not an *official* intolerance,' Alison told the waitress taking her order. 'I have a relative on my mother's side who took a test that identified she carries the gene for it. So, you know... I could become intolerant,' she explained.

Tasman wanted to walk out of the café, leaving his overpriced latte behind, but Alison had already seen him standing there, he was caught in her web once again.

'Good morning,' she smiled as she strode up to Tasman and kissed his cheek.

Tasman fumbled his words, repeatedly asking how she was as she watched him with her signature intense eye contact. It made his stomach twist.

Alison spoke rapidly, giving Tasman a blow-by-blow account of her running workout at the gym, she was dressed in active wear with brand new runners, as bright as the café they stood in. She then seamlessly moved the conversation onto her breakfast order and her suspected intolerance to gluten.

When the barista called Tasman's name, he felt instant relief for the interruption wash over him. But Alison's monologue wasn't over. Tasman tried to continue listening to her as he awkwardly stepped towards the counter to collect his order.

'Anyway, enough about me,' Alison conceded. 'How's everyone at work holding up? It was pretty crazy about what happened to what's her name, Zaylee Edwards, and her car.'

Tasman stared at Alison. How did she know it was Zaylee's car? The paper had only named the victim as being a staff member at the Sapphire Times. How could Alison possibly know, he wondered, instantly suspicious. Could it have been Alison?

'The poor thing, she must've had such a fright. So scary to think there could be someone out there doing all of this to you all,' she said, reaching out to pat Tasman's arm to comfort him. Alison watched him intently, searching for his reaction and trying to read and decipher his response.

'Wow. News really travels fast,' Tasman replied quickly, taking a large sip of his latte. 'She was so shaken up about it all. People are just insane. But we've got the police looking into it now, so hopefully they find something,' he continued.

'Oh, the police are involved?' she asked, surprised. 'Silly me, I mean, of course they are, especially with everything that's happened with your work, like why wouldn't they be involved?' she said, looking back at the counter to check on where her order was.

Tasman carefully observed Alison. She seemed suddenly uneasy, scanning the area around them, as though expecting someone was about to jump out from behind them in the busiest café on this side of the city.

'It's like the Sapphire Times is, I don't know - cursed or something,' she said, fiddling with her hair as she stared into his eyes for far too long.

'So how did you know that it was Zaylee's car?' he asked directly.

Alison paused for a moment, unsure of what to say.

'You know, I think I saw it on social media. I follow Zaylee, and she posted a photo of the damage, or someone did,' she blurted out quickly, before looking towards the door. Alison moved backwards, bumping into a small table crammed into the space, knocking over a glass from the table. The sound of it breaking on the polished concrete floor interrupted the busy conversations filling the café.

'Oh, my goodness, I'm so sorry!' said Alison to the couple at the table, while a waitress rushed by them to clean the glass up.

'Takeaway for Alison,' said the barista pushing her coffee and packaged food towards her at the counter. Tasman knew this was his final opportunity to be absolutely clear with Alison. He wanted nothing to do with her, in fact he would be completely content if he never saw her again.

'I just wanted to say, I really appreciate how kind you have been to me, but I just want to make sure that you understand I don't really see us moving past anything more than friends. I think you are wonderful - but I think we are just two very different people,' said Tasman.

Alison closed her eyes and breathed deeply before opening them again, revealing a piercing stare at Tasman. She wasn't sad; she was furious.

'So, what, that's it then?' she questioned, raising her eyebrows in disbelief. 'Without even giving this a real shot?'

Tasman was taken aback at the reaction.

'I'm sorry,' he said, wishing he had more experience with relationships to know what to say or do to handle the situation better.

Tasman's phone began ringing in his hands. He looked down and felt a wave of relief and comfort - his mother was calling him and he knew it was time to make amends.

'Another important call, right?' she asked, narrowing her eyes.

'It's... my mother,' he replied, silencing the call and putting it into his pocket. He would call her back.

Alison had closed her eyes again, as though she were meditating. Tasman wondered if she wanted him to wait to continue the conversation or to leave, the other customers in the café were now watching them with interest.

'Tasman,' she scoffed bitterly, her neck still a burning red. 'That's totally, totally fine,' she said, her expression softening as she opened her eyes slowly. 'Take care,' she said as she walked out of the café.

Tasman stood for a moment in the bright pink café. The barista exchanged a look of confusion with him. He knew he had made the right call.

CHAPTER THIRTY-FIVE

TWO MONTHS GONE

IT HAD BEEN DAYS and Tasman was no closer to breaking the next big story he so desperately needed. The major national news outlets were long gone from the Ranges, instead they were off covering a triple murderer on the west coast.

After another long day, Tasman was relieved to be back inside his apartment. It was the only thing that was certain in his life at that moment. His stomach rumbled as he searched his fridge and cupboards for food, realising it had been days since he had been to the supermarket.

Tasman didn't bother with his umbrella as he left the house to walk to the store just around the corner. It was close to 9pm, and he knew it would be quiet, isolated. He walked the aisles without a clear sense of what he even wanted, picking up tins and ready-made-meals examining them and replacing them with no conscious thought.

As he threw more into his basket, he let a tin slip through his fingers at the sight of a familiar face, the same face that he had thought of every day since he had met her. It was Cressida Marks standing at the end of the aisle. Tasman was both elated and petrified upon seeing her. She was dressed in khaki cargo pants and a plain white t-shirt. She looked more beautiful than any woman Tasman had ever encountered.

For a moment, he considered whether he should ignore her and leave her alone, but before he could turn around to leave on impulse, the rolling can spilled towards her across the aisle. She picked it up and slowly walked towards him.

'This might be yours,' she said, handing the can of soup to Tasman.

'Thank you, it got away from me,' he replied nervously.

Cressida smiled a little. She was trying to live day-to-day, waiting to hear if her loved one would ever be found.

'How are you doing?' he asked, noticing she was lingering, holding her grocery basket.

'Fine. Thanks,' she blurted. 'I'm sorry I haven't responded to any of your calls. It's all been a lot to handle. But thank you - the interview helped. People stopped calling me a murderous bitch, at least, so that's something,' she shrugged.

'Don't mention it,' he said, immediately regretting his choice of words. Tasman looked into her sad eyes, wanting to say more. Cressida looked past him, as though she had just seen a ghost jump out from the aisle ahead of her. Tasman turned around, but no one was there.

'Sorry, I thought I just saw something,' she said shaking her head. 'Someone watching us from the corner. I'm completely losing it. Anyway, I should keep going.'

'It was good to see you,' he said, wondering if he sounded too pleased. He didn't know what was the right thing to say given the circumstances.

Cressida nodded awkwardly and walked to the checkout.

The entire conversation was a disaster, thought Tasman regretfully. Tasman looked down the empty aisle, as though Harrison's ghost had been the one standing there, watching them, knowing that Tasman was falling for a woman who he could never be with.

Walking out of the grocer, Tasman struggled with his shopping bags to answer his ringing phone. He stared at the screen in disbelief that Alison was calling him.

He ignored the call and walked at a fast pace through the intensifying rain home.

As he dumped the shopping bags on his kitchen bench, she rang again.

The phone calls continued, one after the other, just minutes apart. The woman he wanted was untouchable, unavailable, yet the one he couldn't imagine a future with was becoming obsessed, a stalker.

'Alison?' said Tasman exasperated as he finally answered her eighth call.

'I've been trying to get in touch with you!' said Alison, attempting to hide her distress.

'I'm sorry, I've been busy, Alison... What is this all about?' he asked perplexed.

'I need to see you. We have to talk,' she demanded. 'Can I come see you tonight? It's important,' she pushed, this time her tone was colder, frustrated.

'Look, it's really late. I've got work first thing in the morning. What is all this about?' Tasman pleaded.

'Fine. Meet me tomorrow,' she demanded. Tasman knew she wasn't actually asking him anymore. 'I'll text you the time and the place. And Tasman? Don't let me down.'

'Alison, at least tell me what's going on?' Tasman pleaded. But she had already hung up.

CHAPTER THIRTY-SIX

TASMAN'S HANDS TREMBLED slightly as he leaned against the damp stone wall, waiting at the car park of the Ranges National Park Lookout. He stared out at the breathtaking view, but his unease made him unable to appreciate the beauty of the city skyline and kilometres of bushland and forest below. He waited as the next bucking of rain was forecast to roll through.

The Lookout was the most picturesque part of the city, but the pressure of being there to mysteriously meet with Alison diminished the scene's beauty. It was also impossible to ignore how this same mountain had been the scene of Harrison's disappearance, with the search site just a few kilometres away.

Now, the search and police tents were long gone, with only traces of the disturbed dirt and flattened bushland where they once stood. Tasman had spent hours here, waiting and watching. The blackened forest was a sign that it also hadn't forgotten the search for Harrison Marks, just yet.

Food and coffee vans began to setup in the car park and Tasman felt relieved he was no longer alone when he saw Alison's car finally arrive.

'You're a hard man to get a hold of,' said Alison as she approached Tasman, smiling. Tasman struggled to make sense at what she wanted, her threatening tone from the night before, long gone.

'Alison, what's all of this about?' asked Tasman, cutting straight to the chase. 'What is so urgent that we had to meet up here at the crack of dawn?' His heart was racing, irritated that he was standing on a mountaintop when he should be at work.

Tasman's forwardness had already offended her.

'Wow. Okay,' replied Alison. 'Straight to the point, then. I get it,' she said as she clutched her handbag closely.

Alison looked out at the view, contemplating her words. Tasman instantly felt guilty for being so cold towards her.

'Tasman, I don't think you've given us a real shot,' she began. 'But I'm hoping this might change your mind…'

Reaching into her handbag, Alison produced a thin white box, an identical box to the one she had gifted his pen in. When she handed it to Tasman, he looked back at her, utterly confused.

'What is this?' he asked her as he opened it. Inside was a long blue and white piece of plastic. It was a pregnancy test. And it was positive, Alison was pregnant.

Alison observed Tasman's jaw drop as he looked from the test to her. She took a step closer towards him and smiled hopefully.

'You know, someone once told me that sometimes stupid things drive people apart. And then sometimes fate can push them back together,' she said, holding the test upwards, smiling as Tasman understood the news.

'It's yours, by the way,' she said, staring at Tasman, awaiting his response. She was holding her breath, watching him with her signature intense stare.

'Like I said, you never really gave us a chance, Tasman. But I want you to give *us* a chance,' she said, looking at the test.

Tasman's mouth was agape, he wanted to speak but the words never came.

'Say something Tasman,' she said, touching his arms.

'I'm sorry. I'm just… in shock,' he finally managed. 'You're telling me you're pregnant and that the baby is mine? But how is that even possible? I thought we didn't even…,' he said, holding his head as he calculated again.

'Wow. You really weren't kidding when you said you didn't remember the night we met, weren't you?' she said, disappointed. Alison looked away out at the view for a moment before biting her lip and continuing.

'I know this is a shock, Tasman. Believe me, I was shocked at first too. I did the test. And now… well, now this is what's happening. I don't know what else to tell you. You're going to be a father.'

Tasman doubled over upon hearing the words. He had never wanted a family. He had never wanted to be anything like the father who left him, the father he despised.

'We could be a little family. You know, we could be the parents we both didn't really have,' she said, reaching out to hug Tasman. He moved her hands off of him gently, still in deep thought at the news.

'Alison. It's like you've got this all figured out. How can we just play happy families?' he said, trying to make sense of her proposal.

Her hopeful eyes closed tightly again, Tasman recognised her sweet nature turning.

'So, you're saying you won't even consider this?' she fumed suddenly.

'Alison. I'm sorry, I just need some time to process all of this. It's more than I can manage right now,' he said, backing away from her slowly.

But Alison walked furiously towards him, even closer than before.

'I'm sorry this news isn't convenient for you Tasman,' she sneered. 'Forget I said anything. Don't worry, you can keep pretending to fill the shoes of some missing reporter. See how it all works out for you,' she said getting into her car.

'Alison, just wait a minute - this is a lot to take in. I'm sorry I'm not jumping for joy right this second. I am still processing all of this,' pleaded Tasman.

'You know what? I'm already sick of waiting. Call me when you grow up and can be someone our baby can be proud of,' she hissed out of her car window, the coffee van staff watching the exchange. Alison took out her phone and furiously hit the screen.

'Here's all the proof you need. And Tasman, don't think too long on it. I will not wait for you forever,' she said as she pulled out of the Lookout, leaving Tasman stunned in her dust.

He looked at his phone and opened the message from Alison. It was the ultrasound image of a tiny circular speck. It was their baby, right there in black and white.

IT HAD BEEN 24 HOURS since Tasman had been told that he was going to become a father. And suddenly, the deadlines didn't matter anymore. More than an hour after Alison had left him at the Ranges Lookout, he was still sitting in a state of panic, replaying the life-changing conversation over and over.

Tasman felt like everything in his life was suddenly hanging in the balance. He was facing a pinnacle moment in his career; he must push to succeed now or else return to the night shift. And just as he realised, he had developed feelings for someone he could never have, someone he could never be with, he faced a new, unexpected change – becoming a father.

Doubling over, leaning again on the same stone wall at the Ranges Lookout, Tasman didn't notice the rainfall, the water running through his hair, his clothes becoming saturated.

Thinking over the little time he had spent with Alison that first night was agonising, unable to be reconciled.

'Give us a chance,' Alison had said, the wordings ringing over and over in Tasman's mind.

Tasman had never envisioned having a family. He had sworn off ever having a child, knowing he never wanted to put them in the position he had been, growing up with a workaholic father, a father who left and traded him in for a new start. He would never wish that upon anyone... yet here he was, torn between stepping up to be the man his own father never was, or running away from the responsibility altogether.

LATER THAT DAY, Tasman stared into space, struggling to focus as he sat at Marks' old desk. He looked up to see McAllister staring at him from across the newsroom. Tasman readjusted his laptop screen but couldn't find the energy to work. He was unable to even think about hunting down a new story. His head was a mess with worry and seemingly unsolvable problems.

Zaylee was nowhere to be seen; she had been out working in the field all day and Tasman longed to speak to and confide in his friend. Tasman was instead surrounded by the loud chatter of his colleagues in the bustling newsroom, yet he had never felt more trapped or more alone.

Every half an hour Tasman stepped outside the Sapphire Times and desperately tried calling Alison, hoping she would answer. He sat in the news van, gripping the wheel in frustration as he yelled into his hands. He felt out of control, as though every part of his life was about to slip through his fingers. He had only felt this way twice before in his life. When his father left him, and then when he died.

Tasman didn't blame Alison for screening his calls. His reaction to the news of their baby was devastating, and he did not even know how to begin to make it right.

Exhaling deeply, Tasman ignored his knotted stomach and pulled himself out of the van and dragged himself towards the newsroom. He stopped at Harrison's floral memorial at the entrance. The number of visitors had slowly declined, day after day. The flowers had died, decomposing in the rain.

'Honey, I think it might be time to call it a day,' said Christine the receptionist appearing suddenly, patting Tasman lightly on the back to comfort him in front of the memorial. He pretended to rub his forehead to cover the tears in his eyes. He now realised Christine had sat at her desk and watched as Tasman walked outside dozens of times.

'You go. I'll handle that dickhead,' she said, nodding regarding McAllister.

Tasman was grateful, and stifled a sob as he turned back to the news van to leave. Tasman had intended to drive home, but instead pulled out onto the highway to leave the Ranges. In a long-awaited moment of clarity, he knew there was only one person who could comfort him and give him the advice he needed.

'MUM,' SAID TASMAN, shocked that the phone answered so quickly on the first ring, let alone at all.

'I'm glad you called, darling,' said Tasman's mother, Eileen Hill. The sound of her voice had never been sweeter to Tasman. His stomach that had been in stitches of stress, slowly eased. The tightness around his neck loosened enough for him to breathe again, just a little.

'I'm sorry I haven't called...,' Tasman began, unsure of where to begin. He clutched the steering wheel as he sat on the side of the highway.

'Well, honey, we can talk about that later. I know why you haven't called,' she said warmly.

Tasman was surprised, a wave of relief washing over him. 'You do?' he asked.

'Well, of course. You've been busy with work, all of those big interviews about that poor missing journalist. And of course, you've got yourself a beautiful new girlfriend!' she said with joy that radiated through the phone.

Tasman winced.

'Girlfriend? What are you talking about?' he asked, completely confused. And that was the moment he heard Alison's laughter in the background.

The hairs on the back of Tasman's neck stood tall, and his mouth suddenly dry. Alison was with his mother. Alison was in his mother's home.

'Oh honey, don't play dumb,' Alison's voice called in the background. 'The cat's out of the bag. She knows everything! Don't you Grandma or do you prefer Nan? We'll work it out!' yelled Alison into the phone as Tasman's mother laughed happily.

Tasman felt the enormous shot of adrenaline flood his arms and legs. Alison had forced her way into his life once more. She had somehow found out his mother's address and driven hours from the Ranges just to announce the news that he was having a baby, all without Tasman knowing. The situation made him feel dizzy, he was about to be sick.

'Alison, what are you doing?' Tasman demanded, his state of panic growing.

'Congratulations darling,' his mother continued. 'I won't lie. I would have preferred to have at least met your girlfriend first to welcome her into the family properly, but I know relationships aren't always so traditional these days. It's just all so exciting! I know David will be thrilled when I tell him the news when he comes back from his golfing trip. Our first grandchild!' she shrieked. 'I wish you could have come down together to tell me the news, but Alison explained you've been so busy with work you've not had a chance to stop...'

Tasman had heard enough of the insanity. He wasn't Alison's puppet.

'Mum, I need to speak to Alison, right now, it's ah, about the baby,' said Tasman urgently.

His mother passed the phone to Alison who faked a laugh as she took hold of it.

'I know what you must be thinking,' Alison began quietly. 'Grab those baby albums you told me about Eileen. I can't wait to see baby Tasman!' she said to his mother, before lowering her tone again to speak to Tasman. 'I know you haven't been speaking to your mother, so I thought I would help your reconciliation along. After all, nothing brings two people together like the news of a baby.'

Tasman felt like was about to explode. 'What the hell are you doing?' he spat back in shock. 'Alison, we haven't even bloody discussed any of this. I've been calling you all day! You've only just told me about the baby. Why would you do this?' he yelled.

The silence from Alison made him feel unsettled.

'It's not *the* baby. It's *our* baby, darling,' she said, mimicking Eileen. 'I thought coming to see your mum might really make it clear how important it is to me that we are one big, happy family,' she laughed into the phone, keeping up appearances in front of Tasman's mother. 'I really hope you've thought more about giving us another shot. You wouldn't want to disappoint your mum - you've already put her through so much,' said Alison, menacingly.

Tasman could do nothing but listen. His jaw dropped as he wrangled with understanding the situation he found himself in. Alison was not at all who he had thought she was, in fact this person was a grand manipulator, not a sweet, misunderstood and neglected daughter of a successful politician. He had no idea what this woman was capable of and that thought terrified him.

'But you should also know this, darling Tasman: don't disappoint me. I've already had so many men in my life let me down and I just don't take it well. Don't be one of them, okay?' she said, her tone dead cold. 'Darling, I've got to go. There are these adorable little Tasman photos I can't miss. Love you, mwah,' she said, faking affection as she hung up the phone.

Tasman felt the surge of stress hit him like a punch in the stomach. And just like that, he opened the car door and vomited on the side of the road.

It was unspoken, but it was clear - there was no stopping Alison until she got what we she wanted. Alison was like a spider, gathering up all of the strands of her web, and he was her prey. He had no idea what to do, or how to get free.

CHAPTER THIRTY-SEVEN

ALISON

TWO MONTHS EARLIER

ALISON HADN'T RUN THAT FAR in years. She struggled to catch her breath as she leaned against a large gum tree in the Ranges National Park that towered metres above her head. She checked the burner phone again. Still nothing. She had paid for it in cash just to text Harrison Marks. It was the only way to trap him into meeting her.

Alison did not know if her former lover would actually show at all - but after seeing him on television that night claiming yet another award; it had driven her to a new level of wild.

Calling and messaging Harrison as Alison simply no longer worked, and above all else, Alison did not tolerate being ignored. Tricking him into rushing to meet a secret source to get the scoop on a bogus story was the only way she could see him. To confront him.

The chill in the air hit Alison's face, but she didn't feel it at all. She had been running up the narrow snaking dirt tracks all the way to the Ranges National Park Lookout, recalling her training on the mountain each night, as part of her cross-country running in high school.

It had been so long since she had done it, she couldn't believe she had made it up there so easily. Most people shied away from the mountain, especially at this time of year with so much rainfall about and the risk of landslips. But the adrenaline and rush of knowing she was about to see him was enough to fuel her. Her plan would work perfectly.

Alison knew she couldn't have driven to meet him. The moment Harrison saw her car, he would turn right around and never looked back. And she couldn't let him do that to her again.

She waited in the shadows cast from an old streetlamp positioned near the tourist map at the highest, most picturesque part of the Ranges Lookout.

Its small stone wall served no other purpose than to prevent cars from plunging down the cliff embankment, surrounded by ferns, gumtrees and bush scrub, covering most of the dirt bush tracks she had raced down while training for cross-country on her school holidays visiting her father. Time spend waiting for her father had been some of the loneliest days of her life. And ironically, they continued to this very night.

Alison struggled to regain control of her breathing. She had been on edge for weeks, watching and waiting for Harrison to come back to her. But he had easily tossed her aside once he got what he needed - the next piece of his story.

For one glorious month he had flooded her with adoration and attention - it was blinding, consuming. It convinced Alison it was true love, because Harrison made her believe it too. Until he disappeared. Alison assumed Harrison had wanted to go back to his wife, but it was too late. It was a possibility she couldn't accept.

'After everything we had. After everything I did for him. I don't think so,' she thought. 'He promised me,' she said aloud.

Alison thought of the night she had met Harrison. It was the same night their affair began.

It had only been a few months since she had returned to the Ranges, at her father's request. He had promised to be better to her, to be there for her. But it was all short-lived. It didn't take long before he had done what he always did, he let her down. Leaving her waiting at her own birthday dinner was right on the brand for him. Alison had waited an hour, but she knew deep down that he was never coming. There was always a more important cause, a local business in crisis, a vote her father needed to get over the line. As she waited, her phone pinged, notifying her of money just deposited into her account. A text from her father followed it apologising. She had thrown the phone into her bag furiously and walked from the set table to the bar. It was then that Harrison sat down next to her, and she was immediately charmed. She knew who he was. And that fact that her father despised the journalist made him simply perfect.

The timing of when Harrison broke her heart, disappearing like a ghost from her life, was not lost on her. In fact, it was what she had feared the most when they began their affair.

Harrison had made her *believe* that he loved her. He promised to leave his wife to be with her, but there was always a catch. Harrison always needed something more from Alison. It was all about the documents, the files, the records - the evidence he needed to prove her father, Councillor Glenn Mosca, had siphoned millions from his city skyscraper project, the same building construction that had killed innocent people. It had happened because of him.

Alison photographed the records for Harrison, sending them to him late one night as she worked back in the office. Alison had waited, enthusiastically hoping to hear from Harrison. But his reaction never came. Once he had got what he wanted, Harrison disappeared.

The betrayal sent Alison into a blind rage. She began following Harrison, watching him from afar. She parked outside his home each night, waiting. But he barely came home to Cressida. And that was when Alison realised - she wasn't the only one, Harrison had other lovers.

Harrison was driven and work-obsessed, just like her father. And just like him, all the men in her life had disappointed her. And she would not let them get away with it anymore. That was why Alison was standing there in the shadows on the misty mountain in the early hours of the morning, ready to act out her plan. She needed to stand before Harrison, to end the silence.

Alison re-laced her brightly coloured runners, leaning against the old stone wall of the Lookout as she waited.

Alison's breath quickened as the headlights of Harrison's car slowly crept into the carpark, the light reflecting across the surrounding trees.

'I'm here,' Harrison yelled as he stepped out of the car, looking around the darkness for the person who had called him there in the dead of night. She waited for Harrison to walk a few metres before she finally stepped forward into the spotlight of the overhanging streetlamp. She walked closer into his view.

'You've got to be kidding me,' Harrison scoffed, spotting it was Alison who had called him there. 'This is actually insane, you realise that. So, you're the mysterious anonymous tipoff then?' he stated, shaking his head furiously.

Alison remained silent, standing just a metre before him now, the sound of thunder rumbled in the distance.

'If you want me to pull the story on your old man, you can forget it,' he said, his voice echoing across the mountain.

'Well, you didn't exactly give me a choice,' said Alison coldly. 'You vanished. What was I supposed to do? Knock on your door and ask your wife why you weren't returning my calls? But - it wasn't just me - right? You do this with all your sources,' she said, looking at him with disgust. 'I risked everything for you. You said we were going to be together,' she said, her voice breaking.

Alison stopped speaking as Harrison laughed in her face.

'Oh, no, no,' said Harrison, shaking his head in disbelief. 'Don't come to me now if you're looking for someone to blame for ruining daddy's career, sweetheart. I'm sorry, but that's on you.' Harrison turned around to walk back to his car parked near the old stone wall. He looked back at Alison, following closely behind him, standing inches from him now.

'This story is what you wanted,' Harrison furiously spat. 'You wanted to blow up his career, you surely knew there's going to be consequences, that he's going to end up in prison – that was all your call. I've started writing the story, I've got everything I need, and it's all thanks to you. It's too late,' he said, throwing his hands in the air.

Alison threw herself towards him, she was now so close to him she could smell his alcohol-stained wool coat. She wanted to shake sense into him.

'I never put the gun to your head,' said Harrison. 'You did what you wanted to do. This is all on you, sweetheart,' he said, pointing at her with disdain.

Alison had felt the sting of rejection and humiliation too many times before. 'I'll tell your wife,' she said bluntly, her cheeks burning.

Harrison stopped and turned to look at her with disgust.

'Just so we are clear, Alison, you meant nothing to me,' he shot back. 'You were so desperate to be loved that you handed over your own flesh and blood on a platter to me.' Harrison began to laugh again. 'Daughter of the Year, right here. It must be hard, though. He convinces you to move back to town, and even then, he doesn't want to be around you, too busy fooling around with your colleagues, right?' he said, enjoying the humiliation.

Alison stood, her fists clenched, holding back her furious tears. But Harrison wasn't finished, his fury towards Alison was just beginning.

'The thing that really gets me about you, Alison is that here you are pretending to be the victim. But you're the villain in this, you're not innocent, sweetheart. You're cold and you're calculating.'

Alison stood before him, enraged. Tears streamed down her face and her mind was going to the dark place again, the same one she had been medicated for, for almost all her life. But Harrison never knew that.

Harrison finally reached his car, as thunder rumbled in the distance once more.

'We're done,' he said. 'Don't worry, I'll send you a thank you gift after this story gets me my next award.'

And just like that, Alison raced towards Harrison, her adrenaline surging. Within a second and without another word, Alison pushed Harrison, throwing him off balance over the little stone wall, where he plunged down the bush cliff of the Ranges National Park.

ALISON WAS CERTAIN HARRISON was dead. She had heard his body crashing through the fern-covered forest below. And then there was nothing but silence. The drop had been at least twenty metres, there was no way he could survive a fall from that height, thought Alison.

The truth was Alison hadn't gone there that night planning to kill Harrison. She wasn't against the idea. But she didn't want to have to go through with it. All he needed to say was that he made a mistake, that he wanted to give them another chance. Even an apology would have made all the difference. But things never went to plan. And for Alison, dealing with the consequences of her actions had never been her strong suit.

The cold night wind blew through her hair as she stood on top of the stone wall, staring down into the darkness. Her heart raced. She felt triumphant and deeply justified by what she had just done. Catching her breath, she doubled over, she needed to think.

Alison looked at Harrison's car, the car light on and the door still open from where he had last stood, threatening to leave her, threatening to expose her father.

Moving back to the city, Alison had hoped she would avoid this kind of impulsiveness, but it would be her undoing, again. Alison needed a plan to clean up her new mess, but first, she needed to make sure he was dead.

Still standing on the wall, she looked down. The sound of a faint groaning echoed through the mountains, and the adrenaline immediately returned. Alison could hear him. Harrison was still alive. He was alive somewhere down below, a needle in a haystack. And that was an even bigger problem. Alison needed to find him, there was no going back now - everything depended on it.

Without hesitation, she leapt from the wall and ran through the carpark, locating the entrance to take her down the bush tracks favoured by tourists. She ran down into the darkness towards the groaning sound of Harrison calling for help, the noise interrupted as the thunder rumbled closer and closer, the wind picking up.

Furiously searching with nothing but the spotlight from her phone and the moonlight, Alison found him tangled in branches and scrub at the root of a gumtree, far below the cliff of the Ranges National Park Lookout.

Alison shined the phone's spotlight at Harrison, but he barely moved. She kicked him, rolling him over to reveal the blood on his face and head - he had somehow survived the fall, but he was barely conscious.

Alison gazed down at him. Harrison was at her mercy now. And she wondered how that must feel for him, for the tables to have turned completely, for the great Harrison Marks to suddenly be utterly powerless.

She dragged him by his feet deeper into the forest, across the damp bush and scrub until the track was almost impossible to see. Harrison didn't fight it. It was as though he had already accepted that he had met his end.

'It didn't have to be like this, honey,' she said aloud to Harrison.

Without another moment of hesitation, Alison took a heavy tree branch and smashed it into Harrison's head, a splatter of blood flicking back on her face from the impact.

The forest was silent for a minute before a snap of a stick in the bushland nearby startled Alison, she jumped. She looked back at his body.

Good, he was definitely dead now, she thought.

Alison frantically searched Harrison's coat pockets, stuffing his car keys, phone, and notebook into the front of her hooded jumper. She clutched the silver pen, the same one she had gifted him, tightly. He had kept it, but it all had to go. Alison could not afford to leave a trace.

Alison tried to move his lifeless body, he felt somehow heavier, and more difficult to move. Becoming tired as she slipped and fell through the mud on the damp forest floor. She had only moved his body a few metres and her desperation grew. Out of breath, she stopped to rest, hearing the birds beginning to wake. She was running out of time. It would be daylight soon.

Low on energy and increasingly panicked, she dropped the heavy body in anger. Harrison was already ruining her plans again, in life and even in death.

Covered in mud, Alison leant against an upturned tree. She knew she could not drag his lifeless body any further, her only option was to bury him.

Kicking and pushing Harrison's body, he fell into a muddy hole of a large, uprooted gumtree.

Alison flailed as she searched for tree ferns, branches, and dirt - anything she could find to cover his body, and to conceal her crime.

Thunder rumbled above her now, a light spray of rain hit her face, brought in from the wind. Alison had buried Harrison. And the truth would now stay buried with him, she thought.

Alison returned to the top of the Lookout, knowing her work was not yet over. She looked down at her clothing and runners covered in thick brown mud and debris. Turning Harrison's phone off, she turned her attention to the keys in her hand. One piece of glaring evidence remained - Harrison's car.

Sitting in Harrison's car, she could still smell him. She turned the key and began to slowly creep out of the carpark, careful not to draw any attention to her movements in a strange car in the early hours of the morning from those who lived on the mountain.

Alison drove a few hundred metres, quietly navigating the bends until she pulled off onto a secluded, unsealed and overgrown dirt road. They had known it well. It was the same place she and Harrison would meet at the beginning of their affair - it would be the perfect place to dump the car, it would be poetic even, she thought.

Looking around the backseat, Alison searched for any shred of evidence about her father and the story that threatened to ruin their lives. Spilling over notebook after notebook, Alison screamed through gritted teeth in frustration. Harrison had written in shorthand, every page was impossible to read or understand. She couldn't be certain what any of it revealed about her father's secrets.

Alison began to panic, contemplating her next move. She looked again towards the backseat where copies of the Sapphire Times sat stacked. Staring at the newspaper for just a moment, Alison knew what she had to do. Taking a cigarette lighter from the car she sparked it to life, holding the flame like power in her hands, dangling the notebooks to help fuel the fire that would solve all her problems. Torching the newspapers, she stepped outside the car and opened the fuel tank, shoving them inside. The ignition was immediate.

Alison jumped back, screaming in pain - she had been burned. She winced and bit her arm to suppress her screams as she watched the fuel tank explode, creating a defining crack as the blaze took hold of the car. The thunder rumbled and lightning cracked above; the light falling rain doing nothing to douse the flames.

The fire was creating a large plume of smoke that filled the sky directly above, pinpointing Alison's exact location. She checked over her burned hand, singed by the flames. The pain should have been excruciating, but adrenaline continued to flood her body, urging her to keep moving, to fight for her own survival. There was no time to waste, she needed to run faster than she had ever run before to get off the mountain. Staying any longer meant she would risk being seen by early morning joggers or dog walkers.

As she ran, Alison sucked in the cold night air harder than ever, all while holding Harrison's belongings tight to her chest in her jacket's front pocket, desperate to keep her secret safe.

The vision of the flames filled her mind, along with Harrison's last groans of life before she silenced him. Alison reached the back of her apartment block just after sunrise, she was covered in sweat and dirt, the dried blood splatter still across her face. The sound of sirens rang out from across the city as fire crews sped towards the Ranges National Park. Alison turned to look at the mountain view from her apartment, looking up at the massive plumes of smoke circling above, realising it could all burn because of her.

Without guilt or regret, she carefully opened the door, slipping inside to evade any neighbours. She calmly took off her mud-soaked runners and wet clothes, throwing them methodically into a garbage bag, as though she had worked through a murder before, effortlessly.

Her dog Barkley tugged at the bag, smelling it obsessively before she calmly moved a stool towards her wardrobe, removing a panel from within the roof inside it to place the bag inside, replacing the cover after her. She took out Harrison's belongings, his phone, notebook and pen, placing them delicately into her bedside drawer, ready to be examined later.

Alison treated her burned hand, wrapping it in bandages. She looked at the Sapphire Times website, pleased the leading news headline was just another mundane story.

Alison thought of the story Harrison had wanted to tell, the one that would have destroyed her father, and his reputation. If it wasn't for Alison, the world would have known that it was Councillor Mosca's fault that all of those people had died, crushed by falling skyscraper windows. He had cut costs on the materials, paid-off contractors and safety approvals. Then people died. And he had been the one front and centre calling for support for the victims, yet it had been his fault all along. It wasn't that hard for Alison to work it out. After all, she had worked in her father's office. The documents were all there, if you knew where to look.

Alison had kept her father's secrets buried. Now, all she had to do was keep it that way.

CHAPTER THIRTY-EIGHT

ALISON

NOW

ALISON HAD SPENT TWO HOURS waiting, staked out in her car a short distance in view of Tasman's mother's house. She knew it would only be a matter of time before Tasman would appear after what she had done. Tasman needed to know that she was serious, and now that he did, there would be no going back. Every man in her life had let her down, but Tasman would be different, he still had a chance to make things right.

Alison was well prepared for stalking Tasman, after all, watching him had consumed most of her time since they had met at The Lonely Squire, although that had not been a coincidence. It was what she needed to do to feel control.

Everything she needed was hidden under a blanket in the boot of her car, bottles of alcohol, snacks, blankets and even her long-lensed binoculars — she was prepared to stay for as long as necessary, just in case.

Eileen Hill had been understandably reluctant to open the door to Alison that evening, but as soon as she produced a photoshopped image of Tasman and her together, she could tell the old woman's mind was put at ease. After a cup of tea Alison felt elated, she had recruited another supporter for her new life - her fresh start with Tasman.

Alison gripped the steering wheel tightly, growing impatient. She thought Tasman should have been here by now. She unscrewed the bottle of whiskey and took a long hard swig.

In the beginning, Alison had never actually wanted to be with Tasman - he was a messy, lanky, unpolished version of Harrison. It was essential to her plan that she latch on to someone to stay close to the story. But the moment she had seen his name covering the fire at the Ranges National Park, she knew she had to get close to him. Now with Harrison gone, Tasman was the apple of her eye.

Her mind drifted back to the hours after she had murdered Harrison, how she had scrubbed every trace of dirt and blood from her skin. She had dressed herself, wearing long sleeves and leather gloves, protecting her burned hand. At work Alison sat at her desk, lost in thought. She was there physically, but mentally still floating above the scene of where he was buried the night before and her obsession with her crime being discovered grew. Within hours, news had spread of the fire up at the Ranges National Park.

It was all the City Council staff were talking about by lunch.

'Oh, thank goodness for the rain this morning,' said one woman. 'Can you imagine what would've happened without it? The whole thing could've gone up in flames!'

A group huddled in the kitchen staring at the phone of one worker, showing the Sapphire Times article.

'It's the burning off we postponed. You know this won't play well for the city - all that forest is fire fuel, if you ask me,' said another man Alison had never learned the name of.

Alison sat through another mundane city planning meeting when her paranoia had taken hold. She blatantly ignored her colleagues, their voices just static in the background, as she scrolled her phone, searching for any news about Harrison and the fire, half expecting the police would burst in at any minute to arrest her.

'Did anyone even know he was missing?' Alison wondered as she turned Harrison's pen over and over in her hands later that night. She continued to switch from her calm, calculating persona straight back to an escalating state of paranoia. The only cure was to know every shred of information, to know whether the police would be closing in, she needed to be close to the story, as close as safely possible, and she needed someone with access to information.

Alison needed someone like Harrison. She stared at her laptop screen displaying the latest Sapphire Times article on the fire, the light illuminating her face. And that's when she saw his name, Tasman Hill. He was a nobody journalist covering the story. But a nobody would be perfect.

Alison opened her medicine cabinet and began rapidly reading the labels. She eventually found them - the same strong sedative that her doctor had prescribed her for her rage induced insomnia and inevitable meltdowns.

'Alison, let me be clear - never consume alcohol and take these,' the doctor had warned. 'These types of drugs aren't to be messed with. The side effects can be serious, even potentially fatal. I'm talking about memory loss, nausea, severe headaches. It'll put you to sleep for hours. And that's for starters.'

Alison never took them as prescribed; she had instead been saving them for a situation just like this. And now, more than ever, she needed them. She needed to stay close to the story, and this new crime reporter, Tasman Hill, was her way to do it. Finding Tasman would be easy, Harrison had mentioned once that all the junior reporters gathered at The Lonely Squire most nights.

Alison went to The Lonely Squire every night after Harrison's disappearance, just to find Tasman. She didn't have to wait long before her plan was in action. Alison had broken the tablet in half, spiking Tasman's drink the night they met as soon as the waitress dropped a tray of glasses, smashing them all over the floor.

In his drunken-drugged state, she could barely make out what he was talking about, let alone anything useful that he knew about Harrison's disappearance. He smiled widely at her. The smile had almost made her forget all about Harrison and what he had done to her, or rather, what she had done to him.

'It's in pieces. He just threw it on the ground. Why did he do that?' asked Tasman to Alison. She said nothing, feeling frustrated at Tasman's lack of intel. She had pushed him up the stairs of her apartment, By the time she helped him onto the bed, he had passed out.

Alison's mind was ripped from its daydream when light flickered her face, a car passing her still sitting parked a few metres away from Eileen Hill's home. Ducking for cover, Alison sipped her drink before sitting up to peer above the steering wheel. Another flash of headlights appeared, a car pulling into the driveway she was watching. Tasman had finally arrived. Tasman would reconcile with his mother, and it was all thanks to her. Alison clutched at her stomach in practice. Of course, there was no baby. It was all too easy to fake. There were hundreds of websites full of fake pregnancy tests and sonogram images online. It would help her keep up the lies for as long as she needed to. It would be months before she needed to review the plan and by then, Tasman would know her. He may even love her.

Alison shifted uncomfortably in her car seat, twisting the top of the glass bottle tightly. Of course, Cressida Marks had not been part of the equation. This woman seemed to always be standing in the way of Alison's happily ever after. First with Harrison, and now Tasman. Alison wasn't a fool. She had seen the way Tasman had looked at Cressida during the interview, and again that night at the supermarket.

Cressida was a problem, and she had to be dealt with.

CHAPTER THIRTY-NINE

TASMAN

Tasman had driven two hours on the highway, speeding for the entire journey. From the moment Alison ended the call, he knew he needed to see his mother, unable to shake the feeling that something truly awful was about to happen. His fingers tingled with pins and needles from clenching the steering wheel too hard.

Alison was playing her own game, and Tasman was scrambling to understand the rules. He shook his head in frustration. He had completely underestimated Alison and the manipulation she was capable of - and now she was pregnant with his child.

Tasman had wished he had the opportunity to share the most important news of his life with his mother, but instead she heard it from a stranger who was forcing her way into their lives.

Tasman grabbed his stomach, still unsure if he would be sick again. He leaned forward on the edge of his seat as he reached the long stretching driveway of his mother's new home that she shared with David, her fiancé.

Flower beds surrounded the red brick house - it was the perfect understated home she had always dreamt about. Tasman bit the inside of his cheek. He was reluctantly grateful she had finally got the life she wanted with David after what she went through with his father and her subsequent husbands and boyfriends after him.

Desperate to see her, Tasman scanned the driveway, but Alison's car was nowhere to be seen. She was gone. Tasman exhaled, he stood at the large wooden door, unsure of whether to knock or force his way in, scared of what he may discover inside. But the door opened before him.

'Tasman, darling,' said his mother, her voice instantly comforting. She was safe. She was alive. 'I had a feeling I would see your face sometime soon. Come on in, honey,' said Eileen, embracing her son tightly.

Tasman instantly felt a wave of regret for staying away from her for so long. He had missed the effortless comfort he felt in her presence. He hesitated for a moment before he stepped into the entrance, looking left and right.

'She's not here,' said Eileen, looking over Tasman, reading his demeanour. He followed his mother into the kitchen. 'As lovely as it was to meet your girlfriend and to find out I'm about to become a grandmother... I really thought you might have put your feelings about me and David getting married aside to tell me your special news yourself,' she said facing the kitchen window, turning the kettle on.

Tasman winced. He knew she had every right to be disappointed with him. It was news he could barely grapple with himself. He looked at the dining room table, two empty teacups and a plate of half-eaten biscuits still positioned where Alison had sat. Tasman's baby albums were still open on the table nearby.

'Mum. I'm sorry,' said Tasman. 'But this whole thing is just insane - she is insane,' he began to explain.

'Alison seems perfectly lovely,' Eileen snapped, cutting him off as she turned from the bench to face him. The pain inflected from his silent treatment evident in her tone. 'Tell me the truth. Did you refuse to tell me the news just to punish me some more?' she asked, still standing, leaning on the counter. 'You clearly didn't want me to meet Alison. If she hadn't come here today, would you have even told me about my grandchild?' His mother wiped tears from her eyes.

Tasman hesitated. He had been so wrapped up in his own crisis he hadn't thought about who else the news of a baby would affect.

'Alison said she tried to convince you to tell me, but you refused. She said that I had a right to know about my first grandchild and I tend to agree. I'm not saying I've been a perfect mother, darling. I know you don't approve of David - but I never thought you would freeze me out for so long,' she sobbed.

Tasman rushed to her side to hug her, the regret of what he had done to his mother washing over him. Within hours, Alison had weaved a careful and complex web of lies. He did not know what to say or how to explain away Alison's deception. Unable to speak with a lump in his throat, Tasman choked on his words in his attempt to comfort his mother. Alison had orchestrated the perfect way to pressure him into a life together. And it petrified him over what she might do next if he refused.

'I only just found out about the baby. I'm still... processing it all,' was all he could muster. He held onto her tightly, hoping she knew how much he needed her right now.

Tasman looked at the fridge where his mother had proudly displayed all of his latest Sapphire Times articles. He had hurt his mother, but she still loved him unconditionally.

'Mum, she's not actually my girlfriend. I didn't know she was coming here, or how she even found your address. This whole thing, coming to meet you, to tell you - we had never had that conversation,' he said, sitting back down at the table. His mother's jaw dropped.

'What are you saying?' she asked, utterly bewildered, also sitting down.

'We had only seen each other a couple of times and I broke things off with her. Now she's pregnant, and she wants us to be together - to be a family,' said Tasman, unloading. He couldn't believe how good it felt to finally explain the madness to someone who was on his side.

'Tasman. I think it goes without saying that you should have been more careful,' she said, flicking the back of his head. Tasman stared back at her in disbelief. Her reaction was not what he had expected.

'I should have known that was a sign something wasn't right,' she continued. You have always sworn off having children, especially with the way you felt about your own father...' she said, suddenly looking away from Tasman. Even now, the scars of her husband leaving them still hurt.

'I can't be a dad,' said Tasman, the lump in his throat returning. 'I just can't,' he said, slamming his hands down on the table, rattling the teacups.

His mother didn't jump at the outburst. Instead, she smoothed out the white linen tablecloth and looked at him dead in the eye and sighed.

'Oh, darling... aren't you sick and tired of carrying all of this childhood baggage around?' she asked, leaning forward. 'You're a grown man now. It's time to take some responsibility,' she said, raising her eyebrow as though she was pointing out something obvious. 'I know things were hard, darling. Believe me, I know. Your father leaving was tough, but you make it sound like you were abandoned, that you were all alone. But I was there. I was there for you every step of the way,' she said, her voice breaking slightly. 'When he left and even after his heart attack. I was still there with you. And guess what? I'm still here now,' she said, reaching out to touch Tasman's hand, her hand wrinkled, her skin looking older than Tasman had ever remembered, or ever registered.

'So, are you really considering not being around for your own child, just because your own life wasn't picture perfect?' she asked, stirring her tea before taking a sip.

Tasman considered her words of wisdom. He knew she was right.

'This may shock you to hear, darling, but your father wasn't always such a monster. That's a story you've created to understand the pain,' she said, leaning forward to touch his arm gently.

Tasman scoffed in total disbelief at the comment.

'The work changed him. Looking back now, I can actually pinpoint it. One day my loving husband kissed me goodbye and walked out the door chasing another story - and then the man that returned was a complete stranger, like an evil twin had come home in his place. He was never the same after that day,' she said, staring into space.

Tasman sat up straight, listening intently. 'What do you mean, a complete stranger?' he asked. It was the most his mother had ever spoken about her marriage to his father, ever.

'Darling, the obsession with work, the lies, the drinking, the cheating - all of it started when your father rushed to a fatal crash on the highway to cover a story. He was the first on scene and when he got there, he recognised the car straight away - it was his best friend and it was your father who found him dead.

The police found no evidence of the car attempting to brake or swerve to stop. They ruled it a suicide,' she explained. 'What he saw that day, and the loss of his friend, it utterly broke him, and it changed him forever.'

Eileen flattened the dining tablecloth again, fiddling with its white lace before continuing, 'You were too small to know what was going on, of course darling. And he never spoke a word about it after that day,' she sighed, the wounds of the past still stinging as she recalled the memory.

Tasman envisaged what it would be like to stumble upon a story, to find the subject a close friend, or family member. It made him think of finding Zaylee or Peter killed, and he shuddered.

'But he had a choice to treat us the way he did,' said Tasman, refusing to give the man a free pass for how he treated his son for so many years.

'When you told him you wanted to be a journalist, just like him, he wasn't supportive because he didn't believe in you, darling,' said Eileen gently. 'I think he was actually trying to protect you. He never wanted you to see what he had seen. He used to say that a brilliant news story often involved covering the worst day of someone else's life - and when those two worlds collide - sometimes terrible things happen.'

The revelations felt like explosions in Tasman's mind. His father had suffered some kind of posttraumatic stress disorder. It was possible his father was trying to help him or even protect him, not push him away. Tasman was speechless.

Eileen paused for a moment, reading the shock across her son's face.

'If we're being honest, darling, when your father left us, yes, I was heartbroken. But I was also relieved. The man I had loved, the man I had married, the man I wanted to be an incredible role model for you - was long gone. When he left, I felt like I could finally breathe again. And now with David, it feels like I'm making up for all those lost years.'

Tasman stared down into the teacup, sitting untouched before him on the table.

'I would go through it all again - all of it - to be there for you. I would do anything to be your mother. And look at you,' she said, beaming with pride. 'You're already becoming the man your father couldn't be.'

Tasman's eyes filled with tears, and he began to utter an apology to his mother.

'Don't say another word, darling,' she smiled warmly as she kissed her son's head.

Eileen walked over to the buffet, opening its cupboards and began digging through fine decorative plates and glasses before producing a large, brown leather covered scrapbook, placing it before Tasman.

'I was always meant to give you this,' she said. 'I was waiting for the right time. You might look at it in a different light now.'

Tasman opened it up, realising it was a scrapbook portfolio filled with Eric Gleeson's biggest stories. Hundreds of articles were all carefully preserved, some laminated. A catalogue of his success at the Ranges Advocate, and towards the back, the articles his father had written about his own friend - he had covered the death himself.

As Tasman flicked through pages and pages of headlines, he spotted a familiar face. It was the same article he recalled hanging on the wall in his father's study when he was young. In the black and white image, he recognised a younger, red-haired forensic investigator, it was Dr Monica Sinn, the same person who had warned Tasman up on the mountain that the story he was covering may be a little too close to home, and she was right it was.

Tasman looked at the article in his hands, it was the same serial killer case that Dr Sinn had said made her career, it was her breakthrough moment, and it was all recorded by his father.

'Take it. It's yours,' said his mother. 'Now that I think about it, it was probably always meant for you,' she said, hugging him tightly. And just like that, the world came back into focus.

Tasman kissed his mother on the cheek goodbye, and walked back to his car, carrying the leather-bound scrapbook with him. He left her house feeling a new sense of peace, in at least one part of his life. He spent the drive home lost in thought, unaware of anything else around him, or anyone.

As Tasman fell asleep that night in his apartment, he dreamt of his mother's words. She had said she would go through all of it - the pain and the heartbreak - she would do it all again for him, just to be his mother.

He looked at the sonogram Alison had sent him, staring at the small, tiny speck of a circle that would soon become his baby.

He would go through it all, and he would do it all for them.

CHAPTER FORTY

MELWYN

MELWYN BROWN WAS A MAN OF HABIT. He had not changed his early morning routine in over twenty-five years. Even after his wife June had passed away, he fought any change in his daily rituals. They were who Melwyn was, and he preferred it that way.

June and Melwyn had once jogged together each morning, but now an older man, he walked mostly alone. June had always motivated Melwyn to keep moving, to get outside of their little log cabin they had bought nestled in the now famous Ranges National Park mountain top. They had bought the hideaway for next to nothing when they were young, and now it was worth a fortune. A year didn't go by when Melwyn didn't have a real estate agent knocking at their door, asking how much it would cost for them to give it all up. They had always laughed at the prospect because they knew they had something special. They felt the magic of the rainforest surrounding them, the breathtaking, near never-ending view of green.

Of course, today the Ranges had changed. The winding roads across the mountain, leading up to the lookouts, were almost never free of cars and busloads of tourists. All were hoping to photograph the city skyline below and, on a cloud, free day, the horizon of everything beyond the city - it was truly breathtaking and Melwyn never wanted to give that up. Melwyn had grown to love the sound of the humming from the busy roads. They gave him some comfort in an otherwise mostly quiet place of the world.

When his alarm clock hit 6am, Melwyn was ready to begin the day. And he wasn't entirely alone anymore, either. His children had gifted him a German Shepherd puppy after June's death. They could rarely visit him up in the Ranges, but he loved the quiet life and was content sitting with the pup and his memories day after day.

Melwyn knew June would have never approved of the dog, but he had always wanted one, and he needed the company more than ever. Darcy was all too happy to accompany Melwyn on their morning walks. He looked forward to it too, greeting Melwyn with total excitement each time he glanced in the dog's direction. The love and bond between the pair was mutual. They needed each other just as much as the other. And it was beautiful.

Darcy woke moments before the old dusty alarm clock sounded. It was right before dawn. Melwyn looked out his window while the news played on his dusty radio on the kitchen bench. The rain had poured throughout the night again. He couldn't remember another time in his life when the rain had fallen like that, for weeks and weeks on end. Staying indoors for so long was becoming suffocating. The news had been right; the weather was more extreme than it ever had been.

Melwyn had fallen asleep listening to it hit the tiles on his roof. His wife had loved the rain. He pulled on his old gumboots, the same pair June had begged him to replace for years now.

'Why?' he would protest to her. 'These are perfectly fine. They fit me. They do the job fine,' he would tell her, even when she would surprise him with a new pair in bright white, free from the stains of their walks.

Darcy sat waiting keenly by the door.

'Well old boy, would you look at that,' said Melwyn aloud to the pup, as the smallest beam of sunlight shone through. The break in the rain had finally arrived.

Melwyn threw on his long cattlemen's coat, the same faded waterproof one he had worn for fifteen years or more. He knew there would be the rock and mudslides from the downpour and his favourite tracks would likely see a new collection of scrub and bush washed across them.

His daughter-in-law had bought him a new phone, complete with a boosted satellite signal, so the family could keep in touch with him when he went wandering around the mountains. They all worried for him, a concern which irritated Melwyn on one level, knowing he too was ageing and that he resented having to be babysat by a device. He could get out of almost any situation on his own - at least he used to think so.

He looked at the device that sat on charge, ignored in the corner of the kitchen and rolled his eyes to himself, picturing his son begging him to take it because he had even taught him it was crucial to 'always be prepared'. Stung by his own words, now used against him by his grown baby boy, he pocketed the damn thing anyway.

He trudged across the Inverness Track. It had been June's favourite. It was hard to recognise in parts, with fallen trees and mud covering most of the landmarks that were familiar to him. He had walked it more than ever before in the last few months; it had been right near a forest fire and both the thought of seeing the entire area destroyed called him back to it, to take it in, the off-road dirt track even more.

He had walked past the scene, following the smell of the smoke that had filled the usually fresh mountain air, and his old life had called back to him within seconds. Red and blue lights, sirens and the rush of adrenaline that came with being a police officer never left him, even so many years since his retirement. It had been obvious to Melwyn the fire near the Ranges Lookout was suspicious. A car dumped and torched on the Inverness Track. No-one came to this part of the mountain without a reason.

As Melwyn walked, he breathed in the fresh forest air. He was relieved to be back, free from the indoors and walking, with his canine friend running off-lead ahead with excitement, occasionally reappearing from scrub off the sides of the track to check he was still there. He was still okay.

Melwyn inspected the condition of the tracks, moving fallen branches and trees from the paths nearby, collecting washed down rubbish from the landslides. He liked to think of himself as a kind of caretaker of the mountain.

Although he was certain that with the break in the rain, the tourists would come back within days, erasing that quiet slice of serenity he enjoyed so much. But that was life. These moments of happiness and pleasure were all just temporary and therefore had to be treasured when they appeared.

Within twenty metres uphill, he found already two large fallen gumtrees across the track, right near the off-road section where the blue and white police tape was still visible.

He walked on and longer than he had before, following the sound of a lyrebird calling in the distance, before Darcy dashed towards its sound.

'Back here, boy,' Melwyn instructed to the dog, as it growled.

The last thing we want is to kill a native, thought Melwyn. He knew the dog probably needed to be on the leash, but who was around to know, anyway?

The landslips had destroyed the usual fern tree blanket surrounding the track, above the lookout hundreds of metres vertically above.

He continued to call the dog, but he wouldn't come. Frustrated and muttering to himself, Melwyn knew he would have to go get him and prayed he wouldn't have to drag the mutt back. As he called again, he spotted the dog digging hard at the scrub, circling around and urging Melwyn to come closer. Darcy whined to signal to his owner, something was not right.

Melwyn looked from the dog to the mass before him. His eyes fixed on it. The landslip had brought down tonnes of dirt and scrub from the mountain top above, with skid and roll marks denting the mountain side.

Among it, a large, mud-spun cocoon had travelled downwards in the bush avalanche thanks to the nonstop rainfall that had hammered the region. And as Darcy barked louder and grizzled, it was clear it was something much more than dirt and scrub, and Melwyn's former life flashed before him. His gut instincts reengaged, and he just knew what it was.

He reached down and his heart raced faster than it had in years as he cautiously removed a twisted branch to reveal a mud-stained grey wool coat. Bending down, he touched the figure, pulling at the material to reveal the black and blue decomposed body, the remains of a man.

Darcy lay down next to the dead man. Melwyn looked at his injuries and knew what he had discovered had resulted from something sinister, something evil.

Stunned, Melwyn found it almost impossible to break his stare at the body as he reached into his pocket to take his phone to call the police. The old man and his dog had found Harrison Marks.

CHAPTER FORTY-ONE

TASMAN

TASMAN WALKED INTO THE NEWSROOM just after sunrise. He had barely slept, and the knots in his stomach grew tighter with every minute that passed as he considered what Alison had done.

'Wow, you're here early – for a second I thought you were back on the night shift again,' said Zaylee as she strode in through the doors, glancing at Griffo sleeping in his chair.

Tasman put the sonogram image on his phone, face down on the desk as Zaylee pulled up a chair next to him.

'I've got so much on my plate, I've got to get over to the hospital for an interview later and haven't even filed my other stories, so here I am, no overtime as per usual,' she said as she unwound her scarf from her neck looking at Tasman. 'Wow, you look like absolute shit. Are you okay?' she said, looking at him suspiciously and sliding her chair closer to him.

Tasman sighed. He didn't know how to begin to explain the last twenty-four hours to his friend.

'Hill, what's going on? Are you okay?' she pushed. 'It's Alison, isn't it?' she said, looking down at Tasman's phone. 'Let me guess, Nurse Alison is coming back for another check-up?' she joked, grabbing the phone still displaying with the image of the sonogram in clear view.

'Oh my god,' uttered Zaylee as she looked at Tasman, her eyes in shock.

'She's pregnant,' said Tasman, his tone serious. Zaylee could barely speak in response. He had never seen Zaylee that surprised before, not even after her car's windows were smashed in. He actually felt comforted by Zaylee's reaction. After all, it was a reasonable response to what was one of the biggest things to happen in his entire life. Yet his mother barely batted an eye when the mother of his unborn child appeared unannounced to introduce herself.

'So that night - that's about what - two months ago now?' said Zaylee as she struggled to calculate the timeframe in her head.

'I didn't even know we slept together,' Tasman admitted.

'Fuck,' said Zaylee, holding the phone, zooming in and out of the sonogram image. 'Kids wasn't exactly something you had on the agenda.'

'I sort of froze when she broke the news to me,' replied Tasman. 'She wants us to be together, to be a family,' he continued, staring out the window to avoid Zaylee's judging eyes. 'But then when I tried to tell her I didn't see us being together, she kind of turned. I know I didn't give her the reaction she deserved,' he said, ashamed.

'Wait a second, Hill,' said Zaylee, but Tasman ignored her, continuing to recount the story.

'Then Alison disappeared and turned up at my mother's house to tell her she's pregnant with my child. Can you believe that? And I still can't get hold of her. I just don't know what is happening from one minute to the next. I haven't even thought about work and, well, everything is just... out of control,' he said, pulling at his hair, holding his head in his hands.

Zaylee tapped his shoulder, and Tasman looked up at his friend, her eyes wild.

'You need to see this,' said Zaylee, almost ignoring Tasman entirely as she held up both her own phone and his, the screens displaying sonograms on each device.

'Look at this. Really *look* at it,' she said, handing them to Tasman.

The images looked identical.

'It's a fake! I just googled 'baby sonogram, eight weeks' and this is the first image that appears in the search engine!' said Zaylee, standing from her seat in shock. 'It's the same in almost every way. All that's changed is the hospital, the patient's name and date, all of that has been photoshopped,' she said as she patted his shoulder.

Tasman felt his head spin the same way he felt the morning after he had met Alison.

'But she had a positive pregnancy test!' protested Tasman, trying to piece the deception together.

Victoria peered through the curtains of her office, looking in Tasman's direction before she snapped them down again.

'Just try to stay calm,' said Zaylee, urging Tasman to sit down as he loosened his shirt collar. Without another moment of hesitation, Zaylee sprang into action, taking over the desktop phone and dialling.

'Yes hello, my name is Alison Mosca. I had an ultrasound on... Thursday. Is it possible to please send through my images again for me? I've deleted them by accident, would you believe it? Must be baby brain or something,' she said in a fake South Australian accent. 'Oh, right. Sorry, my mistake, it must have been another clinic. Have a great day,' said Zaylee, before quickly hanging up.

Tasman looked at his friend with hopeful eyes, and she shook her head slowly.

'Hill... Tasman,' she said quietly. 'There's no record of Alison at the clinic. I'm so sorry, I don't know what else to say. This is all just fucking crazy.'

Zaylee sat silently watching Tasman holding his head in his hands, bent over his seat at the desk that did not belong to him. He was shocked to realise how much of himself he had already promised to a child that never was. How much he actually already loved it, despite it never really existing, despite what Alison had done.

Tasman thought he would have been happy and relieved, but all he felt was disbelief, anger and loss. And Alison was still out there, somewhere, allowing Tasman to believe in her lies.

Acting on impulse, Tasman dialled Alison's number again, willing her to answer.

'Wait, stop!' shouted Zaylee, snatching the phone from his hands.

Tasman blinked back tears, his heart pounding with fury.

'I need to speak to her! She can't just play with people's lives like that. This is my life, she -,' yelled Tasman, before looking at Victoria's office door.

'I know you're upset, but just take a minute to think, okay?' said Zaylee, placing her hands on Tasman's shoulders and looking around the newsroom to check who had seen the outburst. 'You know what you need to do?' asked Zaylee, leaning forward in a quiet tone as she smiled at reporters walking past their desk, ready to begin their shift. 'Give that bitch exactly what she deserves. Think about it. She doesn't know that you know. Just wait and see what happens next,' said Zaylee wisely, sitting back down in her chair.

Before Tasman could respond, the police scanner erupted. The loud cracking of static filled the newsroom - someone had turned it up even louder than usual.

'Detective Inspector Watts on scene, speaking with the witness now,' said the voice 'Requesting paramedics to check over the witness – he may be in shock. It appears the dog found the human remains, uncovered after the landslide.'

Tasman looked at Zaylee as he felt a rush of adrenaline wash over him. Alison's lies would have to wait.

'You need to go,' said Zaylee, ushering him towards the door.

Taking his coat and whistling to Lindsay, who had only just walked through the newsroom door, Tasman rushed towards the carpark, passing McAllister's desk.

'I think it's finally happened,' said Tasman with complete urgency, nodding towards the scanner. McAllister stood up, understanding the cryptic message.

'Ring it in as soon as you know, you got it, Hill?' McAllister replied, holding back emotion.

It was the news the Sapphire Ranges and the rest of the country had been waiting for. Harrison Marks had finally been found.

CHAPTER FORTY-TWO

ALEXANDRA

DETECTIVE INSPECTOR ALEXANDRA Watts' eyes shot open as soon as her phone rang just after sunrise. She didn't even need to look at the caller to know that it was important. She had a sixth sense like that. No one ever rang in the early hours of the morning with good news. Her own detective father had taught her that.

It wasn't that Watts was a pessimist; she was simply alive to all the evil in the world. In this job she had seen humanity at its worst, and once you see that, you can't go back.

When she got the call requesting her attendance at the Ranges National Park picnic grounds, her mouth turned dry. Wasting no time, she clambered out of bed, while calling her junior partner, Detective Sergeant Aaron Marshall. He was always awake and always responsive whenever she needed him, as though he was sitting around waiting for moments like this. Watts appreciated that keen quality in the younger detectives.

'It's human remains,' said Watts, without waiting for Marshall to reply who had answered on the second ring. 'It has got to be him,' she said with certainty.

'Copy. I'll be there in five,' said Marshall.

Watts and Marshall lived for moments like these in the force. A case could sit stagnant for weeks, months, or even years. Then one little thing, one landslide, could change it all.

Watts' father used to call detectives truth seekers. And the moment they solved a case, she recalled the feeling as though the equilibrium in the world was restored, if only for a moment, anyway.

Watts needed this solve, the whole damn country was waiting for it, she thought.

She pulled on her navy-blue suit - the same suit that had brought her luck in all her major investigations - and today, it was about to pay off again, she could feel it.

As soon as Watts soared down her apartment stairs and made it out the doors of her complex onto the street Marshall arrived, pulling up to the footpath, his car's engine still humming.

They followed the police patrol cars, zooming to the mountain. As she drove closer, she could see the once pristine fern covered green mountain now streaked brown with landslides that had brought down trees and scrub. Watts had never liked the rain, but now she was grateful for the inundation that had uncovered a body, and possibly answers to the crime that had captivated the country too.

When they arrived at the scene, Watts' heart raced. The lump in her throat emerged, and she tried to contain her nerves. As she approached, with Marshall trailing closely behind her, she saw officers taking the statement of an older man clutching a plastic cup, while an obedient puppy sat at his feet. After flashing her police badge and stepping under the police tape, she snapped into action.

'What have we got?' she asked the senior officer at the scene, watching as his team continued to roll out police tape around the perimeter of the picnic grounds.

'Our witness is a local man, an ex-copper. He lives on the mountain and was out taking his dog for a walk to inspect the tracks after the landslides,' said the officer, summarising for Watts and Marshall. 'The dog disappeared into the scrub and started barking and that's when they found him. The witness called it in straight away.'

Marshall and Watts looked over at the carpark, media were already arriving on scene.

'Bloody police scanners,' she said to Marshall as they both stretched blue plastic gloves over their hands. She recognised the first reporter to the scene immediately.

Tasman Hill approached the police tape and watched them intently, his photographer swapping lenses, to try to capture the mound of dirt where the body still lay around fifteen metres away across the picnic ground.

Watts thanked the officer for the briefing and turned back to Marshall. Together they walked across the disturbed mud and bushland towards the crime scene surrounded by forensic investigators, out of view from the bystanders and Tasman Hill standing at the police tape boundary.

The forensic officers wore bright white disposable coveralls, their feet, hands and faces covered. The small group busily examined the scene, some photographing it. One's fiery red fringe was slightly visible underneath. It was Dr Monica Sinn, the lead forensic investigator. Watts and Monica had worked together on countless jobs and were good friends outside of work. Trauma bonded, Watts often said.

'What condition is the body in?' Watts asked, staring at the white sheet laid out across the mound created by the landslide.

Monica lifted the side of the sheet covering the decomposing body to allow Marshall to look underneath. He covered his mouth and nose with his hand, his eyes watering from the smell of decaying flesh.

'Male, early-to-late forties at a first look. He's in a pretty bad way. All of that rainfall hasn't done him any favours,' replied Monica in a matter-of-fact tone. 'There weren't any personal possessions on him, which is unusual to say the least,' she continued, looking only at Watts.

'It's got to be Harrison Marks,' said Watts positively. 'Do you think we could get an ID on him if we bring a family member in for identification then?' she asked.

'He's still in one piece, if that's what you're asking,' replied Monica. 'There's also a large abrasion to the head, blunt force trauma, for sure,' she continued as Marshall furiously jotted down notes. 'His limbs are all broken. Could be from the weight of the landslide, or another plausible alternative explanation is a fall from a great height.'

Watts and Marshall followed Monica's gaze up at the top of the mountain. A fall from a great height, just like the Ranges National Park Lookout.

'So, a possible fall, followed by a blow to the head?' suggested Watts, taking a coffee from a young officer who had rushed it to her from beyond the police tape.

'Exactly,' agreed Monica, making a note on her clipboard before directing one of her team members to continue to photograph the scene.

'How many times have I told you Alex? No coffee in my crime scenes,' said Monica, only her narrow eyes showing between the coveralls and the mask across her face.

'Of course, I know, I know. I'll just be one more minute,' said Watts, turning back to her partner. 'So, the Lookout might be back in focus after all,' she said, considering the path of the landslide down the mountain.

'Is there anything else of note?' Watts asked Monica, as she watched the paramedics offer the elderly dog walker a foil heat blanket at the carpark in the distance from them.

'There's one more thing. We've found traces of hair,' Monica replied slowly, producing a translucent plastic evidence bag and holding it up to the light for Watts and Marshall to examine. 'It's likely animal fur. It's not uncommon for animals to feed near remains so that could've transferred onto him after death,' said Monica.

The forensic officer looked stone faced at Marshall who was fighting his reaction to gag as the smell stained the air.

'However, we've found traces of this hair all over his coat. It's everywhere, even on the inside lining,' Monica continued, ignoring Marshall, gagging again.

'How long to run the tests?' asked Watts, her eyebrows raised. She needed this to be it, the thing that blows the whole case open.

'It might take a day or so,' nodded Monica. 'But I'll put in a call, and see what I can do.'

Dr Monica Sinn was a saint, thought Watts.

'Thank you. Tell the lab there's no higher priority than this case,' said Watts, beginning to carefully step away from the body. 'We've got a killer to catch.'

Watts and Marshall walked back towards the waiting media pack, the number of journalists, photographers and passers-by had tripled within minutes. And so had the pressure on the detectives to find out who was responsible.

After an hour the remains were placed into a body bag and loaded onto a waiting stretcher, moved into the back of a white unmarked van. Watts and Marshall stood next to it, watching their victim leave.

Cameras flashed in quick succession and television cameras moved in as close as they could to capture the moment. Journalists quickly swarmed Watts and Marshall, shouting questions, demanding information on the new development in the Harrison Marks case.

Marshall stood back behind Watts, alongside the officers guarding the perimeter of the crime scene.

'I'm Sapphire Ranges Police Department Detective Inspector Alexandra Watts,' she began, addressing the reporters and cameras with confidence.

The media pack hung on her every word as she paused, considering her words as the sound of the water running from the creek nearby echoed through the mountain.

'Early this morning, police were called to the Sapphire Ranges National Park Picnic Grounds, after a member of the public discovered human remains while out on a morning walk,' she continued, ignoring the constant flashing of cameras taking in every moment of her press conference. 'It appears the body may have been on the mountain for some time and the intense rainfall has led to a series of landslides that have uncovered these remains today, bringing them down the mountain. Our job is now to piece together what happened, and how this individual sadly died.'

'Detective - do you know the identity of the person - is it a man, a woman?' asked one reporter.

'Is it Harrison Marks?' shouted another journalist from the back of the media pack. Watts took another moment before answering.

'The investigation into the identity of these remains is now underway. I can confirm the deceased person is in fact, a man. However, we won't be jumping to any conclusions about his identity until we can undertake further testing and the identification process with the deceased's family,' said Watts.

'Is the death of this person considered suspicious? And if so, is this now an active murder investigation, Detective?' asked Tasman, standing immediately in front of Watts. She looked at Tasman directly in the eye, surprised at his ability to read between the lines of her statement. She paused before turning back to the cameras.

'What we have uncovered today strongly suggests foul play,' she confirmed as the media pack murmured with excitement.

'If this person is Harrison Marks, do you have any fresh leads or any new suspects now that a body has been recovered?' pushed Tasman.

Watts wondered for a moment how much that old Sapphire Times' photographer had captured on his long-view camera lens, before she answered Tasman's question.

'We will confirm the identity of the victim in due course. All we can say right now is that a person has lost their life. And all we know is that the person responsible for this is calculating... and capable of anything,' she replied frankly. 'It's our job now to find them and bring them to justice. Now if you'll excuse me, I have an investigation to run,' concluded Watts as she stepped back towards the officers under the police tape, while reporters shouted after her in a frenzy, desperate for more information.

Watts and Marshall shook the hand of the witness, the old man and his dog, as he prepared to leave the scene.

Watts looked back at the media and watched distracted as she saw Tasman Hill speaking to Monica near the police tape boundary. She saw him hand her something. Skewing her head behind the witness, Watts was certain he had handed her an old piece of newspaper.

CHAPTER FORTY-THREE

CRESSIDA

IT WAS MID-MORNING when Cressida Marks was jolted awake from her latest nightmare, reliving her last fight with her husband Harrison over and over. She pulled the bedcovers over her face, knocking a nearby wine bottle and box of old photographs off the nightstand and onto the bleach white carpet.

Drinking all night and sleeping during the day had become a new hobby, and it was the only way she was coping. Cressida knew closing the curtains and blocking out the rest of the world to drink her sorrows away was a short-term fix. It was the same thing she couldn't stand to see Harrison do, yet here she was, following directly in his footsteps.

After returning from their beach house, Cressida had only ventured outside for food and essentials. Even the new nurses and carers who came to assist Harrison's elderly parents were concerned about her. With their own poor health, his parents couldn't quite understand what had happened to their only son. Cressida didn't have the heart to re-break the news to them day after day, it felt cruel and easier to lie that Harrison was off on another adventure, chasing another story.

There were still people inside her home, yet there was never anyone around to actually care for Cressida. She felt isolated, and more alone than ever in her life, and deep under her blankets was one of the few comforting places she could find these days.

The phone rang again, another private call. Journalists had made a sport of calling her day and night. She thought they would eventually lose interest - but they hadn't. They had not forgotten Harrison was missing, and neither had she.

Rolling over, she willed it to ring out. There was no one she wanted to speak to. All Cressida wanted was to close her eyes and float away again. But the caller was persistent, ringing again and again. She resisted the urge to throw the phone against the wall, instead throwing the pillow over her head, hoping to fade in and out of consciousness, desperate to go back to that place of nothing - where she existed but led no existence. Yet, the phone continued to ring. She groaned and sat up, surprising herself when she abruptly answered the call saying nothing, just holding the phone to her ear, as though she hoped to hear Harrison's voice down the line. A false moment of hope she had created for herself just to be disappointed. Another fantastical wish.

'Cressida Marks?' asked the dead serious voice. 'It's Detective Sergeant Aaron Marshall from the Sapphire Ranges Police Department. Are you there?' he asked, waiting for a reply.

Cressida clutched the pillow as she wriggled back towards the bedhead, still sitting upright, suddenly more awake than she had been in weeks.

'Yes. Sorry - I'm here,' she said, holding her breath.

'I'm sorry to disturb you. We've been trying to reach you all morning. We have some news,' he continued, pausing briefly. 'We believe we may have a breakthrough in the investigation involving your husband, Harrison Marks.'

This was it. Cressida held onto her chest, waiting for the news. The bad news, she suspected, but needed to hear to know it was all real.

'Sadly, this morning, we located human remains at the base of the Ranges National Park, a good distance south of the search zone near the Lookout. The rainfall caused a landslide, and it appears it's uncovered a body. I'm sorry to say, Ma'am, but there are a few strong indications that this could be your husband, Ms Marks. We are almost certain it's him.'

Cressida let out a loud whine, covering her mouth with her hand. Staring at the side of the bed where Harrison once slept, the truth hit her deep in the chest.

She really would never see him lying there again. She thought of when things had been easy, back when they were in love, but that was never inside this room. It was a long time ago. And now he was somewhere on the side of the mountain, cold and wet. Who could have done this to him, she thought in total despair?

'I understand this is incredibly hard news to hear Ma'am. Would it be an imposition for us to ask you to please come down to police headquarters? We will need to ask you or another family member to please assist us with identification, just to be certain,' asked Marshall delicately.

Cressida was silent, but inside she was screaming, unable to speak or take in what was actually happening. She felt dizzy, as though all the blood in her body had just rushed straight to her head.

'I know this is so much for you to take in right now. Is that something you feel you could do? Can someone drive you down? We can organise a car to be sent to collect you,' he offered.

'It's fine. Thank you. I'll come,' she managed, before hanging up the phone. Cressida cupped her mouth as she cried, sliding off her bed and slumping to the floor.

It was the news she had been bracing for since Harrison disappeared. She had tried to mentally prepare for it, to protect herself, but the waves of shock still hit her harder than she could've imagined. She sat in shock, staring at the bars of shadows and sunlight from the trees outside on her wall. Now she was all alone.

The phone rang again, and she answered, wiping her face in a daze.

'Cressida - it's Tasman Hill - I don't know if you know yet - but the police, they're trying to get in touch with you,' Tasman began, a hesitation in his voice showing he was unsure of how to even continue the conversation. 'Are you alright?' he asked, the kind voice on the other end of the line.

'I know, they just told me,' she sobbed after a moment of silence. 'They found his body. I've got to - I've got to - I've got to see him. They want me to check if it's really him,' she said as she cried.

Her eyes closed against the pain. It was somehow comforting to know that the same reporter who had been kind to her that day on the beach, who had treated her like a human instead of a headline, was there with her on the phone, as the blur of shock surrounded her.

'I don't think I can do it. I can't go, Harrison is all I have. I mean, he's all that I had,' she said, through gasping breaths.

'Cressida - take a deep breath, okay? You can do this. You can get through this, I promise you,' said Tasman. 'Listen, I can come and drive you down, okay? You don't have to do this alone. I'll be outside in ten minutes. I'll take you down there,' he said. Cressida didn't refuse the invitation. Instead, she was silent. She knew she needed to go. She just didn't want to do it alone. She was terrified.

'I'll be there in five minutes,' said Tasman reassuringly. 'Just wait outside and I'll take you down to the police station. Wait for me and I'll be there, okay?'

Cressida agreed. She pulled on the same clothes she had worn for days and began to mentally prepare herself for what was about to happen.

She looked paranoid as she moved the curtain to peer through the windows just to be sure no one was outside. She quietly opened the front door, walking with her umbrella close to the top of her head, to make her way to the nature strip to wait for Tasman.

An old neighbour watched her from across the street and waved to her, half smiling, half concerned. He was the same old man that always made a point about their bins being left out too long after they were emptied.

Domestic chores felt a world away from what she could even consider or care about. Her husband was dead. And now she was about to identify his body.

Cressida wanted to retreat inside and hide from the world. Waves of emotions were crashing down on her all at once – and she felt like she was drowning.

The minutes felt like hours as she waited on the edge of the road. Cressida wrapped her cardigan around herself tightly as she recalled the police interview she gave with the detectives investigating the case months ago. She knew at first they thought she was responsible for Harrison's death, and now, whoever the murderer was, was still out there, free.

'I just feel it in my gut. He would have been chasing a story. It's all he did, well, almost all he did,' she explained to Detective Inspector Watts, at the time.

'He has dozens of phones. He's always disappeared for days or weeks. We aren't sleeping in the same bed or even in the same room, so I never know where he is. We are living separately under the same roof,' Cressida had said.

'Is it possible he was with one of his... other lovers,' asked Detective Inspector Watts.

'How could I possibly keep track? I stopped caring after he had an affair with my friend, Victoria Stanley. You might want to go chat with her too,' said Cressida.

Now, as she stood outside, Cressida imagined what she was about to see. Harrison's purple and black, bloated, decomposed body, covered in dirt and leaves. She wondered if Harrison was still... him.

She looked down at her wrist and rubbed the matching tattoo they had got together one drunken night at university, a small black line resembling a compass that pointed ahead, that was meant to point to each other. They had it done the same night they realised they were in love. Harrison had hidden it with his watch ever since he became a serious reporter. But Cressida had never covered hers.

As she traced the outline of the circle and arrow on her wrist, unaware that it had become a mindless, compulsive comfort, she didn't notice the scream of wheels spinning that had out of nowhere filled the usually quiet, suburban street.

She looked up from her daze when she heard her neighbour yelling, before a rapid screech of car tyres. And that's when she saw it, the car zigzagging out of control towards her on the street. The black vehicle slammed into the car parked next to her, it ricocheted, striking her. Then came the sound of a powerful exhaust and spinning tyres, as the car sped away from the scene.

Cressida's knew that someone had hit her. And her last thought was one of calm, hopeful that perhaps death meant it would be an end to the pain she was feeling. That was all that was left, before her mind went blank and everything around her went dark.

CHAPTER FORTY-FOUR

ALISON

ALISON HAD BEEN SITTING in her car parked in a side street across from Tasman's house all night. She had followed him from a distance as he drove back from visiting his mother. Stalking Tasman made her feel close to him and, more importantly, in control.

At around 2am Alison had passed out drunk in her car, but the sound of sirens from police cars speeding past her on the main road ahead finally woke her. The daylight was blinding, and Alison was covered in sweat from the sunlight that had shone through the car window. She had overslept. In panic, Alison jolted herself upright causing a forgotten open bottle in her lap to clang against the car's dashboard.

Looking at her phone filled with missed calls from Tasman, her frustration with him returned. Tasman really should chase her harder, to fight for her and their baby, she thought. If she were him, she would have shown up on his doorstep begging to make things right by now. But Alison's home security cameras showed nothing at her apartment. Tasman hadn't appeared. And it had felt like another knife twist into her heart. And Tasman would pay for that.

Watching through her windscreen, her eyes bleary, she realised Tasman's car was gone. She had lost her target. Looking at the time, Alison hadn't worried about being late for work, she had barely made it in at all. Her obsession with Tasman was her new priority. In fact, her obsessions always did this to her. It had been the reason she had to move back to this town, after all.

Alison was just another problem her father had tried to hide away in plain sight. He had promised he would be there for her. And now, he spent his nights with his assistant. Alison already couldn't stand her, let alone having to work alongside her, knowing she was screwing her dad. It took all of her self-control not to scream whenever the woman spoke to her.

Alison took another sip of the bottle, turning on the car radio, and that's when she heard the news.

'Breaking news this morning in the Sapphire Ranges, with human remains discovered at the Ranges National Park. There's police and emergency services on scene,' said the radio newsreader. 'One eyewitness confirmed the rainfall has caused multiple landslides on the mountain that brought the remains down to the picnic grounds. The entire area is closed to the public - avoid the area altogether.'

Alison gripped the steering wheel and screamed through gritted teeth. Notifications bombarded her phone's screen. Her mind was still fuzzy, but her intent was clear. Alison threw her phone onto the passenger's seat and stared vacantly ahead into the distance, starting her car, the wipers moving furiously to move the sitting water from the rainfall overnight off the windscreen.

She took another swig from her bottle before wiping her mouth with the back of her hand. She needed to know it was Harrison. There was no way she could show up at the crime scene, but there was only one other way to know for sure.

Alison drove to the most exclusive suburb in the city. The same neighbourhood her father lived in. Navigating the twists and turns, she arrived near Harrison and Cressida Marks' home, so naturally it was as though she lived there herself. Of course she had watched their home for months in the beginning of her affair with the star news reporter.

The thought of Cressida Marks had always driven Alison wild with jealousy. Harrison was gone. But the beautiful bohemian Cressida was still here, lapping up all the attention that Alison had gifted to her by making Harrison disappear. She had done all of that - and now Cressida was practically famous. Her art would probably even be worth more too.

Alison knew that if the police came to Cressida's house, then the body they found was Harrison's. Then she would need to do what she did best, to flee.

Parking just a few doors down from the home, she had the perfect view. She shook her head, still in disbelief. She was certain she would have more time, maybe even years, with Tasman before she had to worry about anyone discovering Harrison's body.

Unscrewing another bottle of gin, she downed the alcohol quickly to calm herself, to numb the growing panic.

The moment she bludgeoned Harrison to death played in her mind. The search called off and the constant rainfall hampering the investigation, Alison had become overconfident that Harrison wouldn't be found.

She had allowed sweet, respectful and kind Tasman to take all of her attention. But Alison was strategic, she had needed to keep Tasman around for other selfish reasons.

She needed someone to pin the whole murder on, and who better than a jealous, overlooked newspaper colleague? And if the police somehow ever traced Harrison to her, then she had her backup plan already in play. But Alison really didn't want it to come to that.

Watching through the windscreen, there was no sign of anyone at the Marks house. It had only been minutes, but it felt like she had waited an eternity.

A fresh sprinkling of rain spotted the windscreen. The dripping sound rang in Alison's ears, echoing. After drinking all night, her adrenaline peaking for hours, she was finally beginning to fade. Her focus was becoming hazier as she willed herself to stay awake.

Alison knew she couldn't afford to pass out now while waiting for a sign of the police to show. She had seen enough crime shows on TV to know how it worked, they would need her to ID the body - and Cressida Marks was practically the only able family Harrison had left.

Closing her eyes, Alison fell into sleep, powerless against her drunken state of exhaustion.

Minutes passed and she gasped loudly, as though she had been drowning, taking her final breaths of air to survive. Her eyes jolted open, and she saw an old man was hitting her driver's side window hard, yelling at her.

'What do you think you're doing?! Get off my lawn you journalist vultures!! Leave the poor people alone, they've been through enough! Get going! Go on, get!' he shouted, continuing to whack the car over and over.

Alison jumped, realising the attention being drawn to her. Disorientated and desperate to move, her eyes were wild and glassy as she started the car. The engine roared as she sped up as fast as she could, zigzagging throughout the street as the man continued yelling from behind.

Then Alison saw her. Cressida Marks stood on the nature strip outside her home, and, at that moment, Alison knew she had the choice to save Cressida's life, or to take it. And she chose the latter.

Cressida Marks had been at the root of all of Alison's problems lately. Alison had seen the way Tasman had looked at her. Alison knew that look because she had done it herself a million times. And so, she continued on the same trajectory, purposely swerving into the parked car and the woman conveniently standing alongside it.

The thing was, taking out Cressida as she stood waiting by the road wasn't really a mistake. It was just an added bonus, thought Alison.

CHAPTER FORTY-FIVE

TASMAN

TASMAN DIDN'T REMEMBER the drive to Cressida's house, only the moment that he turned the corner, expecting to see her standing outside waiting to be whisked safely into his car for what would be one of the most challenging moments of her life.

Instead, he saw Cressida's body laying across the road, crushed black plastic and glass surrounding her, while an expensive black car sped away, charging through the other side of the street.

Without any thought Tasman slammed the brakes of the van, leaving it running as he leapt out of the car, charging towards a motionless Cressida, covered in blood from the force of the hit.

Tasman fumbled with his phone as he called the emergency services, desperately searching from beside Cressida's body if there was anyone around, anyone to help. Tasman began CPR, unsure of whether she was dead or alive. In that moment, Tasman knew he would do anything in his power to save her.

He yelled to the operator as he tried to recall the steps of CPR and the first aid training he had when he started an after-school job at a swimming pool.

'I need an ambulance!' shouted Tasman, hitting the speaker function as the operator responded. 'A woman has been hit by a car, she's unconscious, I'm starting CPR,' he said trembling as he relayed the address and Cressida's visible injuries, checking her airway.

'She was hit by a car, I saw it, I saw it speeding away, they definitely knew they had struck her,' he continued. 'And I think I know the name of the driver, the one that hit her in a black Mercedes – it was Alison Mosca.'

'We've got police and ambulance crews on their way to you, stay where you are and stay with me until they arrive,' replied the operator calmly. 'Now, to begin CPR, follow my instructions exactly...'

As Tasman worked to save Cressida, he felt relief hearing the sound of police and ambulance sirens growing louder as they approached in the distance. He continued to work, pressing onto her chest again and again until the paramedics took over and police officers pulled him aside to take his statement, to understand what he had seen.

It wasn't until Cressida was loaded onto the stretcher of the ambulance, fighting for life, that Tasman wondered if Alison could possibly return, to claim another life.

CHAPTER FORTY-SIX

TASMAN SAT IN THE EMERGENCY department waiting room with no answers. He would never forgive himself if Cressida died because he asked her to wait outside her house.

Zaylee sat down silently next to Tasman in an empty seat, while he stared into space. She had been at the hospital to interview the CEO on the new hospital wing opening, but Tasman had barely noticed her arrival.

His mind was swimming. He had the biggest story of his career to cover, Harrison's body had been discovered – yet all he could think about was Cressida Marks. Suddenly, Victoria's ultimatum and deadline, Alison's lies, the never-to-be-child. All the noise just turned right down.

Tasman had dozens of missed calls from Victoria and McAllister, but he simply didn't care anymore. And suddenly he wondered if he had a simple glimpse of what his own father had gone through, arriving at the scene of his friend's death, all for his own story.

'Have you heard anything?' asked Zaylee after a few moments, breaking the sound of the emergency room television playing news updates of the morning press conference. Detective Inspector Watts' voice blared throughout the room.

'No. Not a word. Relatives only,' said Tasman, snapping out of his daze to acknowledge his friend with a small smile. He was truly glad she was there. Peter and Zaylee were the only real things he knew he could depend on in this town.

Zaylee looked at Tasman's phone on the chair beside him. The screen flashed with eight missed calls from McAllister alone. He knew he could be writing up another big story about Cressida. But he didn't want to. He didn't care anymore. All he could think about, was her.

'She sure has been through some kind of hell none of us could ever imagine,' she said with complete seriousness. 'Don't worry about work. I'll let McAllister know you're tied up and we can get the general news reporters on to sort it. Everyone knows something's gone down. They're all over the scene outside her place,' she said.

As they waited, a heavily pregnant woman wincing in pain burst into the emergency room with her partner. The man rang the bell for the triage nurse to help them, but the nurse seemed unfazed, rolling her eyes despite the woman's active labour. The nurse handed the partner a wooden clipboard as another nurse pushed the woman's wheelchair through the doors towards the maternity ward.

It reminded Tasman that just days ago, he too had begun to consider what it would be like to be that man, rushing Alison to the hospital when it was time for their baby to be born. The reminder of her lies made his cheeks burn red hot.

Zaylee eyed Tasman and moved to the edge of the plastic chair, as though she was about to take action.

'I'll be right back,' she said walking towards the triage counter. 'Hello. I need to speak to someone about Cressida Marks... the hit-and-run victim,' she said to the nurse behind the glass screen wall.

The nurse looked Zaylee over suspiciously. 'Are you family?'

'Yes. I'm her cousin... We're practically sisters,' lied Zaylee. 'I just need to know she's okay. Is she still in surgery,' she asked sweetly, hoping the nurse bought her story.

Zaylee ignored the serious stare the nurse gave her. She was not amused at the attempt.

'Sorry, immediate family only,' the nurse replied curtly as she got up and walked through to the staff kitchen and break room behind her.

'Okay, that didn't work,' said Zaylee to Tasman apologetically, turning around to face him.

The next moment a young man in his early 20s burst through the hospital-side of the two-way doors, his collared shirt drenched in sweat, as though he had just run a marathon.

'Zaylee! You're still here, thank God!' he said loudly to her, almost breathless. 'Listen, I think the Boss might have been referring to old data, you know about the emergency department waiting times...' he said desperately, looking around the waiting room to check who was listening. 'The thing is, he mistakenly said they've dropped, but that's not entirely accurate. Do you think it could be possible to...'

'Leave it out?' suggested Zaylee, realising she could leverage the young, green PR officer who was in over his head.

'Could you?' he asked, unable to hide the fear in his voice. He looked at Tasman, realising he was watching their entire exchange, and then invited her to speak behind the nurse's station.

Zaylee shook her head a little. 'The thing is, Ben, the story really needs those stats. It will go a long way in explaining the new wing - after all the taxpayers have paid for it. I was really hoping we could keep it in there,' she lied again. The hospital employee's face turned white.

'Look, I know you're new, and I wouldn't want us to get off to a rocky start. How about this? Just this once, I'll make an exception,' she said patting him on the shoulder, almost condescendingly. 'You go and get those figures updated and I'll wait here – as long as you give me another exclusive over the Advocate, next time. Deal?' The media advisor nodded in relief.

'I'll wait here, and we'll just let the whole thing go. Never happened, okay?' she smiled.

'Oh, thank you! I truly owe you one,' said Ben. 'The Boss would have killed me if he thought I stuffed another interview up. I'll be right back,' he said, wiping sweat from his brow as he backed through the doors of the hospital towards the corporate office area.

Zaylee lingered around the doors, checking with the media advisor had long gone before stepping behind the moveable barrier to enter the nurse's station.

Zaylee lingered around one of the computer monitors before quickly taking a seat behind the desk, hitting the keyboard. A minute passed before Zaylee rushed back to the waiting area and sat down next to Tasman with a smirk.

Tasman looked at his friend with astonishment. 'How on earth did you do that?' he asked.

'Don't look surprised. I'm amazing and great under pressure,' she beamed. 'Now Cressida is in room twenty-three in the Post-Surgery Wing. Go, now — before they get back,' she said, turning back to the nurse's station that was still empty.

Without a moment of hesitation, Tasman disappeared through the hospital doors.

CHAPTER FORTY-SEVEN

TASMAN RUSHED THROUGH THE HOSPITAL, searching for the post-surgery recovery wing. His phone rang, but he could not face the dozens of missed calls and messages that were waiting for him. Tasman didn't know if he would even have a job to go back to after disappearing during one of the most significant stories the Ranges had ever seen. But for the first time in years, he didn't care about the news.

Passing the maternity ward, it was another unwanted reminder of Alison, her fake pregnancy and what she had done to Cressida. Then followed the thought of what else she was capable of, such as what she might do to Tasman. Was it possible she had accidentally struck Cressida just moments before Tasman were meant to appear by her side? No. Tasman didn't believe in coincidences.

Tasman's phone buzzed again, as he looked from door to door, searching for Cressida's room. An unknown number left a voicemail message. And Tasman's instincts pushed him to listen. At first, he could barely make out who the voice was, then it was clear. It was the forensic investigator he had hoped to hear from, Dr Monica Sinn.

'Tasman – it's Monica Sinn. Thank you for that article your dad wrote. I always wanted a copy and to have it in the flesh means a lot,' she began. 'Listen, this is obviously an active investigation and I know you gave me your card...'

Tasman stopped in his tracks, pretending to look at a vending machine in the busy hospital wing hallway, listening intently.

'Off the record, all I can say is that we've found some unusual hairs on the body and inside the clothing of the deceased. It's looking likely to be some kind of rare canine hair, nothing we have here in Australia. We're running checks against the national breeder databases to be sure, something like an Otterhound.'

Tasman leaned forward onto the machine, his arm holding him upright as his mind raced. There was only one person who he knew in the city who owned such a dog. Alison knew Harrison. Alison's rare, pure-bred imported dog had left its fur all over Harrison's body.

'That's all I've got for you. Consider me, you and your dad square now - okay? Good luck,' she said, ending the message.

Tasman stared at his phone in disbelief at what he had heard. In the same moment, his news notifications appeared - including the Sapphire Times.

Police were searching for the driver of the car that had hit Cressida Marks. A woman in her thirties, brunette and driving a luxury sedan, a Mercedes. It confirmed everything. Alison wasn't just a liar, thought Tasman; she was calculating, dangerous and on the run right now. She could be anywhere. And now he knew, just like the police had warned, that she was capable of anything. It felt like he was living through a scene in a nightmare.

Tasman immediately called Detective Inspector Watts, the call going straight to voicemail. And that's when Tasman stumbled upon room twenty-three in the post-surgery wing, where Cressida Marks was heavily sedated, resting. She was alive.

CHAPTER FORTY-EIGHT

ALISON

ALISON STOOD OVER an unconscious, bruised, bloodied and bandaged Cressida Marks in room twenty-three of the post-surgery recovery ward. Dressed in a nurse's uniform she had found in the hospital's laundry hamper, Alison was surprised at just how easy it was to make her way through the building undetected.

Now that her description was out in the media, she was still deciding her next move, knowing that police could appear at any moment. Alison tucked Cressida's sheet in, looking over the machines, helping her victim survive, keeping her safe.

'It's funny Cressida, you don't even know me. But believe me - I know you,' Alison said aloud to the unconscious patient. 'I've spent hours watching you. I hope you know that I didn't actually plan to hit you, but then when I saw you right there in front of me, I knew it would solve all my problems,' she said sniggering.

Alison moved closer to her unconscious victim, leaning over her face to face, whispering in her ear.

'The thing is Cressida, you've sort of been ruining my life. Whenever things start to go my way, bam, there you are getting in the way. You know, I really get what you saw in Harrison. I mean, I loved him so much I almost sent my own father to prison, all for his deep brown eyes. But then, he left me. So, I had to make him pay,' she shrugged.

'I must admit, though, mistress-to-wife, even I didn't see his affair with the nurse coming. Harrison really didn't deserve either of us,' she laughed as she sat down alongside Cressida's bed, patting her motionless arm.

'You know my first love, Chris Clarkson. That guy was a real piece of shit. He was like Harry, charming, gorgeous, charismatic, no accent though, but you get it,' Alison continued. 'He told me he loved me and then the next minute, he just disappeared. He left me waiting outside for him to pick me up one weekend. I waited, like an idiot... but he never came,' she said, tugging violently at the cord of Cressida's heart rate monitor.

'Do you know what it feels like to feel so crushed, so heartbroken, so humiliated you can't peel yourself off the floor?' she asked Cressida rhetorically. 'The police eventually found him though... he was with his other girlfriend staying at the same hotel we were meant to spend *our* weekend at,' said Alison coldly.

She roughly snatched Cressida's pillow from underneath her head, before lifting it to her face to scream into it in anger for a moment. The sound of the heart rate monitor continued to calmly beep.

Alison was unaware she had gone to the bad place, the same illogical place that unlocked in the back of her mind, the one that broke out at times like this. It was the part of her personality that was unpredictable, that was deeply dangerous.

'And Tasman!' she said, trying to compose herself again, clutching the pillow tightly next to Cressida's motionless body. 'At first, I was only watching him to keep a close eye on the search. But then out of the blue, I really fell for him, don't even know how it happened. And now we're going to have a little family together,' she beamed, patting her stomach lightly, seemingly unaware of her delusion for a moment. 'Everything is going to finally work out for me. Probably not for you though,' she said to Cressida, dropping her lip sarcastically.

'You should have heard the awful things Tasman's little reporter friend Zaylee said about me. I really thought she was going to be a problem, but I was prepared to sort her out,' she continued, simulating a baseball bat smashing car windows. 'But then you kept showing up. At the beach, at the supermarket... and let's not forget your interview together, oh I must've watched that a hundred times. I saw the way he looked at you. So, I just think this would all be easier for me, if you just... went away now,' Alison sighed, standing above Cressida.

'Enough talking, right? I just wanted you to know it isn't your fault. But I can't have you ruin my last shot at happiness. After all, I've got a baby on the way,' she said, pretending to clutch at her stomach for a baby that didn't exist.

'This won't hurt a bit,' said Alison and she raised the pillow, ready to smoother the life out of the innocent woman before her.

CHAPTER FORTY-NINE

TASMAN

TASMAN WAS LOOKING THROUGH the windows of room twenty-three's broken screening blinds when he recognised Alison wearing a nursing uniform, standing above an unconscious Cressida. Tasman had watched Alison whispering to her victim before she raised the pillow in her hands and, it was at that moment without hesitation that he stormed into the room.

'Get away from her!' Tasman yelled.

Alison looked up from Cressida's bed surprised, still clutching the pillow tightly.

'I wondered when you would show up, *darling*,' Alison smiled, imitating Tasman's mother. 'Wow. Rushing to be by Cressida's bedside. That's very romantic. I had a hunch about you and her, and looks like I was right,' she said suddenly frowning like a child.

Alison stood closer to Cressida, in front of the equipment keeping her sedated, keeping her alive.

'What do you think you're doing?!' Tasman demanded again. His eyes darted around the room desperately searching for an emergency button to push to raise the alarm. He could see it, only a few metres from where he stood.

'I would keep your voice down if I were you. Unless you want all of this to be over, really quickly,' she said calmly, looking intensely into Tasman's eyes the same way she had done the night they had met.

Tasman didn't know if Alison was threatening Cressida's life or his, too.

'You ran down Cressida with your car,' said Tasman, his adrenaline flooding his veins.

Alison didn't deny it, instead she looked at him perplexed, as though it surprised her. He wasn't aware of the full story, across all the details already.

'Well, it's not like I'm proud of it. I came to apologise,' she laughed sweetly. 'Apologies are very important to me.'

'Alison, your face is all over the news,' he lied. There's CCTV of you, the police will be searching for you. And now they'll know you're here,' he threatened, still waiting for Alison to come to her senses.

But Alison appeared completely unfazed as she fiddled with the drip providing pain relief to Cressida in her hands, winding and twisting it around her fingers, deep in thought..

'I know you knew Harrison. I know what you did,' said Tasman slowly, watching her every move, searching for any sign of acknowledgement or remorse in her face.

Alison's face dropped, the last piece of her innocent and sweet persona had just fallen away. He was looking at the ugly underside, the murderous person beneath.

'It was you. You killed him,' Tasman spat.

Alison began to laugh hard, as though the entire world wasn't about to crumble beneath her feet.

'Sorry, darling. It's just so strange to see you... so serious,' she said amused. 'Everyone always wants to talk about Harrison. Nothing ever changes after death, right?' she said staring coldly into Tasman's eyes.

'Haven't you worked out yet that I don't let anything, or anyone stand in my way?' she asked, nodding towards Cressida.

'What did you do to Harrison?' Tasman shouted again.

'Shhh. I told you, keep it down,' said Alison, walking towards Tasman. 'I really don't want to make any snap decisions. And you and I have so much to talk about.'

She leaned forward to touch his shoulder as she clutched her stomach. The contact made Tasman feel sick. Alison turned towards the window, staring outside with an enormous smile.

'Harry and I... well, he had it coming, didn't he? He used me and once he got what he wanted, he discarded me. And let me tell you, I am really sick of men thinking they can just use me up,' she smiled confidently. 'At least I know you won't be running off telling anyone about all this.'

'And why is that? You're fucking insane,' said Tasman, his cheeks flushed. Alison laughed, unbothered by the insult.

'Because you're my insurance plan. You didn't think I was into you for you, did you?' she laughed. 'Well, not at first. But you know I grew to love you. That's why I'm still here fighting for you, for us and our family.'

Tasman stood speechless, frozen in place.

'I know you'll go along with what I'm asking of you because you and I are in this together now. Partners in crime,' she said moving even closer to Tasman.

'The police are looking for you, I'll tell them about Harrison,' said Tasman, enraged.

'Remember my little gift to you, that pen? It's beautiful, isn't it? Well, I actually took that from Harry the night I killed him. No doubt your fingerprints are all over it now, that's not going to look very good for you, won't it?' she said dropping her lip sarcastically.

'And wasn't it you who took over his job after rotting away on the night shift while Harrison took all the glory? That sounds like a motive to me, darling,' patting his shoulder sympathetically.

TASMAN HAD TO KEEP ALISON talking for as long as he could. It would only be a matter of time before the hospital staff would come to check on Cressida's condition. The longer he could stall her for, the better chance they all had of making it out of the room alive.

As Alison spoke, he spotted Cressida's feet twitch, she was waking up. Tasman had looked around the room, desperate to identify anything he could use to restrain Alison, to stop her from what she was about to do.

'We really can't start our new life together as long as Cressida Marks is around, darling. She's coming between us, and I really can't have that,' said Alison as she dropped the pillow and reached into her pocket, revealing a knife.

Tasman had only one card left to play to stop her.

'You don't need to do any of this, honey,' he said, moving slowly towards Alison. 'I just wish the timing of all of this was different. I mean, what about us?' he asked calmly, hoping to turn her attention, distract her.

'What about our baby?' he asked, knowing that there wasn't one at all. 'I know I didn't react well when you told me the news.' Tasman watched her intently, ignoring the rage he felt inside at uttering the words.

'It's all happened so fast, and I just didn't have a chance to let the news - our wonderful news - sink in. We could just leave now, you know, run away and be together,' he said, moving closer to Alison as she clutched the knife.

Alison said nothing. She stared at him as though she was stuck in an inner torment, split between desperately wanting to believe his words and suspicion. She turned the knife round in her hands. Tasman could see it was working. Alison was softening.

'Think about what you're about to do. If you hurt Cressida, then the police will find you, and we can't be together, our family can't be together,' he said.

Tasman could see the gears in Alison's mind turning, as though her logic and sanity was slowly returning.

'But they're looking for me. They're already searching for me,' she reasoned, easing her grip on the knife.

'They'll be looking for me too, right? The evidence is all on the pen,' he said reassuringly, hoping to convince her.

Tasman glanced at the doorway and the clock, willing one of the staff to change shifts or come to check on Cressida. They needed to do it now.

'But if we leave right now, we could start over. Change our names. Whatever we need to do, we can work it out. We could do it for our baby,' he said, looking at her stomach, knowing there was no baby at all.

He could see Alison thinking it through. Her personality flicking between the sweet woman who was desperate to be loved and the murderous villain he had uncovered. He wasn't sure what part of her was more dominant.

'What you've done doesn't matter to me. I just want to be with you, Alison. If we leave now, we can leave it all behind us. Come here,' he said, reaching his hands out to her to pull her towards him.

'You really think we could do that, after what I've done?' she asked him as he moved towards her and hugged her tightly.

'No. I can't. I lied,' he said coldly.

'What did you say?' demanded Alison in shock. But it was too late, Tasman had tackled her to the ground, the unexpected force sending the knife flying across the floor.

Tasman wrestled Alison to stop her from reaching for the knife, as Zaylee suddenly appeared in the doorway. Witnessing the struggle, she ran into the room and smacked the emergency alarms, the fire alarm sounding immediately.

Alison screamed as she struggled under Tasman trying to hold her to the floor as the alarm rang out, bellowing throughout the hospital with an urgent buzzing of machines alerting the medical staff to room twenty-three.

'I know the baby isn't real,' Tasman said to Alison in disgust, she continued to struggle, refusing to admit defeat. 'The police will be here any minute. It's over Alison.'

Zaylee scampered on her hands and knees, reaching for the knife underneath Cressida's hospital bed. Zaylee stood over Tasman and Alison; in warning she would take action to protect her friend.

Two nurses finally ran into the room before standing frozen in shock in the doorway at the scene, confronting them. One screamed as two security guards pushed past them, drawing their firearms, realising the standoff before them. Alison raised her hands, in surrender, slowly standing from the floor.

'What in good God is happening in here? This woman isn't a nurse!' screeched one of the nurses standing at the door, the alarm still echoing throughout the hospital.

Watts and Marshall burst into the room, almost out of breath. Watts had heard Tasman's voicemail message after all, thought Tasman.

Alison didn't struggle as Marshall and Watts handcuffed her, as though she was enjoying the spectacle she had created, watching and taking in each face in the room, as though she was proud of a performance she had just given.

Alison finally looked at Tasman and smiled, 'I told you, you're my insurance plan, darling,' she whispered to him.

Tasman stood tall, wiping the blood from his cut lip from the scuffle. He adjusted his shirt and stared at Alison in total disgust.

'Actually. No. That won't be happening either,' Tasman replied. 'I had an insurance plan of my own,' he said to Alison.

Tasman pulled his phone out from his satchel's front pocket. It had been recording their entire conversation live, straight to the Sapphire Times social media sites the whole time.

'I believe I have your entire confession right here for what you did to Harrison. To Cressida. And to me. The whole thing. It's over.'

Alison stared back at Tasman; her smirk wiped away. She had been outplayed and Tasman could see that Alison had underestimated him completely, like many before her.

'Detectives, you'll see on this recording that Alison Mosca just confessed to murdering Harrison Marks and the attempted murder of Cressida Marks,' said Tasman, handing his phone to Watts who looked stunned. 'It also includes Alison confessing to framing me for Harrison's murder.'

As he spoke the words, sealing Alison's fate, she kept her trademark eye contact with Tasman. He was staring into the soul of someone darker, someone who had nothing to lose anymore.

Marshall led Alison out of the room, followed by the hospital security guards. The blaring of the alarms soon stopped and there was a moment of calm in the chaos.

Nurses rushed to check Cressida's vitals - she was still breathing, unharmed.

'You saved us - if it wasn't for you, I do not know what might've happened, Edwards,' said Tasman to Zaylee, his hands still shaking.

'I knew something was up when you didn't come back after a few minutes. I saw her through the crack in the blinds and just waited for you to distract her. You know what they say, never leave a man behind, right?' she joked. 'And look at you finally joining us all in the modern age. Your phone even saved the day!' she said, acknowledging Tasman's genius recording.

Watts finished interviewing a group of nursing staff and returned to Tasman and Zaylee, sitting in chairs near the door of room twenty-three.

'Mr Hill, Ms Edwards, you both should feel incredibly proud of what you did. You saved lives today - possibly even your own,' Watts said seriously. 'You should know that we traced Alison's registration plates from the hit and run to her home. We were actually executing a search warrant there when we got your message. What we found was a treasure trove. We located missing notebooks, mobile phones, mud-stained and fire singed clothing all in the manhole of the apartment. Everything we could hope to locate to piece Harrison Marks' murder together was there. Including the dog...,' she said, looking directly at Tasman.

'I just can't believe it,' sighed Zaylee, still in shock. 'I've got to call Peter. He will be worried sick,' she said, walking away to make the call.

Tasman sat stunned with Watts, as doctors and nurses suddenly flooded Cressida's room.

'Mr Hill, now that we've got a minute, you should know there were a couple of other things we found,' said Watts. 'Alison had really done her research on you Mr Hill. We've found your articles detailing the search for Harrison spread out across one room in her house, along with what looked like surveillance images of you at your apartment at all times of the day and night. It looks like she may have been stalking you for weeks, at least,' she said sternly.

Tasman leaned forward, rubbing his fingers through his hair. 'You know, I thought I was losing my mind. I actually thought someone was watching me, following me - but I told myself I was imagining it, but it was... her,' he said. Watts nodded slowly.

'We also found online receipts for a novelty positive pregnancy test and ultrasound prank kit... I just thought you might need to know that,' she said avoiding eye-contact with Tasman. He stared ahead into blank space. He felt a strange comfort in the revelations. Everything that had happened finally added up, the truth had finally come out.

'Are you okay, Mr Hill?' Watts asked him sincerely.

'Ha! Well, I'm definitely not okay, but at least all of this will make a great story. Well, the Sapphire Times already have their story after all of this I guess,' he said, smiling a little as he thought of Victoria's face when he hijacked the Times' social media feed to confront a murderer.

'Well, I look forward to reading your next story on it, Mr Hill,' said Watts, with a small smile. 'Make sure you make me look good,' she joked as she stood up to continue working the scene. 'Now, we will need to take a formal statement in just a moment, but if you want to take a minute, I'll wait just outside... ' she said as she glanced towards Cressida Marks, who was suddenly surrounded by more nurses and doctors. She was awake.

CHAPTER FIFTY

ONE WEEK LATER

TASMAN HAD BEEN LEANING against the pillar at the entrance of the Ranges City Council Chambers for just over forty minutes, waiting. Lindsay sat on the guardrail smoking his third cigarette while flicking over a copy of the Sapphire Times. The front page showed Alison Mosca being led into the Sapphire Ranges Police Station in handcuffs after being charged with Harrison Marks' murder.

It had been front page news for days as more details emerged about the woman who murdered one of the highest profile reporters in the region. Alison's image had been plastered across every television news screen.

'Lindsay, you ready?' asked Tasman, as he straightened and moved towards the doors at the exact moment they flung open.

Councillor Glenn Mosca and his executive assistant moved through the entryway and stopped, looking to his right at Tasman in surprise, and then to his left, where Detectives Watts and Marshall stood.

'What is this?' demanded Councillor Mosca with disgust, and that was the moment when Tasman moved in, swinging into action.

'Councillor Mosca - what do you have to say about allegations you embezzled money from your building company?' asked Tasman, holding his phone outright, recording as he walked.

'Get out of my way! I have no comment,' shouted Councillor Mosca, spitting with rage as he tried to move forward, while Lindsay took photo after photo of the exchange.

'That's the same company responsible for the deaths of innocent people, crushed by falling industrial glass windows - you've been using inferior materials, paying off inspectors to look the other way and pocketing the cash to fund your own luxury lifestyle, haven't you?' Tasman continued.

Tasman had poured over Harrison's final notebooks and deciphered his shorthand. Harrison had left trails of notes pointing to what would have been his next big story, and it was the very same story that led to his death. Tasman felt a sense of pride in being the one to take it over, to deliver Harrison's final blow to the Mosca family and their crooked enterprises.

'Where's there's smoke, there's fire Councillor Mosca. So, I started doing some extra digging, all thanks to the great Harrison Marks. And it turns out, we've also uncovered some evidence that you allegedly stole from the same donation fund you set up for the skyscraper victims' families... that's low, mate,' said Tasman in disgust.

'I said, no comment,' Councillor Mosca said furiously.

Watts and Marshall stepped forward. While Marshall took the politician's arm and pulled it backwards to handcuff him, while Lindsay snapped away.

'Glenn Mosca, you're under arrest for theft and embezzlement, and serious negligence causing death,' said Detective Watts proudly. As she continued to recite his rights, Councillor Mosca's executive assistant stood back in shock, walking backwards into a run back through the Council doors out of view of Lindsay's camera.

'And finally, Councillor Mosca, what do you say to allegations that your daughter - Alison - murdered Harrison Marks to keep him from publishing documents proving your crimes?' asked Tasman, before stopping directly in front of the Councillor, his expression dark with disgust.

'I have no daughter,' Councillor Mosca spat looking directly into Tasman's eyes. Marshall placed him into the back of the police vehicle, while passers-by stopped and filmed on their phones.

'How was that for timing,' said Lindsay, sarcastically. Almost as though you knew the coppers were going to show up.'

But Tasman did know that they were about to show up. And he looked to Watts to offer her a nod of acknowledgement to thank her. An unspoken contract had been fulfilled, and a new bond of trust created. After all, it was essential for the city's up-and-coming investigative journalist to have their contacts, and their sources, thought Tasman.

'You might make the Golden Quills at this rate for this,' said Lindsay to Tasman tongue-in-cheek. 'Although Harrison would've knocked back a few drinks and a smoke while we worked.'

'Speaking of which,' said Tasman, checking his watch. 'The memorial is about to start.'

TASMAN SAT IN THE NEWSROOM at Harrison's desk, knowing the star reporter would never return. He looked out from the wide glass windows onto the lawns of the Sapphire Times; the sun shining on thousands of flowers from the public memorial placed to honour the man that had made the city a more honest, a more balanced place.

'It's kind of nice and symbolic, isn't it? You finished his story on the same day as his memorial,' said Zaylee as she stood beside the desk dressed in black, arm in arm with Peter who had come to pay his respects.

'If it wasn't for you, Harrison's last story might've stayed buried,' said Peter, patting Tasman on the back.

'I think it's safe to say this desk will belong to you now, Hill,' said Zaylee, glancing at Victoria's office.

Tasman didn't know what to say. He thought of how much he had wanted this life; how much he had wanted to leave the night shift behind. But Tasman didn't feel the same anymore. The entire experience, chasing the story, about the death of one of their own, it had changed him.

The trio sat together, watching a stream of mourners pay their respects to Harrison with more and more flowers to add to the pile. The mood in the entire newsroom was sombre, but the reporters, as they always did, continued to work, preparing for the next deadline.

'Hill - can I have a word, please?' asked Victoria, standing in the doorway of her office.

Tasman sat down opposite her desk and for the first time noticed the framed image of herself and Harrison on her desk from many years ago, celebrating an award win.

'Here you go,' said Victoria, handing him a thick stack of paper. 'It's your new contract. Congratulations, you're about to officially become the Sapphire Times' new investigative reporter,' she smiled gently.

'The executive feel that you've more than proven yourself - even Harrison would be proud,' she said, her eyes darting to the photo of the man she had loved and lost.

Victoria rose from her chair, opening her liquor cabinet and fridge, taking two glasses out in preparation to celebrate the achievement.

Tasman paused. He ran his fingers through his hair, unable to speak as he considered what Victoria was offering him. It was everything he had always wanted, yet he stared at the contract representing everything he had been striving for. He felt nothing.

'It's a small pay rise and the condition of airtime across all of our platforms. Of course, this will be in addition to your usual stories in print and online. I know it sounds like a lot to handle, but I'm sure you'll find a way,' she said, opening the bottle of whiskey and pouring. 'After all, you're one of our rising stars now, locking up murderers and local politicians.'

Victoria stopped pouring and looked at Tasman, screwing the lid back on the bottle.

'Don't think it over too long, Hill... ' she said, noting his silence. 'I've got HQ breathing down my neck to lock you in officially before another paper or television networks tries to snap you up and -.'

Tasman's phone rang as Victoria was speaking. He looked outside the window, hundreds still gathered on the grounds for Harrison, and then back at

Victoria and his ringing phone, showing his mother's smiling face, the same call he had ignored for too long.

'I'm sorry Victoria, I've got to take this,' said Tasman, as he stood up and walked out of the office, leaving the contract on the desk behind him.

CHAPTER FIFTY-ONE

ALISON

ONE YEAR LATER

ALISON SAT IN THE CHAIR closest to the window in the plain white and sterile activities room. Even the windows featured white painted bars across them. Alison spent most days now just staring outside to the plain, dusty courtyard and writing in her diary, simply waiting for time to pass.

She knew she had been lucky to be handed just nine years of imprisonment after the trial. Her lawyer negotiated and got her time at the medium security prison, Camwood House Correctional for Women after they argued she likely suffered from borderline personality disorder. But Alison didn't really care, she was just ready to get out of prison and continue her life.

Alison hated the program. The daily group therapy sessions were a bore to her, a perpetual irritation. The deconstruction of her actions that led her to this facility were endless and would remain so if she wanted to cut her sentence short. It was going to be a long nine years, she thought.

'Hey look! It's your baby Daddy,' yelled one inmate to Alison, who pushed another playfully into her chair.

Alison sat up in her favourite corner chair. She could hear that familiar voice, the same voice that landed both her and her father in prison. She despised that voice.

'It's some awards show. He just won something for his story that put you away!' laughed one uncontrollably as she swung upside down on the couch.

Alison stood up and snatched the remote from the young women now squabbling over the volume. None of them dared to defy her. Alison had quickly established her dominance during their daily group therapy sessions and her sharing had told them all they needed to know about Alison - she wasn't to be messed with.

Alison looked at the screen. On the television, Tasman shone brightly on the podium of a glistening black stage lined with gold. He looked different. Even his suit fit him properly. He didn't seem like the younger green reporter she had met and drugged that first night.

'I cannot thank you enough for this honour,' Tasman began his speech, addressing the crowd who continued applauding him. 'As a journalist, it is in your blood to chase a story, to follow every angle, to uncover the truth. And, unwittingly, I became part of that story. And while it was one of the most terrifying times of my life, it led to some glimmers of light,' he said, as the camera flashed to Cressida Marks, sitting at his table next to Zaylee and Peter all beaming at Tasman.

'It should always be remembered that the truth always comes out, the truth cannot be hidden, and the truth cannot be buried. And perhaps that is just another reminder of why the media is, and always will be, crucial to our life. This all happened because we lost one of our own. And tonight, I would like to honour this man, who also stood here, in this place many times before. Tonight, I dedicate this award to Harrison Marks,' Tasman concluded, holding his Golden Quill Award high in the air.

The audience rose to their feet on the screen, applauding Tasman Hill. He was a success, a shining star.

Alison had seen enough and turned to stare out of her window, ignoring the taunts of her fellow inmates as though the words had no effect.

'Mosca, you have visitors,' called the therapist, escorted by a guard from the doorway.

Alison rose to her feet and smiled, believing she was about to see her father. He had been released after just eight months for his theft, embezzlement charges, and after all, Alison had no one else, not now. He must have finally forgiven her, she thought.

She felt the eyes of the room upon her as she walked into the hallway, staff closing the door behind her.

Alison stopped as soon as she saw them. A man and a woman, each wearing dark tailored suits, stopped talking and looked at her. They were definitely not prison guard staff.

'Alison Mosca, I'm Detective Sergeant Kate Dugan and this is Detective Senior Constable Bradley Moody,' said one officer.

'We'd like to escort you down to the station for a chat,' said Detective Moody as he flipped out his badge and quickly returned it to his suit's inner pocket.'

Alison gave them a smug smile.

'I'm sorry officers, but as you can see, I am here as part of a court ordered rehabilitation program. I can't simply leave,' she replied confidently. She knew how to play this game and without a lawyer, she didn't have to say or do anything.

'Ms Mosca, I think you'll find that you don't have a choice this time,' Detective Dugan responded, rolling her eyes at her partner.

They gestured Alison towards the corridor and direction of the exit.

'I've got no comment about the Marks' case. My lawyer can direct you from there,' Alison pushed, attempting to brush off another interrogation.

Alison had refused to be properly interviewed and never took the stand during her trial. Her lawyer had advised that her stalking and obsession with Harrison and Tasman would not play well for her in front of a jury, so instead she remained silent. She was certain she could have charmed the jurors, if she had of had the chance.

'Actually Ms Mosca, we're here on another matter. This doesn't concern Harrison Marks,' said Detective Moody coldly.

'We're here about Chris Clarkson's cold case. Remember the name? That old ex-boyfriend of yours… you know, the one who went missing all those years ago. You know, his parents never gave up on him. They never stopped searching,' said

Detective Dugan, placing both her hands on her hips as standing in front of Alison, blocking her exit from the conversation.

'We never had your DNA on file until that Harrison Marks case. And it turns out you're a perfect match to the prints we found at the scene of Clarkson's disappearance,' she said triumphantly.

'And we think you might be able to tell us exactly where to find him,' said Detective Moody, showing Alison the door.

ACKNOWLEDGMENTS

Writing *Truth Stays Buried* has been a tremendous experience for me that began shortly after the arrival of my second daughter in 2021. Finishing this story has fulfilled a life-long dream that I had never thought possible.

Thank you to my family, friends and colleagues who have each supported me throughout this journey.

I would like to especially thank those who have given their time as beta readers for this project including Cassandra Boland, Greg Boland, Sam Keller and Maddie Harrington. I would also like to acknowledge editors Ray Braun and Sherryl Clark, along with designer Christian Storm for their excellent work.

I could not write a book about the media without also thanking Natalie Forrest who gave me my first reporting job as a young university graduate desperate to become a television journalist many, many years ago. For that opportunity, I will be forever grateful.

And finally, to the reader of this book, thank you for choosing this story. I hope you loved reading it as much as I loved writing it.

Please feel free to subscribe to my newsletter at alexiabolandherrick.com for my next book, a brand-new tale, coming soon.

ABOUT THE AUTHOR

ALEXIA BOLAND HERRICK is an Australian writer, journalist and media expert based in Melbourne, Victoria, Australia. *Truth Stays Buried* is Alexia's debut thriller novel.

www.ingramcontent.com/pod-product-compliance
Lightning Source LLC
Chambersburg PA
CBHW030546310726
48979CB00010B/2057/J

* 9 7 8 1 7 6 3 6 3 4 0 2 2 *